HIDDEN AMONG THE KILLERS . . .

The owlhoot began shooting with such accuracy that Leif winced as a piece of lead creased his shoulder.

He dropped to his knees and aimed both six-shooters. Movement guided his pistols. He fired three times from each gun—six slugs headed for the outlaw. Leif had no idea which one hit its target, but at least one did. The man grunted and collapsed. The death caused a flurry of firing from the gang.

Leif retreated farther and reloaded, but this let them creep closer to him. He was a crack shot, but being unable to see his targets clearly put him at a disadvantage. Once more he tried to count his opponents. The only two he knew for sure were Luther Simkins and Sally Randall. They called out instructions to the others on how to circle him. Their voices located them, but they remained sheltered by trees, letting the rest of the gang members risk their necks.

With some trepidation, Leif changed tactics. Instead of trying to retreat ahead of the gang, he slipped around the tree and hoped the gang on either flank kept hunting where he wasn't. Leif worked his way toward the tree where Luther Simkins remained hidden. If he was going to die, he'd take the killer down with him.

"Where is he? What's happening?" Sally Randall bellowed out her questions from off to Leif's left. He strained to hear Simkins's reply so he could take him out. Leif's heart hammered louder in his ears. Nothing but silence ahead of him warned that Simkins either was staying quiet or had moved.

"Don't know where he got off to, Sally. He's a slippery one. I think he's a mile away by now."

"No, he's not. He's still here. I feel it in my gut." She moved, making considerable noise as she crashed through dried brush.

Leif suspected a trap. She was trying to draw him out so he'd fire at her. He kept his attention focused toward the last spot where Simkins had taken refuge. Leif raised his six-shooter when he saw a shadow move from a tree to his right. A hundred things raced through his mind. Before he consciously came to a decision, he fired. He hit the shadow—it jerked back, then dropped and lumbered away.

He caught his breath. He had fired on a bear and wounded it. Worse, the flash from his gun had revealed his location to not only Sally Randall but another of the outlaws behind him. Ducking and running got him away from where they had spotted him, but the crunch of his boots on dried leaves made it obvious where he fled. Bullets tore through the forest around him. He flinched when one passed close enough to an ear to deafen him momentarily.

RALPH COMPTON

◇

SHOT TO HELL

A Ralph Compton Western by

JACKSON LOWRY

BERKLEY
New York

BERKLEY

An imprint of Penguin Random House LLC

penguinrandomhouse.com

Copyright © 2021 by The Estate of Ralph Compton

Penguin Random House supports copyright. Copyright fuels creativity, encourages diverse voices, promotes free speech, and creates a vibrant culture. Thank you for buying an authorized edition of this book and for complying with copyright laws by not reproducing, scanning, or distributing any part of it in any form without permission. You are supporting writers and allowing Penguin Random House to continue to publish books for every reader.

BERKLEY and the BERKLEY & B colophon are registered trademarks of Penguin Random House LLC.

ISBN: 9780593333730

First Edition: April 2021

Printed in the United States of America

1   3   5   7   9   10   8   6   4   2

Cover art by Dennis Lyall
Cover design by Steve Meditz
Book design by George Towne

THE IMMORTAL COWBOY

This is respectfully dedicated to the "American Cowboy." His was the saga sparked by the turmoil that followed the Civil War, and the passing of more than a century has by no means diminished the flame.

———◆◆◆———

True, the old days and the old ways are but treasured memories, and the old trails have grown dim with the ravages of time, but the spirit of the cowboy lives on.

———◆◆◆———

In my travels—to Texas, Oklahoma, Kansas, Nebraska, Colorado, Wyoming, New Mexico, and Arizona—I always find something that reminds me of the Old West. While I am walking these plains and mountains for the first time, there is this feeling that a part of me is eternal, that I have known these old trails before. I believe it is the undying spirit of the frontier calling me, through the mind's eye, to step back into time. What is the appeal of the Old West of the American frontier?

———◆◆◆———

It has been epitomized by some as the dark and bloody period in American history. Its heroes—Crockett, Bowie, Hickok, Earp—have been reviled and criticized. Yet the Old West lives on, larger than life.

———◆◆◆———

It has become a symbol of freedom, when there was always another mountain to climb and another river to cross; when a dispute between two men was settled not with expensive lawyers, but with fists, knives, or guns. Barbaric? Maybe. But some things never change. When the cowboy rode into the pages of American history, he left behind a legacy that lives within the hearts of us all.

—*Ralph Compton*

CHAPTER ONE

"SIX GUNMEN," WYOMING Bob Jenks called at the top of his lungs. He thrust an arm high enough in the air to be sure every eye was on him. He need not have worried. The gathered crowd hardly let out a breath as it pressed closer, intent on the show. "Six men, all steely eyed and possessing nerves icier than the Yukon winter. Every last one of them is a marksman of the first water. They never miss. And they are all facing . . . Leif Johann Gunnarson, otherwise known throughout these great United States and across the vast Atlantic Ocean to all the crowned heads of Europe—"

Wyoming Bob paused again to build suspense.

"Known as Trickshot!"

A cheer went up from the crowd.

Leif Gunnarson strode out into the street, shoulders pulled back and chin held high. He wore a ten-gallon hat of the whitest felt. A ring of hammered Mexican silver conchas circled the crown. Wrapped around his right arm writhed a rattlesnake skin. The long rattles hung down and clicked ominously as he moved. Given enough whiskey, he'd tell the story of how he killed that western diamondback rattler, one shot through the mouth. His second shot tore the length of its body, skinning it so he could wrap the distinctively patterned hide around his arm. Leif halted in the middle of the street, hands resting on the butts of his matched pistols, etched elaborately and worth more than anyone in this miserable town would ever pay. As Wyoming Bob continued to laud his reputation, Leif whirled about. His bleached-white buckskin fringe made small snapping noises as he moved. A rehearsed movement with his six-shooter caused the fringe on his right arm to crack like a whip and the snake's rattles to underscore the deadly move.

This always brought the crowd around. Everyone stared at him now. He continued his slow advance into the center of the circle formed by the townspeople. His elaborately tooled boots, crafted by the finest boot maker in Mexico, kicked up delicate clouds of dust. With a practiced eye, Leif stopped where he could face off against the six anxious men at the far side of the ring. Not a one had the look of a real gunslinger. If he had to bet, one or two of them hadn't fired their six-shooter in a month of Sundays. The rest would be lucky not to shoot themselves in the foot—or wound the man standing next to them.

"Ladies and gentlemen, let's give him a royal greeting—the man known far and wide as Trickshot!"

Leif waited a moment, then raised both arms high over his head. This always brought huge cheers. It was no different now. In a way, he felt sorry for the citizens of this town, whose name he couldn't even remember. He was the biggest thing to have come through since the Fourth of July parade the month before. Their lives were dreary, and he was entertainment. Entertainment mixed with a hint of danger. The advance riders from Wyoming Bob's Wild West Show had whispered of the gunfights he had been in, the outlaws he had shot, the owlhoots he'd brought to justice with his accurate six-shooters.

He slowly lowered his arms and rested his hands on the hard leather holsters tied down at either hip. A small shrug of his shoulders produced a lightning draw. The etched silver Peacemakers seemed to appear in his grip as if by magic. Leif was fast and knew it, but he put extra effort into today's show. He wasn't certain why, but it gave the fine citizens something more to whisper about.

"Never seen faster." "Chain lightning!" "I swear the gun vanished from his holster and just showed up in his hand."

He had heard it all. And he enjoyed the adulation.

Leif slowly turned, the pistols leveled at the crowd. His blue eyes rivaled the Wyoming sky above for clarity, for brilliance, for just a touch of ice. As he made a complete turn, he studied the ladies in the crowd. It did no good to build a reputation, mostly fabricated out of whole cloth, if it served no purpose other than to bring customers in for the Wild West Show. Impressing the attractive young ladies made putting on the outrageous getup worthwhile. He had no idea why anyone believed his tall tales when he wore the white buckskins and towering hat and boots that hurt his feet because they were a size too small, but they did.

"Applaud your six gunslingers, daring all to call out Trickshot!" Wyoming Bob motioned. A couple roustabouts pushed a corridor through the crowd to reveal six whiskey bottles sitting on six water barrels. "Your champions, your paladins of the pistol, will each get a single shot in an attempt to break the bottle before them. It should be easy enough. One bottle, one bullet!"

Wyoming Bob herded the six men to a spot thirty feet from their targets. He made sure they were in a line and not too likely to kill one another. Making a sweeping gesture, he took off his hat and held it high.

"When I signal, you gents will draw and fire. Just one round. Only one or it's cheating!" He stirred a little breeze with his hat, then swept it downward.

The six men drew and fired. Leif watched to see if any of them really knew how to shoot. Out on the range, they had skill enough to chase off a coyote or bring down a rabbit. Nothing more.

He tried not to wince when they fired. The reports came as a ragged volley. Two of the bottles cracked and fell over. Four remained unscathed.

"Gentlemen, you killed two and scared the bejesus out of the other four!" Wyoming Bob waited for the guffaws from the men in the crowd and the tiny giggles hidden behind hands from the ladies. "Now you'll see how it's really done. Ladies and gentlemen, boys and girls, I give you the master marksman of the Americas . . . Trickshot."

Leif stepped forward and looked at the barrels, then shook his head.

"What? What's this? The legendary Trickshot is refusing to meet the challenge? I can't believe it. Is he admitting defeat to your town's finest gunmen?"

Leif waited for the shocked reaction. He knew how long to wait. He had seen the same disbelief and even contempt before a dozen times over. At precisely the right instant, he called out, "Twelve!"

"What? What are you saying, Trickshot?"

Wyoming Bob already had others from the show in motion to set up a full dozen old whiskey bottles, two on each of the barrels. Though empty of liquor, the bottles were filled with water.

"I'll shoot twelve, Wyoming Bob, but not from where they stood." Leif reached behind him, not even looking. One of the roustabouts dropped the reins to a snowy-white stallion into his hand. He spun about and easily vaulted into the saddle. With a tug on the reins, he got the powerful horse moving away from the targets.

"Wait, Trickshot—the bottles are over here!" Wyoming Bob pointed. Members of the Wild West Show began circulating through the crowd, taking bets. Putting on a free show was not in Bob Jenks's makeup. He'd rather wrestle a wildcat than let a single dime go uncollected.

Leif tapped his heels against the stallion's flanks and rocketed forward. He drew the six-gun on his left hip and shot across the saddle as the horse pounded along at a full gallop. Six times he shot. Six of the water-filled bottles exploded. The addition of the liquid made each hit look that much more spectacular.

He drew back on the reins. The white stallion dug in its heels, kicked up a cloud of dirt, then wheeled around. Leif drew the pistol on his right hip and, again firing across the saddle, took out the remaining six bottles. He returned his Peacemaker to its holster with a flourish and kicked free of the stirrups so he could stand on the saddle as White Lightning trotted back to the crowd. Hands aloft, Leif whipped off his hat and waved it about to loud cheers from everyone.

His practiced eyes watched the members of the Wild West Show as they raked in their bets. Leif knew within a dollar or two how much they had collected. This wasn't the richest town in Wyoming, certainly not as prosperous as Cheyenne, where they had spent an entire week, but he had earned Wyoming Bob enough to keep the show owner happy.

Happy and provisioned with bottles full of whiskey. Leif wondered how many of those bottles shattered dead center by his bullets had been drained by the show's owner.

He dropped into the saddle, then slid off to stand at the edge of the crowd. It took only a few seconds for his admirers to press close. He shook hands and boldly kissed the extended hand of a particularly pretty young lady. Her mother started to protest, so Leif moved on and planted a kiss on the top of another little girl's bonnet. This produced cheers, and the girl blushed and buried her face in her mother's skirts.

"Accept this trophy, madame," Leif said, reaching to his gun belt and drawing out a golden bullet. He handed it to the woman. Startled, she took it, then passed it to her daughter. By then Leif had winked broadly at the lovely lass whose hand he had kissed. He hoped he could make the woman's acquaintance later on, after she'd had a brief glimpse at the acts the Wild West Show would present in a couple nights. It was about all that kept the grinding routine of the show from driving him plumb loco. Even with feminine company . . .

"You really good, or was that some kinda sneaky trick?" The man asking caused Leif to stand a little straighter. Every now and then, he came across a real gunfighter. This one had the look. His rough clothing was dusty from the trail. The six-shooter slung in a cross-draw holster showed hard use and good care for all that. The way the gunman stood hid the handle of his six-gun. It wouldn't have surprised Leif to see a few notches carved into it.

From the man's attitude, any notches were likely to have been earned with a slower man's life. Leif wished he had taken time to reload. Even the golden bullet he had given the little girl's mother slipped into an empty chamber would have made him feel a mite easier. Both his pistols were empty.

"What do you mean by calling it a trick?"

"I've seen cheats before," the man said. He stroked a stubbled chin. His dark eyes never left Leif's. As if thinking on the matter, he added, "A man with a rifle some distance off can take out the bottle and make it look as if you're better than you claim." He cleared his throat, then hawked a dark gob into the dirt an inch in front of Leif's fancy boots.

"There wasn't any cheating going on," Leif said. "Why don't you come on out to the show this weekend and see for yourself? Lots of trick roping, fancy riding, and—"

"I can do all that. Where's the thrill?" He gave Leif a long, hard look from his toes to the white crown of the ten-gallon hat. The sneer told exactly what he thought of the goat-roping imitation cowboy. Leif didn't much care for it, but picking a fight with a killer was something he avoided. Men like this enjoyed watching death all around them, and, as quick and accurate as he was, Leif had never shot it out with another gunman. The notion of killing an opponent made him a bit queasy.

"I'll get you free tickets. You and—"

"You're not very good with those hoglegs, are you? You're all show and no go." The cowboy squared off, ready to go for his holstered pistol.

Leif had seen plenty of killers in his day. Gun handlers, men with sharp eyes and perfect aim. He'd avoided them all.

"You're right about one thing, mister. I shoot targets, not men." Leif was aware of the crowd gathering around him. Such an admission might destroy any box office the next day. Who wanted to see a gunslick and trickshot artist who confessed to being nothing more than a gussied-up actor?

"I'll shoot you for them two six-shooters of yours. I've taken a fancy to the etching. And they're .45s. All I got is a trusty Colt Navy." The man turned slightly to show the butt of his six-gun in its cross-draw holster. He twitched his hip just a little.

Leif hated himself for it, but he flinched, expecting the gunman's fist to fill up with the pistol's handle. He got a mocking laugh.

"Give me the guns since you ain't got any more

use for them." The man's tone came cold and level. He brooked no argument. He was going to take Leif's pistols and humiliate him in front of everyone in town. By now whispers rose to an almost audible level. Leif was sure everyone overhearing the exchange damned him for being a coward. But what was he to do? Was it worth someone—maybe him—dying over a set of fancy pistols?

"Now, you can't expect a master gunman like Trickshot here to bet *both* of his pieces," Wyoming Bob said, coming up and interposing himself between the two.

"Why not? He ain't intendin' on usin' them for anything worthwhile." The gunman tried to move around Wyoming Bob, but the ringmaster was a born showman. He cut him off and took control of the crowd.

"One pistol. That'll be the bet. You and the best marksman on this or any other continent will shoot it out. There, boys, over there. Set up more bottles. Lots of them. And make the range something worthy of our competitors!"

A cheer went up from the crowd. Leif watched the gunman closely. The man had blood in his eye and didn't cotton to being thwarted like this. The tenseness in his face changed as Leif studied every rut and cut on the tanned face. He went from a readiness to kill to a determination that approached plumb loco.

"There you gents are. Six bottles each, set on barrels all the way down the street. First one's only twenty feet off. The sixth bottle's sitting on a rain barrel close to a hundred feet away. Just getting close enough to scare that bottle a mite will take some fancy shooting." Wyoming Bob let the two adversaries take their places, side by side.

Leif stared down the impromptu range. If he took his time and aimed, this wasn't a difficult chore for him, but the rules were being made up as they went.

"You'll both draw at the signal, blaze away at your targets, and the first one to break all six of his bottles wins!"

"Both of his fancy guns," the man said.

"One of them," Bob Jenks countered. "Why, if you lose, you'll get a rematch. And if you win one of Trickshot's fine pieces of ordnance, you can try and take away his other sidearm."

The gunman started to object, but Wyoming Bob rattled on. "Saturday. Our grand finale, the two of you once more facing off." This brought a loud cheer from the crowd. Leif took the opportunity to reload both his six-shooters.

The man turned to Leif and said in a low voice, "I can humble you twice. Let's get this over with. I got some serious drinkin' to do tonight." He turned and squared off, his hand hanging at his right side. A small turn brought his cross-draw holster around a bit to the front.

Leif took a deep breath to settle his nerves. He had made shots like this repeatedly over the years. There wasn't a thing to worry over. This saddle tramp wasn't going to take one of his finely balanced matched pistols.

"Both of you turn this way now. This here little lady'll drop her hanky. When she does, you two spin around, go for your weapons, and fire away. May the best man win!" Wyoming Bob pushed a lovely girl toward them. She giggled, then took out a fancy lace handkerchief.

Leif thought the girl gave him a special smile, a tiny wink. He was a fraction of a second slow realizing it was a nervous tic. She released the bit of cloth to flutter down.

He spun and slapped leather. The gunman had already gotten off his first shot. The nearest bottle shattered. Leif whipped out his right-hand Peacemaker and began fanning the hammer. His first shot was dead-on, and his second and third raced downrange, ahead of his opponent. Then the air filled with gun smoke and hid the rest of the match until both of their six-shooters clicked on spent chambers.

A small breeze kicked up and blew away the white smoke, like drawing back a curtain. A gasp went up in the crowd.

All six of the gunman's target bottles were shattered. Leif had missed the final one.

"You've been bested, Trickshot. Bested right now." Wyoming Bob reached over and took the Peacemaker from his nerveless fingers. "You won fair and square, mister. Here's your prize. You can use it to try and win the matched pistol Saturday night!"

The gunman jeered. He cocked Leif's Peacemaker, aimed it between his defeated opponent's eyes, then sneered. He pulled the trigger. Even though Leif knew the hammer fell on a spent cartridge, he still flinched. This brought out a deep, nasty laugh. The man thrust the etched silver six-gun into his belt and walked off.

"Saturday evening, ladies and gents, in a mere three

nights. At the special weekend Wyoming Bob's Wild
West Show! See if Trickshot can regain his title as the
fastest, most accurate shooter on this or any other continent!"

The members of the crowd began drifting away,
murmuring about the rematch and how they had to
tell their neighbors about it. No one in town would
miss such a show. No one!

Wyoming Bob gripped Leif's arm, pulled him
close, and whispered, "That was about the finest lure
I ever did see, son. You're a natural. If I didn't know
better, I'd think you'd actually missed." The show
owner slapped him on the shoulder. "We've got three
days to sell tickets and make sure there's not a single
living soul in this hick town that won't be there.
Good. Good work, Gunnarson." Wyoming Bob went
off to corral his roustabouts and prepare the upcoming show.

Leif Johann Gunnarson stood alone in the street,
his right holster empty. That made the Peacemaker in
his left holster seem all the more burdensome. He
looked after the showman. His lips moved just a little
as he said to the rising wind, "He beat me fair and
square."

CHAPTER TWO

L EIF GUNNARSON USUALLY targeted the prettiest
  filly in the crowd after his exhibition, but not tonight. He stood alone in the center of the street, arms
like lead and his legs refusing to budge. Something
inside had gone along with his Peacemaker. He had
been working the crowds for a full ten years and had
gotten used to it, but this evening was different somehow. The thrill was missing from hearing the cheers
and gasps from the crowd. It was as if he had grown
old and tired of doing what he did best.

"You all right, Mr. Gunnarson?"

Leif turned slowly to face a short man with a han-
dlebar mustache and long greasy brown hair poking
out all around from under his floppy-brimmed felt
hat. His clothing was about what Leif expected from
someone in a nothing Wyoming town. When the man
pulled back his frock coat, a silver star pinned on his

vest gleamed in the fading light. Instinctively, Leif looked down at the man's sidearm. He carried it up high on his waist in a soft leather holster. If the marshal started drawing today, he might clear leather by noon tomorrow. This wasn't a man who expected to use that smoke wagon anytime soon—or at all.

"Just tired from a day on the trail," Leif lied. He had gotten plenty of sleep before they rolled into town sometime in the early afternoon.

"Reckon that explains why you got yourself whupped by the likes of Will Harding." The marshal looked a bit sheepish, then thrust out his hand. "I'm the law in Newell Bluff. Name's Phillip Denny, and it surely is an honor to meet up with you. I've heard your name mentioned for years."

"How's that? I've been traveling. The Continent, England, shows back East." Leif was slow on the uptake at the moment.

"Before I took the job here, I was deputy over in Cheyenne. Ten years back, it was. I heard about the tragedy that befell you and your family." The marshal put his hand on Leif's shoulder and steered him out of the middle of the street so a buckboard creaking under the weight of supplies could rattle past. "Why don't you come on over to the Merry Maid? That's only one of the half dozen saloons we got here in Newell Bluff, but for my money, it's the best. Ole the barkeep doesn't water down his whiskey like the rest do. And if you'll let me, I'd be privileged to buy you a drink."

The marshal's hand guided Leif in a way that was more insistent than friendly. Leif started to turn down the offer. That wasn't something Wyoming Bob would ever approve of. They had troubles enough with the law in many towns, the marshals wanting a cut of the gate as their due, their "business license fee" before the Wild West Show moved on. Leif thought some money ought to stay in the town where the show garnered revenue from tickets—and gambling. Leaving behind ill feelings and empty pockets wasn't good for a return engagement, not that Wyoming Bob sought to return to any but the biggest cities.

There was only so much blood even a master showman like him could squeeze out of the small towns.

"Yes, sir, you're quite the gun handler. I was mighty impressed." Marshal Denny steered him up the steps of the saloon, hardly more than a shack. The door was a dangling tattered strip of canvas to be pushed aside, and the bar that ran the length of the narrow saloon was nothing more than a rough plank balanced on sawhorses. The dirt floor was more mud than solid in places where beer and probably blood had been spilled. The brass spittoons were the only thing Leif saw that the Merry Maid had going for it. They were polished so bright that the dim light reflecting off them from the coal oil lamps was almost painful. In the sunlight, they'd have burned holes in his eyes.

"Ole, bring over a bottle for me and my good friend here, Mr. Gunnarson."

"The sharpshooter, eh?" The heavyset blond barkeep hitched up his canvas apron, grabbed a half bottle of whiskey and two shot glasses. With agility surprising in one so corpulent, he ducked under the bar and came over. "Set yourselves down anywhere."

Leif looked around. The tiny saloon was full. That didn't deter the bartender. He walked to the nearest table, hooked a booted toe around the back leg of a chair, and kicked out. The chair upended and dumped the drunk onto the packed-dirt floor.

"This suit you, Marshal?"

Phillip Denny nodded once, righted the chair, stepped over the drunk, and settled down. He pointed to a chair across the beer-stained table. Leif sat, wondering if the lawman only wanted to soak up reflected glory or had something more on his mind. Considering the outcome of the match with—what was the name?—Will Harding, and the way he'd gotten his ass whipped when he'd intended to win, there was barely any fame to share.

"Yes, sir, I heard you'd left the territory after . . . after the slaughter." The marshal fixed muddy-brown eyes on Leif. Those cow eyes should have been reassuring and peaceable. Leif felt under such scrutiny that he wanted to cry out.

"How is it you know about my family, Marshal?"

"Call me Phil. My friends all do, and it'd please me to count you among them." The marshal cleared his throat, then proceeded to hawk a gob in the direction of a shiny spittoon. He missed by a foot and contributed to the muddy floor.

"Thanks for the confidence, Phil. How is it you know about me?"

"I was deputy to Marshal Beltrane back then. It never seemed right the way he ignored what I thought was real obvious murder and arson. And maybe kidnapping. Did you ever find your sisters?"

The emptiness grew in his heart. Leif sometimes went weeks without thinking of his lost sisters, but depression always ground down hard on him when something reminded him of what he'd lost.

"I found Flora and Daisy, but Petunia vanished without a trace."

"Dead?" The marshal scooted his chair a little closer to pour a shot of whiskey for himself and Leif. He downed his drink and poured another, waiting for Leif to sample the tarantula juice. Leif did, hardly tasting it. The marshal refilled his glass and leaned forward, elbows pressed hard onto the table.

"Both my younger sisters. They had their throats slit." His mouth turned dry. "I never found Petunia."

"Could never understand why Beltrane never wanted to track them down. I never heard you'd found your sisters. Well, two of them. You think Petunia's dead, too?"

"She was close to seven years older than I was and knew how to take care of herself. I still hope she's out there somewhere, but chances are better that I never found her body." Leif knocked back a shot. Denny immediately refilled the glass. "Not like I found my ma and pa."

"They burned up in the fire. Marshal Beltrane said a lamp got knocked over and they couldn't get out. How'd you survive? You were inside the house, weren't you?"

The saloon disappeared around Leif, replaced with a ghostly image of his family home's kitchen. His ma and pa were tied to chairs, facing each other. They'd been tortured and then choked with strands of barbed wire. Leif had arrived at the house already on fire, had dashed in and found them. His mother was gruesomely dead. His pa was barely alive and had croaked out a single name: Simkins. Before Leif could unwind the fang wire from his pa's neck, the second floor collapsed, forcing him to seek refuge in the root cellar below the house or die trying to escape. Leif lost all track of time huddling in the cellar, a fifteen-year-old terrified for his own life and haunted by the tableau of his murdered parents.

Nearby neighbors had come to put out the fire. He had crawled from his refuge. Shock had deepened when Marshal Beltrane declared that the elder Gunnarsons had died in the fire one of them had started by accident. Arguing with the lawman had done no good. Beltrane hadn't even sent out a search party to find the three Gunnarson girls. He'd claimed they had run off in fright and would return on their own.

Leif had found two of them less than a mile away later that day. Before he had a chance to hunt more for his third, older sister, he had been hurried off to an orphanage by the sitting judge in Cheyenne. His pa had been a powerful, prominent attorney and often locked legal horns with the judge. As soon as Leif was sent off to the Black Hills Orphanage outside Cheyenne, the judge had sold all the Gunnarson property to a rancher who had craved to buy the spread but had been turned down repeatedly by the elder Gunnarson.

"Simkins," Leif said.

"How's that? Somebody named Simkins rescued you?" Surprise caused the marshal's long mustache to buck up and down.

"My pa named Simkins as the one who killed him and my ma and likely my sisters."

"That's a coincidence," Denny said, frowning in thought. "You remember Cable Crane? Crane's the one who bought your pa's spread for a real good price. I seem to remember him having a gent by the name of

Luther Simkins in his employ. Yes, sir, that's quite a coincidence." Denny's words said one thing; his eyes said another.

"Last I heard, about the time I left Wyoming, Simkins had moved on. I tried running him down for what he did to my family, but he's a slippery character."

"The Simkins gang cut quite a wide swath back then," Denny said. "Train robbery, more than one stagecoach holdup, thievery like that. Nobody could get close to catching him and his gang. I never saw Marshal Beltrane put much effort into running down those outlaws, either. He said his job keeping the peace in Cheyenne was hard enough. It likely was. We had freighters coming through all the time, raising Cain and keeping us jumping."

"When did you leave Cheyenne?"

"Well now, I took a job as town marshal here in Newell Bluff a month or two after your family was killed. I heard now and again about goings-on in Cheyenne, but my interest waned. I do remember hearing you hightailed it from the orphanage. I reckon you turned out all right, you being Trickshot and all."

Leif hadn't spent a week in the orphanage before sneaking off in the night. His intent had been to find Petunia. He had spun tall tales about finding her and the two of them avenging the rest of the family's deaths. A week of almost freezing, starving, and not being sure what direction he headed had sapped his determination. Wyoming Bob's Wild West Show had given him a needed refuge. He'd worked hard and recovered some of his determination. The sharpshooter traveling with Wyoming Bob at the time had been flattered the itinerant young lad had followed him around so adoringly. Leif Gunnarson quickly learned the trade and had become better than his teacher.

He thought Wyoming Bob had sent the sharp-shooter packing, probably because of his drunken rages, but it was as likely that Leif afforded a cheaper alternative. Moreover, by the time he was twenty-one, he was a handsome young man who drew appreciative gazes from the ladies. Their money for admission tickets was as good as for any saddle bum cowboy—and they were more inclined to see the show a second or third time because of the better-looking blond gun handler.

"I found a place that'd take me." Leif sucked in a deep breath and held it. He had drunk too much too fast. That was what the marshal wanted. This slowly sank in through the whiskey fog. He pushed away another full shot and fixed his gaze on the marshal. "What is it you want from me?"

"What I said. You're quite a celebrity, and you're almost a local boy. It's not more than a week's worth of travel, if you ride hard, to get to Cheyenne." Denny sampled his own whiskey, as if getting up some Dutch courage. "You're right, though. I wanted to be sure it was really you."

"What do you mean? Of course it's me." Leif let the man's words soak in. "You wanted to be sure I was the boy who found his parents and lost his sisters? Why?"

"I don't want you taking the law into your own hands, but there's good evidence that Luther Simkins has moved back into the territory. He was gone for years. Most folks thought he was dead. I never did, but it hardly mattered."

"Has he been seen?" Leif sobered fast.

"Nobody I'd trust, mind you, but Will Harding's rumored to ride with that gang."

"There's more, isn't there? You'd never ply me with liquor otherwise." Leif tapped the shot glass on the table, spilling a few drops. He resisted the urge to knock back the contents. Whatever more Marshal Denny had to say was important—suddenly important after a decade.

"Let's say I saw your folks' bodies. Burned, as you'd expect. But Beltrane blew up when I asked about the barbed wire nooses. He accused me of drinking on duty. That's something I never did." Denny hiccupped. "Not then, not when I was a deputy."

"You knew they'd been murdered? How'd you come to think Simkins was responsible?"

"Simkins made no secret of his crimes. And it wasn't much of a secret that Beltrane took a wad of greenbacks under the table from Cable Crane. Simkins worked for Crane doing odd jobs, if you catch my meaning."

"You afraid I'll go after Crane?" This wasn't anything he hadn't considered over long, cold nights.

"Crane died six years back, or so I heard from a Wells Fargo driver that makes the run 'tween here and Cheyenne. Got kicked in the head by a horse he was trying to break. From the sound of it, that was the only decent thing that bronco ever did." Denny licked the rim of his shot glass, then poured himself another. His hand was a trifle shaky now from so much liquor in such a short time. "Look, Mr. Gunnarson, I had to be sure you were who I thought you were before I revealed all my suspicions about Harding and his connection to Simkins."

"You want me to do your job for you?" Leif's hand twitched and rested on the Peacemaker on his left hip. He didn't need both six-shooters to take on the likes of Harding. The man had outshot him, but next time it'd be different. He had the motivation now that he knew Harding rode with that murderous snake Luther Simkins.

Or so said the marshal in a Podunk town. Leif knew better than to take any man's words as gospel. For all he knew, Denny had a bone to pick with Harding and saw a way of getting revenge without drawing his own pistol. The way he carried it so high on his hip showed he wasn't gun sharp enough to use it. Even if he was as good a shot as Harding, Denny would be slower than molasses pulling it out. While there were ways around that, maybe he wasn't up to shooting Harding in the back.

"Not that. Nobody upholds the law in Newell Bluff but me. I wanted to check some facts with you before I said my piece."

Leif waited. When the marshal told him the rest of his story, he went cold all over.

CHAPTER THREE

I T'S NOT MUCH, but it's better than trying to live in the shed behind her house, what's left of it," Marshal Phillip Denny said. He wiped his mouth and was a little unsteady on his feet.

Leif hadn't downed anywhere near as much whiskey, and he was sharp. The cold night breeze whipping down from the Tetons gave him goose bumps. Or was it anticipation of talking to the woman? Denny had built up the story to the point that Leif was both excited and scared that his tale sounded eerily close to his past. The marshal hadn't shown much inclination to spin tall tales, but Leif didn't know him. The man had displayed a certain level of cunning the way he had sidled up and claimed to be a fan of his, of Trickshot. But it carried the ring of sincerity with every word.

The marshal wasn't the bravest lawman who ever

pinned on a badge, but he kept the peace in Newell Bluff. If five hundred people lived within ten miles of the city limits, it would be a surprise. The marshal's big chore was dragging dead animals off the streets—that and maybe locking up a few drunk cowboys on Saturday night, sobering them enough for church service on Sunday morning, and . . . nothing else.

Leif stared at the tumbledown shack. The door had been propped up because the hinges were pulled free from the jamb. Some planks in the wall showed gaps big enough for him to run his fingers along. From inside came the wan glow of a guttering candle. The light sneaking past the wall planks caused crazy shadows to dance on the ground near the shack.

"Come on along," Denny said. "You're not losing your nerve, are you?"

Leif silently followed the marshal to the door. Denny didn't knock. If he had, the door might have broken under his knuckles. Instead, he called out, "You decent, Miss Esquivel? It's me, Marshal Denny. I got somebody here who wants to talk to you."

"Go away." The voice from inside was muffled, perhaps choked with emotion. "There is nothing anyone can do."

"If anyone can help you out, it's this fellow. His name's, uh . . ."

"I'm Leif Johann Gunnarson, Miss Esquivel. From what the marshal's told me, we got something in common."

"What? Your family was murdered cruelly?" The woman's voice cracked with emotion now. She began sobbing.

"Yes," Leif said. He glanced at Denny. The marshal gripped the door and moved it to the side, revealing the single room inside. Rough-hewn planks had been put down to form a crude floor. From the way they shifted when the small woman came to the door, they weren't nailed down.

He wasn't able to make out her face with the candle guttering behind her on a low table. A single tin plate and cup had been pushed to the center, showing she had barely eaten dinner. The aroma of beans filled the small room and made Leif's mouth water. It reminded him that he had missed eating since noontime. With the load of liquor sloshing around in his gut, he needed food, but seeing the distraught woman made him forget that quickly.

As he and the marshal stepped into the shack, she turned enough so he got a look at her face. Long black hair pulled back in a severe bun did nothing for her looks. Tears caked her dusty cheeks, and her dark eyes were sunken pits. Even if her attitude didn't show it, her expression told of suffering and despair.

"Please, sit. Be careful. The chair is wobbly." She managed a small weak smile.

Leif settled down in it. She wasn't lying. He tried not to move about nervously, fearing the legs would collapse and dump him onto the flooring. Denny settled on the bed. Tiny bugs scampered away from under the thin blanket and vanished through the walls.

"Tell Mr. Gunnarson what happened to your family, Miss Esquivel."

"It has been almost a week, and it is still like a knife in my heart." She seemed to collapse within herself and become even smaller. Leif started to reach out to her, then checked himself. She wanted to disappear, not to be held in this world.

"Your ma and pa were murdered," he said. "Strangled with barbed wire nooses."

"The marshal, he told you this?" She looked at him. Fire came into her dark eyes, showing her soul had not been completely crushed.

"No," Leif said. "All he told me was that your parents died the same way mine did ten years ago. And then your house was set on fire."

Her head bobbed.

"My pa lived long enough to tell me Simkins did the crime."

She perked up at this. She started pacing, though she could take only a pair of steps before having to retrace her path.

"I had no name to put to the terrible man who did this," she said. "You have given me hope. Marshal, will you—?"

"Tell him the rest, Miss Esquivel." Denny sounded apologetic. Leif realized why when the woman spoke.

"I came back to find my *padre y madre* dead and the house on fire. And Consuela was gone."

"Your sister?" Leif half stood. "My three sisters were also . . . gone," he finished lamely. He had almost blurted out that they were murdered, too. If she hadn't located her sister, a chance, though a slim one, remained that Consuela was not dead. The idea that Consuela was murdered like their parents had to be foremost in her mind.

"So?" She looked at him with fear-bright eyes.

"The same men are responsible? The ones who killed my family also killed yours?"

"Well, Miss Esquivel, it's looking that way," Marshal Denny cut in. "I've heard from others how Luther Simkins might be the son of a—" He stopped and cleared his throat. "Luther Simkins might be responsible. There's a reward already on his head."

"You are the law. You must bring him to justice, or God will. But chasing this ghost of a man wastes time now when there is something more important. Can you get my sister back? Can you find her?" She looked from Denny to Leif.

"The reward ought to bring in news from folks spotting him and his gang. It takes time, but he can't hide forever." The marshal looked uncomfortable at the woman's growing anger and impatience.

"I agree with her, Marshal," Leif said. "When I tried to track him down, he had hideouts where he was able to just vanish. You need to get a posse out after him."

Denny had reached the end of his patience and snapped, "Don't you go tellin' me how to do my job. I know how serious this is, but Simkins is a special case and needs special consideration." He settled down a mite.

"My sister—" Marta Esquivel started. Denny cut her off with a dismissive shake of his head.

"We're going to try our best to bring him to justice and look around for her. You rest up now, Miss Esquivel. Me and Mr. Gunnarson'll go now. If we find anything, I'll let you know first off."

"So? This is what you will do?" She glared at the

marshal, then turned and said, "Thank you, Mr. Gunnarson. I see that *you* share my urgency." She came around the table and clung to him. Leif felt her hot tears soaking into his fancy ruffled shirt. He disengaged her and gently pushed her down into the chair he had vacated with a pat on the shoulder.

He and Denny edged out of the shack. Once they were in the cool night, wind evaporated the woman's tears and left a cold spot over his heart.

"Where's the Esquivel house?"

Denny looked at him out of the corner of his eye, pursed his lips, then nodded slowly. "I was right that you'd be interested. You want to start at the house?"

"Where else?" Leif's mind raced. The only other possible thread to tug at, a thread he hoped ran back to Luther Simkins, was Will Harding.

"It's up to you. I got a town to watch over." Denny sounded glad to wash his hands of the crimes laid at Simkins's feet.

"You can't arrest anyone outside Newell Bluff," Leif said. He had seen men like Phillip Denny before. In a way, Wyoming Bob was the same. They talked big and got others to do the work for them. Leif had no doubt that if he brought Simkins and his gang to justice, the marshal would take credit.

He didn't care. If he found Luther Simkins, there wasn't going to be a need for a judge, jury, and trial. Marshal Denny wouldn't have to lock up any of the outlaws or feed them in his jailhouse. Leif's fast hands and accurate shots would bring down the men who had murdered his family. He sucked in a deep breath and exhaled slowly. Vengeance would be his, for both his family and that of Miss Esquivel.

* * *

L EIF JOHANN GUNNARSON sat astride his stallion,
White Lightning, and stared at the burned black
pile that had been the Esquivel house. The construc-
tion surprised him. He had expected brick or perhaps
adobe. It had been wood frame, and there wasn't a
single wall standing unscorched.

He blinked hard. For a moment, tears blurred his
vision, and he saw a different house—his family's
home outside Cheyenne.

"Marta," Denny said unexpectedly.

"What's that?" Leif forced himself to look away
from the destruction. A barn remained standing, but
a shed a few yards from the house had been destroyed. In the dark, he made out a shadowy out-
house. The door hung on one hinge.

"Her name's Marta. Marta Esquivel. You never
asked, but I saw the question was eating away at you."
Denny laughed easily. "She's a whole lot more so-
ciable when she's not mourning. Her pa had to ride
herd on her to keep the suitors away. He intended to
marry her away to someone with a big spread and
give her a good future."

"How long?" Leif rode forward slowly. The embers were long extinguished. "When was the house
burned down?" He drew rein and stared. Out by the
cottonwood tree growing near the shed were two
mounds of dirt. The older Esquivels, or what was left
of them, had been buried on their property. He had
seen how awful burned corpses looked.

"Been close to four days."

"You examined the bodies?"

Denny was silent for a moment, then said in a small voice, "I did. There wasn't a question how they died." He pantomimed being hanged.

Leif rode in a wide circle around the house, getting the lay of the land. The darkness kept real details hidden and secret, but a gut feeling grew. He stopped and looked toward the dark hills in the distance.

"That where you reckon they went after they done their . . . dirty work?" Denny edged up beside him. "You going after them now?"

"I'm not taking the chance they hightail it now. I've got a couple days before the show. If I can't find them before the show, I'll have another chance to find them if Harding shows his face." He wondered if he would abandon Wyoming Bob and the show if he actually found the outlaws' trail. His right hand touched the empty holster at his side. Only one six-gun was needed to bring Simkins and his henchmen to heel. Either hand proved deadly. Once upon a time, a German professor had called him ambidextrous. Leif liked the sound of that, but he enjoyed being able to handle two six-shooters at the same time using both hands.

"I wish you luck, Mr. Gunnarson. If anybody's deserving of catching them varmints, it's you." Denny spat. "And you got the skill to outshoot the lot of them. Except maybe for Harding."

"He bested me once. There won't be a second time." Leif wished he had changed into trail clothes, because the bleached-white buckskins made him stand out like a sore thumb. A tap of his reins sent White Lightning walking toward the distant hills.

After Simkins had killed his ma and pa, he had

found his dead sisters off in the direction of the low hills. Leif doubted the outlaw changed his tactics. He had learned from traveling in the Wild West Show that the performers were loath to vary their act once they learned it. Even if the crowds demanded something more, the performers resisted. That was what made Leif so different. Over ten years, he had practiced constantly and innovated. Watching other marksmen had given him ideas. The crack shot Captain Adam Bogardus had shown him new ways to captivate the paying customers' attention. He had learned even more showmanship from Annie Oakley, perhaps the finest gun handler he'd ever seen.

The accuracy and speed that were his own special gifts would be put to the test. He felt it.

Leif rode steadily, finding a narrow path leading into the hills. Assuming the gang had come this way, he dropped down more than once to hunt for hoof-prints but found nothing. There had been a light rain since the murders. He found old piles of horse drop-pings and estimated four or five horses had left so much behind. How long ago they had been there was something he couldn't determine. He was a gun han-dler, not a trailsman.

He slipped his Peacemaker from its holster and checked to be sure he carried rounds in all six cham-bers. With a quick motion, he spun the weapon around and sent it back into his holster. He rested his left hand on the butt, considered moving it to his right holster, and then decided against doing it. The six-shooters were always kept in the same holsters and had worn distinctive outlines in the hard leather. The left Peacemaker wouldn't sit securely in the right holster. He depended on everything being comfortable when he threw down.

If he even found anyone.

He began climbing into the hills, choosing to walk and let his horse rest a spell. Not being mounted also removed the shining white of his buckskins from his elevated position. White Lightning was enough of a target, so white he almost glowed in the moonlight. Leif patted the horse's neck as the trail turned steeper. They wended their way back and forth between increasingly large boulders until Leif was panting from exertion.

"Let's take a rest, old fellow." Leif settled on a rock and caught his breath. He stared up into the night sky, following the constellations. The one in the southern sky that looked like a scorpion drew his attention. "Sting like a scorpion. That's what I have to do."

He started to stand, then froze. Turning slowly, he homed in on the sound of horses' whinnying. The sound came from farther uphill. At first, he wasn't sure he'd actually heard anything, but then came loud neighing and the sound of hooves clacking against rock. More than one horse was ahead.

He secured White Lightning's reins, then hiked up the trail another two hundred yards. The trail suddenly opened onto a sandy spit where two campfires had burned down. Off to one side, a rope stretched between two gnarled, stunted trees had five sets of reins fastened to it, forming a crude corral. Leif stood stock-still and studied the camp. Dark lumps hinted at sleeping men covered with blankets.

Four. But there were five horses. He continued to

study the way the camp was laid out. It was like the one he'd discovered when he'd tracked down Luther Simkins ten years before. There were three ways out of the sandy spit, giving the outlaws plenty of directions to escape. Then he saw a fifth shadowy figure. This one was huddled in a crevice. He made out long hair dangling down over drawn-up knees. He silently circled the camp and stopped a yard away from the crevice.

A girl looked up, eyes so black and hidden in darkness, they might have been burned out with only charred sockets left behind. She lifted a drawn face to him. He pressed his right forefinger to his lips to silence her. There wasn't any reaction. Leif could only imagine the horrors she'd seen beyond her parents' murders.

"Consuela? Your sister sent me. Marta."

There wasn't any reaction. He feared she was injured; then she stretched out her legs and pressed her hands into the sides of the crevice. She moved slowly and with some reluctance, but he saw nothing to hint that she was injured.

"Can you stand? We'll take their horses and get out of here."

"Are you one of them?" She pointed an accusing finger toward the four men near the dead campfires.

"Your sister sent me to take you back. Marta's worried about you."

"Marta?" She shook her head as if she couldn't believe it. For a moment, Leif worried this was someone else the gang had taken hostage. It didn't matter. She wasn't here of her own free will. He had to get her out of there. After he got her away, if she wasn't

Consuela Esquivel, she must have information he could use to find Marta's sister.

"Stand up. Come on." He motioned to her.

Leif saw her eyes dart toward the sleeping men. Or men who had been sleeping. One had stirred and overheard the rescue attempt.

Leif spun, went into a gunfighter's crouch, slapped leather, and drew his six-gun. Holding it firmly in his left hand, he fanned off two rounds using his right hand. Trickshot was fast. Trickshot didn't miss. The outlaw straightened, cried out, and triggered the six-shooter he had drawn from his gear. He fell back and sat heavily in the dead fire.

Leif's third shot snapped his foe's head back. The owlhoot flopped flat on his back. But by now, the other three had come awake. One grabbed his rifle. The other two filled the air with lead from their six-guns. Leif dropped to his knees and took his time firing. The fourth shot drilled deep into the second outlaw's chest, knocking him down. The fifth shot spun another outlaw about.

Leif cursed. He used his final shot on the third outlaw, making sure there'd be no more fight. But the fourth man fired one round after another from his rifle. His shots went wide and wild, forcing Leif to flop belly down.

"Consuela, the horses. Go to the horses!"

The girl stepped over him and walked as if in a trance. Leif rolled onto his back, fumbling for bullets held in leather loops on his gun belt. Dexterously pulling two out, he rolled again onto his belly. He snapped open the gate and ejected two spent rounds. He shoved the two live bullets in. He had to make them count, but he had practiced so many hours, he was up for the task.

Even more, he had run to ground the Simkins gang. After ten years, he had found the men who had killed his family. That they had kidnapped Consuela Esquivel proved their guilt. He rested the butt on the ground and looked around the spit.

The outlaw had disappeared. Leif rose to his knees and squinted, the moonlight concentrated a little more when he did so. Nowhere did he see the outlaw. Then horses protested. He whirled around, knees grinding into the sand. He couldn't make out the outlaw. Worse, he had lost sight of Consuela.

Then he had to worry about saving himself as three horses reared and pawed the air above him. Hooves crashed down around him. He was forced back into the rocky crevice where the girl had been imprisoned. Ducking and weaving around, he tried to see past the angry, bucking horses. When he did, his heart sank.

Consuela and the last outlaw had vanished.

CHAPTER FOUR

T HE FIRST THING he did was reload his Peacemaker. Leif had developed some fancy ways of
tossing the cartridges in the air, snaring them, and
thrusting them home to make reloading in front of a
crowd entertaining. He did this now despite the absence
of a crowd. The dead bodies on the ground around
the campfires weren't appreciative of his dexterity. Leif
slid the sixth bullet home, closed the gate, and spun
the pistol around. It slid easily into his holster. Then
he circled the camp, collecting fallen six-shooters and
a rifle.

"Never leave a gun behind," he said to himself. He
checked the bodies for ammunition and took what fit
his weapons. One Smith & Wesson seemed to be in
good enough shape for him to use. It went into his
empty right holster. With the rifle, he felt ready to
whip his weight in wildcats.

He trooped back down the trail to where he'd tethered White Lightning. The horse tugged hard at the reins and snorted before pawing at the ground.

"Sorry, old friend. No apples or carrots. After we get back to town. I promise." He swung into the saddle, settled down, and began his continued quest to rescue Consuela Esquivel. For all his quick reflexes and sharp eye, his fast trigger finger and deadly aim, Leif knew better than to rush ahead blindly. The outlaw had a hostage, but he was more inclined to lie in wait to ambush the man who had killed his partners.

Leif rode through the sandy spit. White Lightning did a little crow-hopping when he scented the spilled blood. His rider kept him moving and onto the narrow dirt track leading higher into the hills. The moon was beginning to sink in the west and cast long, dim shadows. He tried to make out hoofprints, but the ground was too hard. The biggest worry he had was how he rode through a rocky chute that could become a shooting gallery. Before he had to deal with exchanging gunfire in such a stone coffin, the trail stretched out around the mountain rather than continuing upward.

He picked up the pace. It would be dawn soon enough, and he would have the sun in his eyes. The nature of the rock began to change. Here and there he saw cascades from above that weren't natural. Although he couldn't see them, he suspected mines dotted the upper slopes. What he edged around on the trail were tailings that had finally washed down from higher elevations.

The sound of horses ahead caused him to reach for his Peacemaker. He rounded a boulder and whipped out his six-gun. Leif had it cocked and aimed but held off firing. Consuela rode behind the outlaw. Shooting past her in the dim moonlight would endanger her life. He would have had confidence in making the shot if there'd been enough light. If only she saw him and knew to slide off the horse's rump so he could take a clear shot.

The kidnapper turned to begin a steep uphill climb. Leif took aim. He had the man's profile in his sights. Then he lost his target when Consuela leaned forward. Her wrists were tied together, and her arms circled the outlaw's waist. Even if she had seen him, she was pinned astride the horse unless she took her captor along in a futile escape attempt.

"Let the girl go, and I won't kill you!" Leif's command rang out, loud and strong.

The outlaw jerked around, took a second to find the man on his trail, and then bent low to give as small a target as possible.

"You hightail it, and I won't harm her. You . . . you killed my partners. I'll forget that if you leave now." The outlaw's voice was shrill with fear. That fear made him even more dangerous.

Leif had to separate Consuela from her bonds before anything more could be done.

"There's nowhere to run. Give up. You'll get a better deal from the town marshal than from me if you try to run. And harm the girl and I'll leave your stinking corpse for the buzzards, if they'll have it after I fill you with lead."

"Go away!"

Leif edged closer. The outlaw worked his way up the steep trail. A broken sign proclaimed this to be the trail leading to the Gold Heart Mine. The lack of recent traffic along this dirt track told Leif the mine was long since abandoned. Other, bigger roads might stretch along the mountainside, but he had a sense that years back, the entire area had seen a boom and was now in decline.

"Go!" The outlaw drew his six-shooter and fired wildly. The bullets went wide when his horse reared and Consuela jerked around to spoil his aim. The outlaw elbowed her in the face, tried to get off a better shot at Leif, and finally forced his struggling horse uphill.

Leif reached the trail to the abandoned mine and took careful aim. If the owlhoot showed so much as a hair, he'd be dead. With Consuela tied behind him, he had a perfect shield guaranteed to stay Leif's shot. They finally rounded a boulder and disappeared.

He could ride after the man and his captive, but Leif didn't want to expose White Lightning to gunfire. Hopping to the ground, he secured the reins, drew the rifle, and started up the trail on foot. The rifle weighed him down, but he resisted the urge to use it as a walking stick. Stones turned under his fancy boots, making a clatter that worried him. So much noise drew attention and gave away his progress.

Try as he might, Leif couldn't walk along any more quietly. He stopped trying to be stealthy and opted to hurry as fast as possible. If he ran the outlaw down before he had time to hunker down in a natural rock fortress, he could rescue the girl and be halfway back to Newell Bluff by noon.

Leif snapped off a rifle shot when he saw the outlaw's back. The man was pushing Consuela into the mine, intending to make his stand from inside. The bullet spanged off a rocky wall and whistled away into the mine shaft, but Leif had done nothing but make the man scamper along even faster. His one chance to end the kidnapping had failed.

"You won't ever get her back," the outlaw shouted. "I'll kill her before it comes to that. You turn around and get out of here. Do it now, and she won't get hurt."

Leif ignored the threat. With men such as this, with the cutthroats who rode with Luther Simkins, promises meant nothing. Consuela's life was only a bargaining chip. Making his way closer to the mine proved dangerous. The outlaw laid down a hail of lead, and Leif wasn't able to even see the man's hat. He had sought refuge in the mine and had found it, much to Leif's disgust.

He should have been quicker back at the sandy spit. If he had ended this foul kidnapper's life then, Consuela would be safe and sound. Leif settled down and drew a bead on the mouth of the mine. He had learned how to relax to get the best shot, but now he felt tenseness in his shoulders and arms. Hitting a bull's-eye or bottle filled with water was spectacular, but usually no one's life rode on the shot. It did now. If he made any mistakes, Consuela would die.

Like his sisters. Like his parents. Like the Esquivel family. He had the chance to right a terrible series of crimes. Failure meant more than missing a target to the crowd's displeasure.

"Did you kill her parents?" Leif shouted. "Were you responsible for strangling them and burning their house to the ground?" He didn't care if the man answered. Guilt wasn't in question. Leif wanted a shot he could take.

Movement. He forced himself to relax so he wouldn't jerk the trigger and miss. Leif was glad he controlled his instincts to fire. The outlaw had pushed Consuela up to draw his fire. A lesser man would have shot at the first sign of movement and killed the hostage.

"Hiding behind her skirts won't save you," Leif called. "Did you ride with Luther Simkins ten years ago? How many people have you murdered by strangling them and then burning down their houses? Do you like doing that?"

Leif judged angles and distances. From this spot, he had only a limited cone of fire. He moved to his right. This gave a smaller target in the mouth of the mine but better visibility along the ground leading to the shaft. Mounds of dross gave some protection to anyone hiding inside the mine, but Leif eliminated some of that advantage with the new angle.

He tensed and forced himself to relax again. Once more, the kidnapper tried to gull him into firing at Consuela. That trick hadn't worked either time, but Leif hoped the man tried a third time. Consuela might wrest herself free and dash down the slope. Once that happened, Leif could fill the mine with a hail of bullets until one had to hit the outlaw.

"What are you talking about? I only been with Simkins for a few months. Ten years? That's a powerful long time."

"Ten years, ten minutes, you're still a killer and will pay for it."

"I've had enough of this," the outlaw cried. "You

leave now, or I'll plug this girl. I don't want to, but you're wearing on my nerves something fierce."

Consuela sobbed when the outlaw shoved her forward. She stood a few feet in front of the mouth of the mine, head down and her body racked by sobs. Leif willed her to drop, to run, to get away from the man with a gun pointed at her. She didn't budge. He slid back down the hill a few paces and got a different view. Consuela couldn't run. She was securely tied to the rusted iron ore cart tracks.

Seeing the tracks got Leif thinking, calculating angles and distances and the bullets he had in the rifle. He laid the rifle aside and slid his Peacemaker from its holster, then switched to his right hand. This required the utmost accuracy. Using his trusty six-gun with bullets of known quality in it went a ways toward making the shot possible.

He settled himself and sighted at the girl's feet. She half turned to plead with her captor. This gave Leif his chance. The outlaw rose just a little. Leif's finger drew back on the trigger. The pistol spat its precious bullet outward to smash into the iron ore cart track. The lead left a bright streak as it ran along the track straight back to the outlaw's foot. The man yelped and fell forward.

Leif stood but didn't bother sighting along the pistol barrel. This was an easy shot now. The outlaw had been wounded in the foot, surprised when a bullet tore through his boot. That made him careless, because what man could make the next shot?

Leif Johann Gunnarson drew back on the trigger. The killing shot hit the outlaw in the cheek and drove into his head. As if everything moved in cold molasses, the kidnapper's head snapped back so he seemed to be looking up into the faint dawn lighting the distant sky. Like a screw turning, he pivoted around until his back was to Leif. There was no call to send another bullet winging toward its target.

Trickshot pulled the trigger anyway. The man deserved to be hanged, but it was long past time when such justice could be meted out. The outlaw slumped across the tracks, his face pressing into the bright silver scar on the iron that had set his death into motion.

Leif scrambled up the hill to where Consuela still stood, sobbing.

"He won't bother you anymore," he said lamely. No matter what words rattled about in his head, whatever came out would sound weak and wouldn't be what the girl wanted to hear.

"He . . . he . . . the others . . . ," Consuela cried openly now.

Not knowing what else to do, Leif held out his Peacemaker. She reached for it, then drew back and shook her head.

"He's dead. Shooting him again won't do a thing." She looked up at him, her dark eyes bloodshot and rimmed with new tears. "Thank you."

Leif had no words. If there had been the opportunity, he would have saved his own sisters from Luther Simkins. That had been denied him, but somehow killing this man—was he even in Simkins's gang?—did nothing to sate his bloodlust.

"He's alive!" Consuela jumped back, came to the end of her tether, and fell heavily.

Leif swung his Peacemaker around, ready to fire.

He doubted the man was actually alive. He was like a snake that never stopped wiggling until sundown. Only this snake in human form was alive. Feeble fingers groped for his fallen six-gun. Leif kicked it away.

"It looks as if you will swing. I'm taking you back to town. The marshal's got a cell waiting for you."

The man half rolled over. His face had turned a disturbing white from lack of blood.

"Can't feel anything. You busted my spine," he grated out. His lips curled in a sneer. "He'll get you for certain sure. He will."

"Who's that?" Leif kept his six-shooter aimed at the dying man.

An evil grin spread on the man's bloodless lips. "Harding. He's more 'n a match for you. He'll take . . . care . . . of you." With that, he finally died. Leif had seen enough corpses in his day to know. He still poked the man in the ribs to be sure. No reaction. A quick kick sent the man's six-shooter spinning away into the mine, clattering metallically against the tracks as it went.

"Is he . . . dead?" Consuela had untied the rope around her ankles and balanced on her knees to peer at the unmoving outlaw.

"Dead," Leif confirmed. He started to discuss with her how he had failed to kill the man with the gunfire they'd exchanged. The ricochet had only set up the target. Every shot after that should have been deadly. He stared at his Peacemaker and shook his head. Had he rushed his shot? That wasn't like him, but then he usually shot paper or glass targets, not flesh-and-blood men.

"You shouldn't have played with him."

"What?" Leif looked at her, startled. "What do you mean?"

"A cat plays with a mouse. That was the way you were with him. You teased him; then you killed him." Consuela wrapped her arms around her thin body and twisted from side to side. "That was cruel. You should have put him down like a mad dog."

"Come on. Let's get back to town. Your sister's worried sick about you." He reached out to help her down the steep slope, but she pulled away. Leif pointed to a trail being illuminated in the fresh light of a new day. Consuela made her way down to where the outlaw's horse nervously pawed at the rocky ground. She stepped up and waited for him.

As distasteful as it was, Leif dragged the corpse down the hill. White Lightning let his displeasure be known if his master tried tying the deadweight over *his* back. Leif silently promised the snowy-white stallion a bushel of apples to make up for such a notion as he made his way back to the outlaw camp.

There he secured the other three bodies over their horses. It took some doing, but he added the body from the mine to the load so White Lightning was relieved of that burden. He fastened the horses together and led them down the side of the mountain, a grisly packtrain.

He and Consuela rode back to Newell Bluff, saying nothing the entire way. For his part, that was all right. The name Luther Simkins burned in his brain. That, and another name: Will Harding.

CHAPTER FIVE

LEIF GUNNARSON WISHED Marta hadn't come rush-
ing to the marshal's office when he rode into town.
But she must have had some special sense that her sister
was returning to her. Consuela rode to the side of the
jail and jumped to the ground, stumbled, and fell into
her older sister's arms. Leif watched them for a moment. Homecoming. A family reunited—reunited as
much as possible after Luther Simkins had torn apart
their family the way he had.

The way he had destroyed Leif's family, too.

He rode at a more sedate pace, not wanting to attract attention. He was only halfway to the jailhouse
when a huge crowd formed. Silent, pointing, some
whispering behind their hands, but they had all come
to see the spectacle. He grinned without humor. If
Wyoming Bob could have sold tickets, he'd have
made a fortune. Even more watched as he led the

train of horses with the dead bodies tied over the saddles than had seen him go down in defeat to Will Harding.

Leif scanned the faces, wondering if the outlaw was there hiding out among the citizens. He had no proof that Harding had anything to do with Consuela's kidnapping, much less the deaths of her ma and pa, but the last outlaw's dying words had condemned Harding.

"Well, lookee here. Ain't you the conquering hero?" Marshal Phillip Denny lifted the head of one outlaw and gave it a good look. "You bagged your limit, Mr. Gunnarson. But then, it's what I expected from a man with your gun-fighting skills." He worked his way down, looking at each face flaccid in death. The bodies had started to putrefy. Leif was glad to be off the trail and back in town.

"Is there any bounty on them? I can't prove it but I think they're all in Luther Simkins's gang."

"Can't rightly say until I do some checking, but this one's certainly got a few dollars riding on his head." Denny lifted the head of the last outlaw Leif had shot. "It looks like it took more 'n one shot for some of them. Are you losing your touch, Mr. Gunnarson?"

"Every last one of them was killed by a fancy shot. I ricocheted the bullets off the moon."

Denny started to laugh, then sobered as if considering the matter. He motioned to the horses loaded with the dead bodies.

"Get them into the shed behind the calaboose so I can identify them for your reward money."

Leif started to tell the lawman to keep any blood

money, then changed his mind. He led the horses around to the rear of the jailhouse and wrestled the uncooperative bodies down to the ground before dragging them into the shed. A small table provided a work space. By the time Leif was finished displaying the outlaws, Denny came in with a coal oil lamp and a stack of wanted posters.

"You already searched them for money and jewelry?"

Leif shook his head.

"That's a surprise. You don't seem the squeamish sort to me." Denny emptied pockets and made a pile of three watches and close to fifty dollars in greenbacks and small coins. From the way he kept tapping his fingers at the edge of the pile, the marshal would have swept it all into his own pocket if Leif hadn't watched.

Giving up on the notion of keeping the money and watches, Denny started comparing faces with posters. Every time he identified one of the dead men, he laid the poster on the unmoving chest. Leif took the discarded posters and went through them on his own. Two of the men had more than one reward out on their heads.

"This is all," Denny said. He fanned the air in front of his face. Flies buzzed around. The stench became overpowering. "You've got, uh, close to five hundred dollars in reward."

Leif fixed the man with a hard stare. He took the identifying posters and spread them out. He tapped each one and mouthed the amount.

"I never was too good at ciphering," the lawman said. "Eleven hundred dollars?"

Leif had come to the same sum. "Use the fifty dollars to bury them. It doesn't matter what you do with the watches."

Denny laughed harshly. "They're not needing them where they're going. You have any need to keep their horses, tack, and guns?"

"All yours," Leif decided. Keeping the marshal happy, or at least not antagonistic, was a good thing until the Wild West Show moved on.

"Well now, it technically belongs to the township. Newell Bluff needs some work done, and selling the gear and horses might cover some of it." Denny motioned Leif to follow.

They went into the marshal's office, Leif going through the wanted posters a final time. Denny took the posters from Leif and tossed them on his desk. He said, "You looking for another one? Anything in particular?"

"Not really," Leif lied. Denny smirked.

"Finding one for Will Harding would get you out of being beat again, wouldn't it?"

"You peg him as a road agent?"

"He blowed into town recently, about the time I started hearing rumors about Luther Simkins and his boys. There's not been anything to tie them together, but he has the look. You know what I mean?"

Leif knew the look. He also had heard the last outlaw at the mine invoke Harding as a curse, but he gained nothing by mentioning it. Consuela wasn't in any condition to back up the accusation, and the marshal only thought he sought a way to avoid facing off with the gunman.

The lawman collapsed into his desk chair, took out a book with blank checks, and started scribbling.

"How do you spell your name?" He looked up. "You can take this check over to the bank and get specie or scrip, however you like. The town's good for it, and I can send in a request to the governor for reimbursement."

"It's not hard to spell," Leif said. "Marta Esquivel." He carefully enunciated each letter.

Denny rocked back and looked surprised.

"All of it? You're giving the Esquivels the whole eleven hundred dollars? Not even keeping a few dollars for your trouble?" He looked Leif over from head to toe. The once-immaculate fringed buckskin jacket hung in tatters. Only if someone had seen how snowy white it had been before could they have guessed the color now. Black soot and brown trail dust had turned it into a dirty rainbow of filth. "Not even a few dollars to replace the bullets?"

Denny laughed and went back to writing the check. "But then, you didn't use that much ammo because you bounced the slugs off the moon."

"Good thing it's almost full. That's a lot harder shot when it's a new moon."

Denny looked up sharply. It took a second, but he finally laughed. He wasn't sure if Leif joshed him or not. He pushed the check across the desk.

"I'll see that the Esquivels get it," Leif said. He made sure the ink was dry before tucking it into his pocket.

"Mr. Gunnarson," the lawman called to him. "You're not intending to stick around town much longer, are you?"

Leif didn't bother to turn, and only shook his head and left. As he stepped out into the street, he saw that those in the crowd hadn't drifted away. They no longer pushed their way forward, but the boardwalks and storefronts were filled with silent, awestruck faces.

Though he was used to being center stage and having so many people watching his every move, this made him a tad uneasy. He walked faster than usual, though he tried to look confident and stride along like he owned the world. Whatever he did would go back to Will Harding. He had a shoot-out on tap with the man in a couple days. Being confident now took away some of Harding's thunder.

Leif caught White Lightning's reins and led the horse to the livery stables. He tipped his hat to some of the women and waved to the children. By the time he got to the stable, he felt as if he had gone a hundred rounds with the bare-knuckle champion of the world. Worse, it hit him that he had killed those men. Never before had he faced down another gunman and shot it out. More than a gunfight, he had killed them.

For the first time, he had taken lives with his gun-handling skills. The weight of that made him light-headed.

"You want me to give your stallion some oats, Mr. Gunnarson?" The stable boy looked at him as if he had two heads.

"Much obliged. Take real good care of him. He's a champion."

"Just like you, sir, just like you!" The towheaded boy grinned now and led the horse to a stall. Did being a champion also feel like being a killer?

Leif waited but not long. Marta came from the interior of the livery stable, her dark eyes flashing.

"You rescued her. I owe you."

Leif took the marshal's check from his pocket and handed it to her. She blinked and shook her head, not understanding.

"Use it to clear out of town. Get away from the bad memories."

"I have talked it over with Consuela. She will stay with our mother's sister in Kansas City. You are right. It is best that she be away from here." Marta fixed him with her lovely eyes. Leif saw how they hardened. "These men weren't the only ones, were they? There are others in the gang?"

"It might be Luther Simkins. It might not. I don't know. These were the ones holding your sister captive. Don't push any harder to find out more."

"You think a few dollars will make all this go away? You are wrong!" She waved the check about.

Leif closed his eyes and remembered finding his ma and pa, and the barbed wire nooses around their necks. Blood hammered in his eyes, but he heard his pa damning Luther Simkins for the crime—the crime that looked for all the world like the one that had befallen the Esquivel family. Had he extracted enough justice?

"Nothing makes the pain go away," he said. "I know."

"Vengeance! I want revenge!" She began rattling off curses in Spanish. He turned away. There was nothing more he could do for her or her sister. Consuela was better off as far from Newell Bluff as possible. Kansas City seemed like a good place. As he walked off, the woman's tirade fading behind him, he wondered if Wyoming Bob would consider a stop in

Kansas City in the near future. Or Chicago. Or New York City. Leif hadn't wanted to return to Europe, but now it was worth thinking on. Anywhere that took him far, far away turned into a worthwhile destination.

He headed for the town gunsmith, thinking there wasn't anywhere on Earth far enough away to escape his memories or the knowledge of what he had just done. Leif stopped in front of the shop window. A young man bent over a bench with a pistol dismantled and spread out on a cloth in front of him. His face crunched down around a jeweler's loupe as he poked and prodded with a tiny screwdriver. Leif went into the shop.

"Be right with you," the young man said. He looked up, went back to his work, then dropped the loupe and sat straighter. "I didn't know it was you, Mr. Gunnarson. Pleased to have you come by my store. What can I do for you?"

Leif drew the Smith & Wesson he had taken off one of the outlaws and laid it on the counter. "What can you give me for this?"

"Well now, it's not in the best condition." The gunsmith looked up curiously. "You have the look of a man who takes real good care of your firearms. This might have been . . ." His voice trailed off.

"The prior owner won't be needing it any longer," Leif said. "I'd like to swap it for ammunition. I need to do some practicing before the big match this weekend."

"You took this off an outlaw? One of them fellows you brought in all slung over their horses?" Veneration like Leif expected to see in church made the man's face positively glow. "Can I put this on display? I heard already how you used your fancy shooting to bring all four of them down. Having one of their six-shooters to show off is a real honor." He spun the cylinder, checked the loads, and tested its balance.

"Don't believe everything you hear," Leif said.

"Four owlhoots, four shots. That's what I heard."

"Not that I shot them all by bouncing my bullets off the moon?" Leif's voice carried just a hint of sarcasm. He was too tuckered out to make it sound any less plausible.

"Really?"

Leif saw the gunsmith wasn't joking. This was the way legends started. First came something danger-ous, maybe deadly; then tall tales told around camp-fires were spun. When the story got old, details were added, details that had never happened. If ricochet-ing bullets off the moon were too outrageous, the story would soon be that he drilled all four with a single bullet.

"A couple boxes of .45 shells? Is that a fair trade?"

The gunsmith searched under the worktable and came out with four boxes of shells. He dropped them on the top.

"These do you, Mr. Gunnarson? They're .45 Long Colt, with twenty-eight grains of powder and two-hundred-thirty-grain bullet. They're real manstop-pers, but if you're only going to practice on targets, maybe a lighter load will do you?"

"These are fine," Leif said. "I never use anything else during the show. It gives the audience what they paid for."

"Lots of gun smoke," the gunsmith said, nodding.

"And these are as accurate a round as you'll find in these parts. You'll win back your other Peacemaker easy with these. I guarantee it."

Leif scooped up the boxes and stuck them into his pockets. They bulged and looked ridiculous, but as filthy as he was, such a minor fashion flaw would go unnoticed.

"Are you going to come see the shoot-out?" Leif wasn't sure he wanted to hear the answer, and yet he did.

"Yes, sir, I am. Good doing business with you, sir. It really is." The young man hefted the S&W and looked around. Leif knew he intended to frame it and hang it on a wall as advertising. He left the shop. In a reverent tone, the gunsmith said, "Come on back anytime, Trickshot!"

Leif got his bearings and turned toward the road leading from Newell Bluff. Wyoming Bob had intended to set up the show north of town, but Leif had ridden in that direction, tracking down Consuela's kidnappers and hadn't seen any evidence of the show. The next obvious direction was along the broad main road leading west toward the Tetons. Even if he didn't find the encampment, the towering purple-clad mountains soothed him and let him think of something other than finding Luther Simkins.

And facing down Will Harding.

The latter bothered him more than it should. He had lost one of his Peacemakers, but only he knew he had been outshot—and by Harding. Harding had to know he'd bested Trickshot. Too much was wrapped up in the forthcoming shoot-out, and that caused Leif to worry uncharacteristically. The Peacemaker meant something to him. It was special, and it was his. Having a road agent steal it away from him galled him. Or worse, having Harding win it fair and square.

He turned down the road leading from town. His steps slowed. Then he edged toward a laundry to take refuge in the doorway. Across the street, Will Harding stood in the afternoon sun, waving his arms around angrily. Leif couldn't make out the man's words, but Harding was powerful mad over something.

The man he upbraided stepped out where his face was visible. Leif started to cry out, then clamped his mouth shut. The short, red-bearded man wasn't taking guff from Harding, but neither man had the look of being ready to throw down on the other. Whatever they argued over was important, but not life-and-death important.

The man facing Harding finally threw his arms up in disgust, spun around, and stalked off. Harding watched for a few seconds, then headed back toward the center of town. Leif watched him go. When he was out of sight, he ran to find the other man.

Looking around, Leif saw nothing of him. Recognition gnawed away at his memory. He wasn't sure, but he thought that right after his family was murdered, he had seen a wanted poster for the man. He had ridden with Luther Simkins then.

Leif wasn't sure, but he couldn't shake the feeling that he was right.

CHAPTER SIX

L EIF GUNNARSON STOOD slowly and stared into emptiness. He was bone-tired and not thinking straight.
He turned and started toward the marshal's office, then
slowed and turned away. Thoughts jumbled up. If the
man he had seen talking to Harding rode with Luther
Simkins ten years ago, there was a good chance he still
did. The outlaw at the mine had cursed him and
claimed Will Harding would bring vengeance crashing
down on his head for rescuing Consuela.

Were they all riding with Luther Simkins? The
more he peeled back the layers in Newell Bluff, the
more it seemed that way. Marshal Denny hadn't positively identified any of the dead outlaws as being
with the Simkins gang, but they weren't on the trail
by their lonesome. What Leif couldn't forget was the
way the Esquivel family had been treated. The elder
man and woman had died exactly the way his parents

had. A fire had been set to cover the evidence. A
young girl had been taken. Leif's three sisters were
gone, long gone. Though he'd found the two younger
ones, his older sister's body hadn't turned up, but after such a long time, he had no reason to think she
was anything but another victim of Luther Simkins.
At least he had rescued Consuela Esquivel before she
met the same fate.

He turned in a full circle, taking in the entire town
and residents milling about on their way home to
hearth and family or to the saloons to drink away the
woes of the day. The marshal wasn't going to help
him. He had made that clear. All the lawman wanted
was to collect rewards on the outlaws' heads, and he
didn't even try to steal the money cleverly. His trick
might have worked on someone unable to add and
subtract, but Leif Gunnarson lived and died by the
box office sales. He had to claim his share from Wyoming Bob and keep on top of the revenue collected.
The owner of the Wild West Show wasn't a thief, but
he always cut the take as thin as possible for his performers, even his star gun handler.

Finding Harding in town was easier than tracking
the red-bearded man as he lit out across the prairie,
but there wasn't much Leif could do to get information from the gunman. If he ran down the fleeing
man, he had a chance of questioning him and finding
answers. He wouldn't have the power that taking one
of Trickshot's Peacemakers gave Harding.

Leif took a wrong turn and went the way opposite
from the stables. He rubbed his eyes and held back a
massive yawn. He tried to remember when he had
slept last. His belly rumbled from lack of food, and

his hand trembled. None of that mattered if he finally found a way to bring Simkins to justice.

The more he thought, the more certain he was that the red-bearded man had shown up on a wanted poster back in Cheyenne ten years ago.

He corrected his direction and went to the stables. The stable boy popped up like a prairie dog, grinning ear to ear.

"Mr. Gunnarson, sir, I got your horse all taken care of. He's a fine animal. Best I ever did see."

"Is he ready for the trail?" Leif went to the first stall. White Lightning's nose bag was empty. The horse had eaten quickly and well. It was almost a shame to awaken the poor animal and get back on the hunt so soon after their trek.

"Well now, he needs to rest. You can't push a horse, even one as strong as yours, and not expect him to balk. Maybe even die under you if you exert the horse too much."

Leif took off his filthy buckskins and hung the jacket over the stall. He yawned again, then worked his way around the horse. The boy had done a fine job getting White Lightning curried and groomed. He took off the nose bag and tossed it aside. The stallion awoke and fixed a large accusing eye on him.

"We've got some more riding to do right now, old boy." He patted the horse's powerful neck. He turned to the stable hand. "You have any apples or carrots I can give him?"

"Well, yes, sir, I do. You don't want to give too many of these apples. They're sour apples, and too many will give even the biggest horse a bellyache." The boy came back with a half dozen apples.

"Put them in a gunnysack. Then saddle him up."

"Well, all right, if you say so, Mr. Gunnarson."

"You don't approve?"

"It's not my place to say, but you can push yourself a whole lot harder than you can a horse. Gallop for three or four miles, and most horses will collapse under you." The stable hand carefully rattled on and detailed all the bad things that happened to a horse when pushed past the point of exhaustion.

Leif sat on a hay bale and leaned back. He closed his eyes to snatch just a few minutes of sleep. He snapped upright, hand going to his Peacemaker when the boy gently nudged him.

"Your horse is all saddled." The boy's tone had changed. Before, he had been cheerful, even reverential. His disdain for anyone, even the famous Trick-shot, who abused his horse came through loud and clear.

Leif rocked to his feet and caught himself when he lost his balance. He took the reins from the boy and led White Lightning outside. The twilight turned the town into a paradise. It had been hot before. The wind made him come alive, invigorated him, tore away the lethargy. Leif wanted to gallop away but remembered what the boy had said and contented himself with a quick walk to the edge of town and the road taken by the red-bearded man.

The cool breeze felt good against his face, lifting the brim of his Stetson and working its way under his vest. He was glad he had left his ragged buckskin jacket back at the stable. He needed to connect with the night, and the feel of air breezing past his body worked. The road out of town was deserted, giving

Leif a chance to study the faint tracks in the dirt and guess which might belong to the red-bearded man's horse.

When he discovered a pile of fresh horse manure, he reckoned he was on the right track. But how far along the road would the man go? Leif rubbed his eyes and focused on the hoofprints the best he could. The chance that red-beard would keep on riding wasn't all that good if the Simkins gang had moved into the territory. The rumors that Harding was one of the gang added to the evidence of Luther Simkins's scouting out something in Newell Bluff. Leif considered the Esquivel deaths as Simkins filling the time as he waited for—what?

He shook himself awake again. Leif had drifted and almost missed freshly crushed brush alongside the road. A quick dismount let him examine the trail more closely. These were definitely new. Leif saw the stand of trees ahead, dark and sinister in the early night. The moon wouldn't rise for some time. Only starlight filtering past nighttime clouds lit the landscape, turning it into an alien world where he knew death would strike the instant he dropped his guard.

A quick move touched the butt of his Peacemaker. He was ready. Leif advanced, jumping at every sound, every tree limb stirred by the breeze. Animals moved about in the forest, hunting and being hunted.

Leif tethered White Lightning and slipped into the cool darkness. He shivered a little and wished now he hadn't left his buckskin jacket back in town. Cocking his head to one side, he listened hard. The sound of a horse ahead drew him. In a small clearing blazed a campfire. Off to one side, a hobbled horse nibbled away on a clump of dry cheatgrass. Leif heard someone quietly butchering "Camptown Races" but couldn't find the songbird in the dark. He crouched and waited. Bulling ahead only got him into trouble.

A few minutes later, the hobbled horse raised its head and looked off into the woods. Leif heard "Doodah, doodah" and knew the singer was returning to his camp. Shadow hid the man's identity until he reached his fire. The dancing flames cast light for Leif to see the beard and enough of the man's face to assure himself his tracking had been successful. This was the red-bearded man who had argued with Harding back in town.

The man had clubbed a rabbit for his dinner. He set about skinning and gutting the rabbit and paid no attention to anything around him. Leif took the chance to silently approach. Moving slowly, he didn't frighten the horse. A quick sniff of smoke from the fire assured him that he moved from downwind. Even so, something gave him away.

The man, bloody knife in his hand, looked up suddenly. His singing stopped, and he half rose. With a looping move, he heaved the knife at Leif.

Leif twisted lithely and avoided the knife as it sailed past. Dodging like this gave his quarry time to slap leather. The bullet that followed the bloody blade came closer. Whether the bearded man was a crack shot or just lucky didn't matter. Leif winced as the hot lead ripped his right biceps.

A quick border shift moved the six-gun from his right hand to his left. Leif had trained himself to be as accurate shooting left-handed as he was using his right. He triggered a round. His shot wasn't as accu-

rate as the bearded man's. He missed. Years of practice had taught him to understand not only that he
missed, but how and why. His round had gone to the
left because he jerked back on the trigger rather than
squeezing it.

Still, his shot had an effect. It panicked the man into
firing wildly. While his first shot had drawn blood,
none of the four following came within a country mile
of Leif's body. He set his feet, aimed, and fired. Leif
took no pleasure in the loud yelp of pain from his target. A minor wound wasn't good enough to stop the
outlaw. Leif fired again, but the man had lit out across
the clearing, heading for the woods.

Leif fired twice more and missed in the dark. He
heard the man bungling through the undergrowth,
not trying to keep quiet. Before heading after his target, he reached around to reload, using bullets from
leather loops in his gun belt. He hadn't bothered re-
plenishing the spares.

A sinking feeling hit him. He had bought four
boxes of cartridges—and had stuffed them into the
pockets of his buckskins. That buckskin jacket was
still draped over the first stall in the livery stable. He
had six shots left, and that was all.

Trickshot had to make every round count or die
since he never once considered retreat. He had too
much to prove, to find out.

A bullet kicked up dirt in front of him. He dodged
to the side, hunting for the place in the woods where
a muzzle flash would betray the shooter. A quick cut
back allowed him to avoid a couple more shots.

"Give up," he called. "Surrender and I won't kill
you."

"Who are you, you sneaking varmint? If you're trying to rob me, you gotta try harder than that."

"I want to know where to find Simkins." Leif waited for a response. Nothing came. The lack of response was better than a howl of denial. He dashed forward a few more paces and gave in to intuition. Leif flopped forward onto his belly and began wiggling like a snake. His sixth sense screamed at him again.

He fired four quick rounds straight ahead just as a foot-long tongue of orange flame exploded from the woods. He was rewarded with a grunt. The bearded man had taken a round, but how bad was the injury? Leif doubted it was as bad as the one he had suffered. His right arm throbbed now, and blood oozed constantly. For a minor wound, it threatened to distract him when he could least afford it.

"You the law? I ain't givin' up, no sir. You'd have my neck in a noose before sunrise."

Leif followed the sound of the voice. The bearded outlaw was on the move. With a quick twist, he rolled over and over on the ground, going in the opposite direction. He dug his toes into the dirt and crab-walked for the woods. Two more rounds ripped past before he reached the safety of a thick-boled tree. Pressing against it got sticky sap on his vest and shirt. Sounds from his adversary were muffled by the thunder of blood in his ears.

"You just ride on out and let me be. Whoever you think I am, you're wrong. I ain't nothing but a poor pilgrim, drifting from town to town."

"Well now, I'm inclined to disbelieve that, but I

know one thing for sure. You can't carry a tune in a bucket."

"You'd arrest me for that?"

"I'm not a lawman," Leif said. He held his Peacemaker and stared at it. Two rounds left. Just two, but he had located the bearded man. While he had been sheltered behind the tree, the outlaw had snuck forward.

Hardly thinking about what he was doing, Leif whirled around the tree, went into a crouch, and fired into the brush, one round to the right and the last one to the left. He wanted to hear the outlaw scream in pain as a slug ripped through his gut. Instead, Leif heard what could have been a stampede coming through the forest. Twigs broke, brush was crushed, and a man huffed and puffed like a locomotive.

Leif stood upright, his empty six-shooter in his hand. He waited.

"Gotcha!" The bearded man fanned off two more rounds. Then the hammer fell on a spent chamber. The outlaw crashed to a halt in a thicket, stumbled, and dropped to one knee.

Leif stepped forward, cocked his Peacemaker, and pointed it at the man.

"You're out of ammo," Leif said in a firm voice. "I will drill you right between the eyes if you don't get those hands up. High! Reach!"

The outlaw lifted his pistol, cocked it, and said, "I got one more round, and it's got your name on it."

"You're going to die. I'm the world's best marksman. At this range, there's no way I can miss. You want me to shoot through your left eye or your right?"

"What?"

"It doesn't matter since either way splatters your brains over half the forest. Think of all the little animals coming to lap up your brains. Maybe the coyotes will take most of them. You won't care. You'll be flat on your back, staring up at the trees. Staring with the one eye I left you!"

Leif stepped closer and aimed so the outlaw couldn't possibly miss where the bullet would blast through his head.

"I heard how you and Harding shot it out. He beat you." The confidence wavered.

"I let him," Leif lied. "It's all show business to get the marks to come see our final shoot-out this weekend. Now drop the six-gun." Leif kept moving forward. By now, he knew the barrel looked like a train tunnel, dark and deadly, and promising a hurtling slug at any instant.

"Don't shoot!" The outlaw tossed his six-shooter in front of him and lifted his hands.

"Stand up and turn around. Keep your hands up." Leif made a beeline for the fallen pistol. Clumsily, he opened the gate and looked. Conflicting emotions poured through him. There was one live round in the chamber. He dropped his Peacemaker into his left holster and aimed the captured six-shooter. One shot trumped having an empty cylinder.

Leif herded the bearded man back to his camp. The outlaw's horse looked up sleepily, then let its head droop back. It had eaten as much as possible and now wanted to sleep. Leif shared the urge. His vision blurred from lack of sleep, and he looked at the skinned, half-gutted rabbit. His belly demanded food, but the carcass already furnished fodder for bugs and, from the flesh ripped away in places, what looked like a rat or two.

"How long you been riding with Luther Simkins?"

"What's it to you?"

"Was it you or Simkins who killed the Esquivels?" Leif rummaged through the outlaw's gear, hunting for spare ammunition. He didn't find even spent brass. Disheartened, he tossed the saddlebags to the ground.

"Wasn't me. I was busy elsewhere. But Luther's got this yen. I don't understand it, but ever since I first rode with him, he's enjoyed tyin' up a husband and wife and seein' how much they love each other." The outlaw laughed hard. "You'd be surprised what they'll say with wire nooses around their necks."

Leif felt light-headed as the blood drained from his face. Wire nooses? His parents! He lifted the pistol. One shot. He was not likely to miss. At this range, he might even set fire to the man's coat from the fiery powder discharged from the muzzle.

The outlaw saw how it galled him and kept up a steady description. Leif had no idea if any of it referred to his own ma and pa. Then he snapped alert when the outlaw said, "Why, Luther even got hisself a girl from one rendezvous, as he calls 'em, over in Cheyenne."

"What do you mean, 'got himself a girl'?"

"Figure it out, gunman. Figure it out for yourself."

"Get on your horse." Leif got the man astride his horse, then looped a lariat around his neck and led him away. Every time the bearded man tried to speak, Leif jerked hard enough to get a choked gasp.

Leif mounted White Lightning and cinched the end of the rope around his saddle horn.

"Keep up. You don't have much slack, and I'm not giving you another inch."

Leif urged White Lightning to a quicker pace. The rope tightened. He almost gave a little more slack and then didn't. The man didn't deserve it. If he hadn't felt like he'd been pulled through a knothole backward, he'd have continued questioning him. The man admitted to riding with the Simkins gang and knowing Harding. In Leif's mind, that confession was evidence enough. While he doubted Marshal Denny had the stomach to interrogate the man and find out what the Simkins gang was up to, he might get the bearded man to repeat what he'd said about the Esquivels.

They reached the road back to Newell Bluff. The moon slid across the sky and turned everything a shining silver. Leif fell into the rhythm of the trail and drifted to sleep. He came awake when a shot destroyed the silence.

He whipped out the captured six-gun and looked around wildly. He saw nothing ahead or to the sides. "Did you see who fired?" His question went unanswered. Leif twisted about to cover his prisoner.

The man sat slumped forward in the saddle. Leif tugged on the rope and pulled him off his horse to flop lifelessly on the ground.

Once more he looked around. Someone had taken a single shot, but had it been intended for him or the outlaw?

And if it was intended to kill him, why shoot only once?

CHAPTER SEVEN

LEIF GUNNARSON WALKED his horse into Newell Bluff just before sunrise. Every step he took felt as if his muscles had turned to water. His eyelids drooped until he forced them back open. Try as he might, he couldn't remember when last he had slept or eaten. As he trudged alongside White Lightning, the stallion jerked its head about and tried to pull away. They passed the stable. The horse remembered food and water—and sleep.

"Come on. In a while, old boy. In a while." As if the horse understood, it stopped dead in the middle of the street and refused to budge. Leif looked around. The town was beginning to stir. Some shopkeepers had already opened their doors and swept off the walks in front of their establishments. Some citizens hurried in twos and threes to their jobs. Smoke billowed from the café stovepipe. The cook had been hard at work preparing for the first of the workers. The saloons had closed just a little while before he reached town.

"Go on," Leif said, giving the horse a couple swats on the rump. It reared, turned a huge baleful eye on him, then dropped back to all fours and trotted to the stable. The stable hand popped out, rubbing his eyes. Leif waved. The boy waved back and grabbed White Lightning's reins.

"I got your buckskins," the boy called. "You left them hanging inside."

"I'll claim them in a while." Leif stewed over how four boxes of cartridges weighed down those filthy buckskins, bullets he could have used and not risked his own hide with a bluff. His hand touched the Peacemaker in its holster. One round rested there now, taken from the outlaw's gun.

He jerked on the reins of the red-bearded man's horse. It dutifully followed him, bearing its burden. Its rider was tied belly down over the saddle. Leif reached the marshal's office and started to knock on the door, thinking Denny would be inside sleeping. The door opened before he had a chance to put knuckle to wood.

"Now, aren't you up early?" The marshal looked past him to the horse and its dead cargo. "You're going to make the town wonder if they need me anymore. That the only one you got for me today?"

"One of Luther Simkins's gang," Leif said. His mouth had filled with cotton, but the marshal understood him well enough to motion him into the office to start leafing through a stack of wanted posters.

Leif found one matching the dead man after glancing at six posters. He held it up.

"Well now, you're right about that being one of the Simkins gang. Garland Brothers, it says his name is, but we know they change names more often than they take a bath." Denny flipped through the rest of the pile and slid another wanted poster aside. When Leif tried to get a look at it, the marshal shoved it into a drawer. "You got yourself a hundred-dollar reward."

Leif wondered if the other poster was also on Brothers and the marshal would claim it for himself. His earlier dealings with Phillip Denny weren't the most aboveboard and honest, but he was so bone-tired, he didn't care.

"Here's a check for the varmint's scalp. You can cash it in over at the bank when it opens." Denny cleared his throat. "You want to contribute the man's horse for sale so he can have a proper burial?"

Leif considered for a moment. Garland Brothers might have been one of the gang who had savagely killed his parents ten years ago. He almost certainly had taken part in killing the Esquivels. He deserved to be left out for the buzzards, only that might make the carrion birds puke.

"Yeah, do it." Leif tucked the check into a vest pocket. He wobbled as he turned to go.

"You look plumb tuckered out. You want to stretch out in the back? Don't have any prisoners in the cells."

Leif wondered at such generosity. Denny was as likely to slam the door and charge him a hundred dollars for the privilege of using the cot. He shook his head. It felt as if something came loose inside.

"I have to see to my horse at the stables."

"Wondered if that fine horse of yours was around somewhere. You go on now, Mr. Gunnarson. I'll take care of the little *billet-doux* you brought me." Denny cleared his throat. "I read that in a book." Denny seemed proud of his command of the French phrase.

All Leif could do was nod tiredly and leave. Somehow, he got to the stable, found an empty stall, and stretched out on the clean straw, White Lightning in the stall next to him. Leif wasn't sure how long he slept, but it was dark outside when he stirred. He rolled onto his back, then heard someone moving quietly. His Peacemaker came to hand, and he had it pointed as a dark figure loomed at the mouth of the stall.

A thousand things raced through his mind. His eyes were still blurred from sleep. He hadn't bothered to reload his six-shooter. And the only one who'd sneak up on him was likely to avenge Garland Brothers's death.

"Wait! I mean you no harm!"

The voice was soft and insistent. Leif lowered his six-gun and sat up.

"Miss Esquivel?"

"Marta. Call me Marta." The woman dropped to her knees. A ray of light from a gaslight out in the street fell across her lovely face. She looked intent and wasn't armed.

"What are you doing here?"

"I sought you, Mr. Gunnarson."

"If I'm to call you Marta, you can call me Leif."

"Not Trickshot?" Her voice carried a hint of laughter. Then she turned somber again. "I heard you killed the man who murdered my parents. Is that true?"

"It might be. He didn't confess, not exactly." He scooted around and propped himself up in the stall. She came in and sat beside him. "I think he rode with the gang responsible."

"The Simkins gang, yes. You are not sure, though, that he killed my parents and . . . and kidnapped my sister."

"Where is Consuela? I thought you and she were already on a stage for Cheyenne. Isn't she going to stay with relatives?"

"She is, but I stayed in Newell Bluff to bring those murderers to justice. I do not see the marshal doing anything to find them. I sent a telegram to the sheriff but have heard nothing from him. I am not certain the cavalry would enforce the law when they are out on patrol hunting Indians."

"There is an army post a day's ride to the west," Leif said. "I had forgotten that."

"You are the only one hunting for these terrible men. Is the one you killed the last of them?" She pressed closer. Both her nearness and what he had to answer made him uncomfortable.

"You shouldn't get involved. Brothers isn't the last of them. Luther Simkins is still out there, I suspect." He remembered what Brothers had said about Will Harding. "I have my suspicions about some others, too."

"Harding," she said bitterly. "He came to town only weeks ago and made no secret of his contempt for the marshal. You must outshoot him."

"Tomorrow?" Leif scratched his head. He had lost track of the days.

"At the Wild West Show. Your boss has sold tickets to everyone in town. He claims it will be the most famous gunfight since Wild Bill Hickok shot Davis Tutt." Marta paused, frowned, and shook her head. "I do not know of this fight."

Leif did. The last thing he intended to do was face down Will Harding like Hickok had done with Tutt in Springfield, Missouri. It was one thing having bottles and paper targets. It was something else squaring off against a man intent on filling your belly full of lead.

Considering the past couple days, Leif had already had his fill of killing. Sweat popped out on his head when he realized he was more than a little scared of Harding. The man had outshot him fair and square once. If Wyoming Bob pushed the rematch into a real gunfight, Harding had an even bigger advantage. The men Leif had killed hadn't been facing him with the intent to outdraw him when he shot them. He was Trickshot, certainly, but Harding was a killer. From what Leif had seen, another notch on the man's gun would make the butt look like a termite's feast.

"I heard Harding boasting that he can outdraw you and that a woman can outshoot you."

Leif still pictured facing Harding and going to his gun—and Harding going for the Peacemaker matching the one Leif used. He had won it fair and square. Leif had no desire to be shot with his own six-gun.

"What's that? A woman?" He forced himself to concentrate on what Marta was saying.

"He calls her Randall." Marta averted her eyes and lowered her voice. "He claims she is called 'Randy Sally Randall.'" She reached out and put her hand on his arm. "You do not kill women, do you? Even one who is as evil as Harding claims this one to be."

"It won't come to that. I've met women who were crack shots." He smiled ruefully. "One was a far better shot than I will ever be. Annie Oakley. Wyoming Bob tried to set up a match between her and me, but Bill Cody dodged him. He packed up his entire show and left Chicago in the dark of night rather than allow the two of us to have a shoot-out, but that's what Wyoming Bob said. I'm not sure he ever talked with Wild Bill."

"She is better than you?" Awe tinged Marta's voice. "You admit this? A woman is better than you? You, Trickshot? But you are the best!"

"Don't believe everything Wyoming Bob says." He laughed harshly. "Don't believe much of anything he tells you, especially if he swears that it's true. But yes, I saw her shoot years ago. She is more than a match for any man I've ever seen."

Marta muttered to herself.

"Is it surprising that I know there are gun handlers out there who can best me?" Leif smiled with a touch of sorrow. "There's always somebody better than you, no matter what you do."

"You sound like a failure, not the best gunman in the whole world."

He mentally replayed the defeat at Harding's hand.

"I can always do better. When I face Harding again, I won't make the same mistake I did before." Resolve turned to ice in his veins. Harding was the end of the rope leading to Luther Simkins. He knew it. Every time he crossed an outlaw, they all led to Simkins—before they died by his hand.

"You should sleep. Rest. It's only a few hours until dawn." She backed away.

This shocked Leif. He hadn't realized he'd slept for so long. It was nearly dawn of the day when he had to win back his Peacemaker—and learn if Harding rode with Simkins. Doing the former was a matter of skill. He held out his hand. It was steady and ready to grip his second Peacemaker. But getting Harding to spill his guts about Luther Simkins and his gang took more than a steady hand and steely eye. It'd take luck. Of late, his luck had been mighty poor.

As Marta slipped away, he called after her, "You steer clear of Harding. You ought to join your sister. You've done all you can. Leave it to me."

Mocking laughter came from the direction of the door leading to the street. "Leave it to a man who is not as good as a woman? Perhaps *I* am that woman, too!"

Leif cursed himself for being so honest. His reputation as a gunslick depended on bragging 'til the cows came home. He seldom had to do much. Wyoming Bob did a fine job of puffing up his star's shooting accuracy, and not many in any crowd knew if Trickshot was all that fast a hand. He made it look like he was, and with his marksmanship, he seldom failed to awe and entertain.

Leif stretched out and laced his fingers under his head. He ached all over, but his long sleep had taken the edge off his exhaustion. He strained to hear the tiny sounds all around him. Horses snoring and shifting in their stalls. A mouse squeaking as it raced through the stable. He blinked at the gray shadow racing after it. The cat failed to jump on its prey before the mouse slipped through a hole in the outer wall and escaped.

Leif wondered whether he was the cat or the mouse. He groaned as he sat up, then pulled himself to his feet. Stretching erased some of the aches. So far, he hadn't gotten the lead needed to locate Simkins, but he had a decent reward for Garland Brothers riding in his pocket. Giving the other bounty money to Marta to take care of her sister had been the right thing to do. If he offered Marta the hundred in his pocket, would she leave and join Consuela?

He knew she wouldn't. Revenge burned as brightly in her breast as it did in his heart. Such cruelty and death had to be punished.

Walking slowly, he left the stable. He held up his arm to block the rising sun. If Marta was right, he had a showdown with Will Harding in a few hours. The town wouldn't stir for a while. That gave him time to find where Wyoming Bob's Wild West Show had camped without having to answer questions from any of the townspeople. He had already shown with Marta that his responses weren't what they wanted to hear.

Leif had no idea why he was so honest with her. They shared the same sorrow, but he'd had fully ten years to develop calluses on his feelings. Something about her liquid brown eyes and fleeting, sad smile drilled through his excuses.

"Hello there, Mr. Gunnarson," came a cheery call from the marshal. He hitched up his gun belt and stepped out into the street to walk alongside Leif. "You're up mighty early. Thinking on getting some practice in for the big shoot-out this afternoon?"

"I need to find out what Wyoming Bob has advertised. Three-gun is possible. Shotgun, rifle, and pistol, one after the other until the magazines are spent," he explained when the lawman frowned.

"That's not how the rumors have it. I want to tell you I don't approve, but there's not a whole lot I can do to stop you."

Leif looked sharply at Denny. "What do you mean?"

"Rumor has it you and Harding aren't going to shoot bottles or targets." The marshal coughed politely. "I mean paper targets."

Leif stared at him. What on earth had the Wild West Show owner been spreading around town to sell tickets?

"I'd advise you to back down, even if it means losing your other fancy iron." Denny looked significantly at the Peacemaker in Leif's holster. "The six-gun's not worth the two of you squaring off and using each other as targets."

Denny slapped him on the shoulder and cut down an alley, whistling off-key as if he didn't have a care in the world. All Leif could do was stand in stunned silence. The town was expecting him to face Harding in a real gunfight. That'd be to the death. The gunman wouldn't have it any other way.

CHAPTER EIGHT

"YOU'RE MAKING TOO much out of this, Gunnarson," Wyoming Bob said. He shook his head in dismay. "You know how we make money with the show. If the rubes don't line up with money in their hand, demanding to see something that'll amaze them and brighten their dull days, we go out of business."

"This. Look at this. Explain why you put this broadside up on every wall in town." Leif held up a flyer he'd torn down. He shook it under Wyoming Bob's nose.

"It may be a *little* bit of an exaggeration," the show owner confessed.

"A little? A little! You are claiming we're going to shoot it out. To the death!"

"Not exactly. If anyone reads that and gets the wrong idea, that's not my fault. All you have to do is outshoot him on the stationary targets, and there won't be a head-to-head gunfight. You'll do that, Gunnarson; you will. Don't get so worked up. It's making you red in the face. Calm yourself, or your hands'll shake."

A steam calliope drowned out Leif's furious reply. When the loud music died down, Wyoming Bob was still talking.

"It's simple enough. You're expert at hitting targets. We'll make sure the glass spheres with the feathers in 'em all have the little fins to give you an edge. That's how Bogardus did it. His glass targets were puny ole things, and his opponents all had hard glass that required a dead-center hit."

"So you're saying I can't win honestly?"

Wyoming Bob shook his head sadly. "What's wrong with you, man? First you think it's a crime you and this Harding fellow will shoot it out to the death, and now you're complaining that I'm saving you from having to do it? There's no blood going to be spilled. He will never hit as many targets as you. Or are you admitting to me he's a better shot?"

Leif swallowed some of his anger. It only made him more determined than ever to walk away from the Wild West Show. Wyoming Bob had no right to put up such flyers or to promise bloodshed just to get a crowd when it was Leif's life on the line.

"You might as well hand over your Peacemaker right now," Wyoming Bob said. He held out his hand. "You show a yellow streak up your back, and you don't deserve such a fine six-shooter. I'll present it to Harding in front of the crowd. Maybe I'll even offer him your job. Would you like seeing his name in big letters on a canvas banner in place of yours?"

"I don't need you as much as you need me to draw the crowds, Bob."

"Hand over your six-shooter, Gunnarson. Hand it over now. Get on that fancy white horse of yours and clear out. You ought to be out of town before the show starts." He took on a cagey look and added, "Unless you're as good as I think you are. As good as I *know* you are. I've seen you bust every target when you had a fever so bad you could hardly stand. Remember when you got that dust in your face? You were nigh on blind and never missed a bottle at twenty-five yards. *That's* the Leif Gunnarson the crowd loves." In a voice almost too low to hear, he finished, "Think of the applause. What'll it be, Leif? What's your decision?"

Leif thought for a moment, weighing the risks. "If I bust more targets than Harding, it'll be over? We won't try to kill each other?"

Wyoming Bob slapped him on the shoulder. "You got it, my good man. I knew I could count on you. This is going to be the best show we ever put on. Wait and see. When they stop talking about it, there won't be a town in the entire US of A that won't pay us to come and entertain them. And you wait and see if I don't find that treasure train!"

"What treasure train?" Leif reeled from the sudden change in topic. "What else do you have in the works?"

"Not yours to worry over. I heard things back in Fargo that will suit us all. Providing a glimpse of the Wild West to a select audience riding along on a special train's going to make us all rich. What do they know, anyway, coming halfway around the world just to see a few buffaloes?"

Leif stared at the show's owner, wondering what he was going on about.

"And," Wyoming Bob said in a confidential tone, "I also heard rumors of someone of interest to you coming back into Wyoming. You'll thank me for this precious gift once you settle accounts."

Leif had other concerns than Bob Jenks's vague words, concerns he had to focus on. Harding was the last thread to be pulled that would unravel the Simkins gang. Until now, he had brought all the outlaws to a sudden, final end and had denied himself the evidence he needed to bring Luther Simkins to justice.

"In an hour. Be ready for the shoot-out of your life!" Whooping with glee, Wyoming Bob set off, bellowing and waving to everyone he saw that the show was about to begin.

Leif watched and wondered if it was going to be as easy as his boss said. He slid the fancy-etched Peacemaker from its holster and checked to be sure he carried a full load. Spare ammo hung in loops on the belt around his middle. The only thing that unbalanced him a mite was the missing six-shooter in his right holster. He'd win it back. If Harding showed up.

Panic gripped him for a moment. Will Harding could skitter away like a lizard if his courage faded even a tad. Leif began planning how to track him down. Harding wasn't going to escape that easily when opportunity had finally presented itself to Leif after a full decade.

Returning to the wilds of Wyoming wasn't something he anticipated. The Wild West Show had closed in Fargo and hightailed it all the way into the territory when more profitable towns beckoned. Leif hadn't asked Wyoming Bob why they'd come back after touring the world, but it had paid off. It *would* pay off if he ran down Simkins. Let Wyoming Bob go after that mysterious treasure train. He had revenge to keep him occupied.

He wandered the streets for a half hour, waving to people who cheered him on. Leif's footsteps finally turned toward the show's encampment, where a large box attached to the rear of a wagon held all his equipment. Not caring to waste time with the other performers, he edged in past the knots of men and women preparing for the upcoming show. The few performers who saw him recognized his desire to settle his mind and prepare himself.

It took a few minutes to unlock the box and rummage through the contents. His buckskins were filthy. Cleaning and patching the jacket was out of the question in the short time he had. Leif hung it up and studied the other two coats in the box. He decided on a black broadcloth frock coat that jingled with medals as he took it out. Sunlight caught the fancy engraved medals and colorful ribbons won over the years. He touched one that the king of Prussia had awarded him for breaking an even thousand targets, never missing a single shot over a five-hour marathon shoot.

"Not a single miss," he said softly. He laid the jacket down and shucked off his vest. A flashy red brocade vest replaced it. It drew attention. Leif considered how it would help Harding center on his body as easily as if there had been a bull's-eye drawn on the chest. Bright silver buttons and a chain attached to an expensive watch some prince or count or whoever had given him in England also provided targets. But not as effectively as the huge ceramic watch fob dangling from the chain. He had won that in New York City.

"Hurry it up, Gunnarson. The show's about to begin!"

He looked over his shoulder. Wyoming Bob strutted around in his own gaudy ringmaster outfit. The show's owner was better suited to a circus, but Leif had to really think hard to figure out the difference between their Wild West Show and a circus. An elephant or tiger and that was it. He walked past the bison and a cage with a snarling, snapping gray timber wolf in it. They'd had a dancing bear, but it had pulled free of its chains a month earlier and vanished outside Fargo. Leif felt sorry about that. He and the bear's handler were the only two who had gotten on with the ursine monster. Leif always tossed a few fruits into the cage because the bear liked them and often rejected the slop it received regularly.

"Here you go, Mr. Gunnarson." A young boy held White Lightning's reins. "Lookin' like we've got a packed house this afternoon."

He looked out across the arena. Wyoming Bob had set up twice the number of plank seats.

"The smell of blood always draws a crowd," Leif said. The boy looked confused. Leif wasn't going to explain. He'd either figure it out for himself or be forever lost in a maze of confusion about why usually peaceable folks came out in droves at the hint of bloodshed.

Leif checked his six-shooter, made sure the magazine on his Winchester was loaded to capacity, and then vaulted into the saddle. White Lightning reared, paws slashing at the air. The instant the horse righted itself, Leif tapped the animal's flanks. They galloped out amid calliope music and a huge cheer as Wyoming Bob continued to talk Leif up to the crowd.

Swinging around in the saddle, he pulled his rifle from its sheath, levered in a round, and fired. At a dead run across the arena, he emptied the rifle's magazine and destroyed fifteen bottles with the .44 WCF rounds. At the far side of the arena, White Lightning again reared. Leif sheathed his smoking-hot rifle, yanked off his huge Stetson, and waved it in the air. Sunlight glinted off the band of silver conchas strung as a hatband. If the crowd's response before at his entry had been tumultuous, this time it rolled out in a deafening wave like the very ocean.

Leif paid no attention to Wyoming Bob setting up the next stunt. Wheeling around, he galloped back. This time he fired his six-gun until it was empty. Bottles had been set atop crates hung with bunting, so six rows of three gleamed in the sunlight.

"Eighteen bottles with only six shots!" Wyoming Bob whipped the crowd into a renewed frenzy of cheering.

Leif reloaded, pleased with himself. That was quite a feat he'd just accomplished. Riding full speed and hitting anything was close to a miracle for most men, but using his pistol, he had sent one slug through three bottles all lined up just right. Doing that once was accurate shooting. Repeating it for all six rounds was what put his name at the top of every Wild West Show banner.

He watched as a half dozen Newell Bluff boys rushed out to pick up the bigger pieces of glass and cart them away. He had a few minutes respite as other acts paraded out, but he had warmed up the crowd. Trick riders, experts with the lariat, the display of their animals—all went well. He caught hints of how Wyoming Bob teased the crowd with what had to be the finale.

Leif looked around, but Will Harding was nowhere to be seen. That suited him just fine. He could put on a demonstration of marksmanship that would awe the locals. There wasn't any need for the challenge of a man shooting it out against another. Losing his Peacemaker was an annoyance, but he earned enough from the show to have a gunsmith back in Denver gussy up a plain Peacemaker to match the one he still carried.

"You ever get nervous, Mr. Gunnarson?" The boy who had tended his horse looked up at him with worshipful eyes.

"That's the way to miss. I have to fire every round between heartbeats, between breaths. That's how you don't miss."

"Gosh, I'd be huffin' 'nd puffin' like a steam engine to face down the likes of him."

"What's that?" Leif spun and saw Harding walking up. The gunman whipped out the Peacemaker he'd won and spun it around his trigger finger a few times, then shifted from hand to hand, tossing the gun around until it turned into a silver wheel in the sunlight. With a final toss, he sent it spinning into the air. Harding thrust out his hip. The six-gun dropped into his holster as if it had been pulled down with a string.

"Seein' him do all that fancy gun handlin' would put the fear into me. You gonna win back your Peacemaker, Mr. Gunnarson?"

He nodded once, curt, firm. Thinking about anything now but hitting every target was going to do him in. All he needed to do was . . . not miss. Then there wouldn't be any call for the two of them to face each other for the finale, the showdown, the reason the stands were jammed with paying customers.

Not a person in the audience would admit to wanting to see him and Harding throw down on each other, but that was why they'd come. Leif closed his eyes and began imagining the targets. Every time he pictured a bottle in his mind, it exploded as his lead blasted it apart. He opened his eyes slowly. The boy held his Winchester in both hands, as if offering a peace pipe. Leif snatched it, held it aloft, and strode briskly into the arena. A slight wind caught at his long hair and pulled it back from his collar. He stopped in the middle of the arena. The wind tugged more insistently at his black frock coat and made the medals bounce about and sound like wind chimes.

Will Harding came out and stood beside him, a carbine in his hand. For the close-range work, the shorter barrel wasn't going to hinder him at all. Wyoming Bob explained that the first round required each sharpshooter to fire and, hopefully, break one hundred glass balls. Leif had learned Captain Bogardus's secret. His feather-filled glass balls were made of thinner glass and had tiny fins on the exterior. From a distance, no one in the crowd could spot them. Even a near miss was enough to break the glass as the globe spun above the arena.

"Begin the shoot-off!" Wyoming Bob pumped up the crowd until Leif wanted to clap his hands over his ears.

"Pull," he called to the man with a basket of glass balls in front of him.

The glass sphere soared above. Leif swung through, firing at the precise instant it reached its apex. Colored feathers cascaded down and then fluttered off on the wind.

Harding broke his, too. Then the match began in earnest. After fifty targets each, Leif wondered if Harding was ever going to miss.

"Let's speed this up," he called to Harding. "Two at a time?"

The gunman laughed and said, "Make it three!"

"Start tossing as fast as you can," Leif ordered.

He broke fifteen of the globes in as many seconds, then took a rifle shoved into his hand and continued firing. Sweat beaded on his forehead as the strain of sending so much lead into the air accurately took its toll. He was ready for another when Wyoming Bob called out, "That there's one hundred each! No misses! Neither of these sharpshooters missed a single glass ball!"

"Ready for another hundred?" Leif stretched his cramped right hand. "Want to do it left-handed?"

"We can do this all day long," Harding said. "Set up the next challenge."

"Next?" Leif started to protest but cut off his words as men set out twelve barrels in a wide circle and put a whiskey bottle on each.

"Each of you has to break every other bottle in the circle and do it as fast as you can. The one who finishes the fastest wins!"

Leif wanted to back out. He'd never been in a shoot-off like this. They had to each spin in a complete circle, taking out alternate bottles.

"In our challenger's bottle is white sand; in our champion's is red so everyone can know who's the winner!"

Leif saw the sneer on his opponent's lips. Breaking bottles wasn't as likely as blasting apart Leif's heart. Before he had a chance to object, Harding turned his back and began firing. He fanned off the rounds and swung around the circle. More from reaction than thought, Leif responded. He shot faster. They ended up facing each other.

"Die" came to Harding's lips as he fired.

Leif jerked violently and felt the hot trail of the gunman's slug break the ceramic disk on his key chain. The heat on his belly occupied his thoughts more than taking his last shot. Leif stumbled back, hand going to the bloody crease across his stomach.

For the first time, he noticed something amiss. The crowd stared in utter silence. He expected wild cheers. Then he turned in a full circle. Every single one of his bottles had been shattered.

The last one had been broken after his slug tore through Harding's body. The gunman lay on his back, staring up into the bright blue Wyoming sky.

Will Harding strained to look at Leif. His lips moved, but no sound came out before the gunman died.

With a sinking feeling and a fiery burning in his stomach, Leif Gunnarson realized his chance of finding out Luther Simkins's whereabouts died with Harding.

CHAPTER NINE

"THIS IS 'BOUT the first time I ever saw so many witnesses and so few of them willing to step up and tell what happened." Marshal Denny cleared his throat and spat. He wiped his mouth with his sleeve. "Fact is, I saw it myself. Your boss set me up real good with a front-row seat."

"It was an accident," Leif Gunnarson said. He stared at Harding's body stretched out in the middle of the arena. Clumps of grass had been cut up all around as riders came over and let their horses paw the ground. Dozens of others had tromped down the entire area, trying to get a better look.

"Can't dispute that, Mr. Gunnarson, no siree. Cannot say that it wasn't." Denny squinted just a little as he studied Leif like a flea on a hot griddle. "Is that the way you saw it? Being part of the shoot-out and all?"

"He never said a word after I shot him." Leif felt a smidgen of regret, not for ending the man's life but for not finding out if Harding knew the first thing about Luther Simkins's whereabouts.

"You exchanged an insult or two before the match? No? You wouldn't do a thing like that, would you, not after he took this from you a couple days ago?" The lawman picked up the Peacemaker on the ground from where it had fallen beside Harding. He spun it around, opened it, and checked the cylinder. "All fired." Denny knocked out the brass onto the ground, closed the gate, and ran his finger along the barrel. "A nice six-gun." He held it out for Leif. "Go on; take it. That was the bet, wasn't it? You won."

Leif took the Peacemaker matching the one resting in his left holster. He tossed it back and forth between his hands, stopped when it fit nicely in his right hand, then spun it around into the holster that had been irritatingly empty since he'd first shot against Harding. It felt better than normal. It felt good.

"From what Wyoming Bob says, your show's moving on right away. If you'll take a bit of advice . . ." Marshal Denny squinted at Leif again with his intent, studious gaze. "My advice is for you to be out front of all the wagons, leading the way to wherever the show's going. I don't want to see you around Newell Bluff again. I won't have you gunning down anyone just to please a payin' crowd."

Marshal Denny spat again, turned, and sauntered off, waving to people who had remained to see whatever remained of the show. A couple cowboys engaged the lawman, and they left the arena together.

Leif stared back at Harding stretched out on the ground.

"You cheated me. You knew something about Simkins, and you died before you told me."

"Hey, mister, you want to get out of the way?" The undertaker and an assistant rolled up with a handcart. Leif stepped back to let them turn over Harding's corpse onto a filthy blanket, then hoist him to the cart. The assistant took the handles and grunted as he began pulling. The undertaker marched alongside, a constant flood of invective gushing out about his do-nothing assistant.

Alone in the middle of the field, Leif began reloading both his six-shooters. As the last cartridge slid into its chamber, Wyoming Bob came riding up.

"Get your gear packed. The marshal's made it clear we're not welcome here anymore. The ingrate." Wyoming Bob mumbled a bit and then complained, "After I gave him ten percent of the gate. I can't stand a crook who won't stay bought." He made a sweeping gesture with his arm, snorted, and then wheeled about and rode away.

Once more, Leif stood alone in the middle of the field that had been an arena of death.

He tried to convince himself that Harding had been a member of the Simkins gang and that he'd done the world a service. Somehow, that wasn't good enough.

With slow steps he returned to the wagon with the box holding his belongings. Two roustabouts worked on the axle, greasing it down with lard and grumbling. Nobody in the show was happy with being kicked out of a town. After the work setting up everything and getting the animals settled, they should have had another two or three performances before rolling on.

"Don't know why he brung us to this forsaken town in the first place," one man half-hidden under the wagon groused. "We'd a' been better off in Denver or even down in Texas. Heard tell of San Antone bein' as close to a gold mine for people like us there as anywhere."

Leif had wondered about Wyoming Bob's return to the state. Ten years earlier, he had joined the Wild West Show. Not once in that decade had the owner even hinted at wanting to return to his namesake territory. And there wasn't any call to come to Newell Bluff when more people, richer folks, populated Cheyenne or Laramie. Leif looked around the empty field one last time. Still, they had done well. He touched the handles of both six-guns. The show had done well because of him.

He changed out of his show costume and put on sturdier trail gear. The buckskin coat hung from a hook inside, mocking him. It was ruined. If he'd stayed in Newell Bluff a week or two longer, he might have found a seamstress to whip up a new coat or, less likely, discovered someone able to do a miracle cleaning. The hide might be bleached white again and the tears patched.

He closed and locked the door on the box. Those were chores to take on when they reached their next stop, wherever that was.

"Has anyone seen the stable boy? I want to be sure my horse is ready to travel."

When neither of the men under the wagon answered, Leif spun and started to find the youngster responsible for tending the horses. He stopped dead in his tracks. Marta Esquivel blocked his way. In her hand lay White Lightning's reins. The stallion snorted and tugged but made no real effort to break free.

"You have a way with him," Leif said. "He doesn't cotton much to strangers leading him around."

"I've got a way with animals," she said.

Leif started to take the reins, but she pulled away. His anger rose. Playing silly games after the time he'd had only made him madder.

"The show is leaving. Give me the reins." He held out his hand. She still refused. With a movement faster than a striking rattler, he caught her wrist and pulled her off-balance, causing her to release the reins. He snared them with his left, but to his further irritation, White Lightning took her side and backed away.

"He said something. I saw him talking with a man, and I was able to find out what they talked about. Harding bragged about how he knew the notorious Luther Simkins and his woman."

"How did you find this out?"

"He was drunk. It was easy to get him to talk." Marta blocked his attempt to mount. "He bragged he knew Simkins and the woman he called his pet. Maybe if we can find her, we can get to him."

Leif stared deep into Marta's eyes. Her limpid brown pools showed no hint of deceit. Whatever she had overheard she believed to be true.

"Harding said she is a lovely woman except for the scar."

Leif stopped trying to mount. "What scar is that?" His heart sped up. His sister Petunia had a scar, but it was too incredible to believe she had ridden with the outlaws for all these years—that she was even alive. She would have escaped or, more likely, fallen prey to their savage desires and been left for dead.

"Your expression," Marta said, concerned. "You turned pale. Do you know this woman, Simkins's woman?"

"It's been ten years. I can't believe it's my sister, but it might be. Petunia was always a wild one, but to join Simkins like that after all that happened? I can't believe it."

"The name? Yours is different. He spoke of Sally. How can it be her?" Marta looked open and honest in her question.

"Outlaws use summer names. But I've never seen a wanted poster for a woman outlaw, especially one riding with Simkins."

"What will you do?"

Leif tried to deny his feelings. This was pure chance, and the woman could not be his sister. But it did not matter who she was if she rode with Luther Simkins.

"Who is this man that told you all of this? Was it anyone special or just someone hanging out at the saloon?" He saw the two roustabouts slide from under the wagon and wipe their filthy hands on their overalls. They exchanged a few words, then went in different directions.

The wagon was repaired, and the team would be hitched up soon enough. The show was almost ready to hit the road.

Leif tried to move, but his feet might as well have

been stuck in buckets. Since coming to Newell Bluff, he had killed for the first time and found no pleasure in it. The dead outlaws were scum. Even if they weren't Simkins's henchmen, he had done society a favor, but he had spent ten years telling himself what he would do if—when—he found Simkins. He saw now it had been false bravado. Skill with a six-shooter meant nothing when facing a gunman. Skill and determination to take a life were different. The gunfights had happened fast and had given no time to think about what drawing back on the trigger, a man's heart in the sights, meant.

Cutting down Harding had been another kill-or-be-killed situation, but it only now began to eat away at his gut. Luther Simkins might kill from cruelty and the joy of watching another suffer, but Leif Gunnarson wasn't cut from that cloth.

He looked at the wagon as it rattled off. The gaily painted box fastened to the rear with all his belongings bobbed, bounced about, and then vanished from sight as the driver took a bend in the road. Leaving his life during the past decade was not as easy as letting the wagon drive on without him.

"You turn paler yet," Marta said. "What is wrong?"

Leif wished his decision were as simple as everything had been for him before reaching this town. Line up targets, draw, and fire. Watch the lead rip through paper targets or glass balls filled with bright feathers explode and slowly flutter down. Then wait for the hushed crowd to erupt in applause. While the memory of his murdered family had been a constant thorn in his conscience, he had come to discount what he could do.

Coming to Newell Bluff had changed that. He had killed his first man—and had felt he was an avenging angel doing what the law had not over the years.

"Who was that man, Marta?" Leif felt a chill settle on him. He glanced down the road. The wagon and the rest of the Wild West Show were gone, the dust from their departure already settled. It was as if they had never been to town.

"Some cowboy," Marta said. "In a saloon. He wore a black hat with a rattlesnake hatband. The rattles sounded as he moved about. They were fastened to the brim at the back of the hat." She touched the back of her head, then motioned vaguely in the direction of a trio of saloons. "I went to many. I don't know which of the saloons since they all look alike. No decent woman goes into a cantina like those." She lowered her eyes. "I had never been in one before. Papa forbade even coming to this part of town."

He handed her his horse's reins and set off for the nearest gin mill. Somehow his mind had come loose from his body. Each saloon looked like the next to him, the smells and sights and even the customers and barkeeps all the same. After four saloons, he found one with a garrulous barkeep who greeted him heartily.

"I do declare, it's Trickshot hisself. Come on over and have a drink on the house. Ain't often we get famous folks like you bellyin' up to the bar." The bartender poured a shot of dubious-looking whiskey. Clouds swirled in the amber fluid. Leif picked up the shot glass and studied the liquor. He put the glass back on the bar, untasted.

"You're a generous fellow," Leif said. "You have

the look of someone who doesn't let anything slip by him."

"Well now, I've heard others say that, but I'm a mite too modest to speak it 'bout myself."

Leif knocked back the whiskey in a single gulp. It burned and came close to choking him as surely as if a noose had been dropped around his neck. He couldn't help making a face.

"I brew that rotgut myself. A few rusty nails in alcohol to give color, a drop or two of nitric acid to give it kick. Yes, sir, that's the best whiskey in town, if I do say so myself."

"Much obliged," Leif said, his voice ragged. "Generous and clever, that's you."

The barkeep beamed.

"Tell me about Will Harding. Heard tell he drank here and sometimes talked to one particular gent. A cowboy with a rattlesnake-hide hatband. The rattles hung down in back." Leif swallowed hard and wished for a glass of milk to quell the fire in his gut.

"Harding? The one you cut down in the show?" The barkeep turned cagey. "I might know a little about him and his partner. They spent a good deal of time back there, yeah, that table, their heads together, whispering like conspirators. But now and again they raised their voices."

"What'd you hear them saying?"

The barkeep looked around the room. A half dozen customers had edged closer when they saw a celebrity in their midst.

"You ever put on a show for . . . friends?"

Leif understood he was being extorted. If this was what it took for him to find out more, so be it. He looked around the room, estimated angles, and came to his decision.

"You willing to have an apple shot off your head?"

The barkeep opened his mouth, then clamped it shut. He shook his head slowly.

"I'll do it. I seen how you never miss. It'd be somethin' to tell the boys about back on the Jolly J spread." The cowboy speaking was so drunk, he hardly stood without wobbling about.

"Yeah, go on, Max. Let him use you as a target." The small crowd egged on the cowboy, who seemed more willing by the minute to be part of Leif's performance.

Leif looked around and judged distances. He pointed to the bar and said, "Sit there, up on the bar in front of the mirror. And put that beer mug on your head."

"He can hardly sit up straight," muttered the barkeep. "There's no way he'll keep it balanced on top of his pointy head more 'n a few seconds."

"That's all this will take. Set it there, on top of his head. He can hold it in place," Leif said. He took five long strides that put him on the far side of the room. He drew the six-shooter in his left holster and rested the barrel on his right shoulder. A quick glance and then he pulled the trigger.

The man on the bar toppled over onto his side, laughing so hard he could hardly be stopped. The barkeep shook him hard enough to rattle his teeth.

"Max, you fool. He missed. He missed you by a country mile. Sit up!" The bartender glared at Leif. "You didn't even bust the beer mug." He held it up, unscratched. The others in the saloon muttered among themselves. A man who had been passed out at a table in the rear stirred, put on his hat, and came over on unsteady feet.

Leif stared at him. The man wore a hat exactly as Marta had described. A quick scowl in the barkeep's direction confirmed his guess. This was the man Leif wanted to get the information from.

"You got to admit you didn't come close." The man rubbed his chin and shook his head. "No, sir, you missed by a country mile."

"How'd you know, you ole drunk? You was passed out and missed every second of it." The man speaking from among the crowd found himself shuffled aside as Leif moved between them. Like a cowboy cutting a calf from the herd, he was separating his quarry from the others.

"Sit him back where he was and put the beer mug on his head again. Then come over here and take a gander," Leif said.

There was some grumbling, but Max was repositioned. The man in the rattlesnake-banded hat crowded close. Leif silently pointed. It took him a few seconds to understand what the trickshot artist had done. The cowboy burst out, "He drilled the mirror smack-dab where the mug was reflected. Lookee there! He shot the reflection dead center!"

"What?" The barkeep let the drunk flop onto his side again and whirled around. He leaned over the back bar and put his finger into the hole Leif had shot through the mirror. "You weren't aiming at old Max? You intended to put a hole in my mirror?"

"Where the reflection was. I can do it for real to prove it wasn't a fluke, if you guarantee you won't wobble all around like he's doing." Leif pointed to Max. The drunk was kicking and laughing and carrying on.

"You ain't puttin' a hole through any of my mugs," the barkeep said. "And you're not doing it with it sitting on *my* head."

Leif let the man rage about how much the mirror cost and how hard it was to replace it. He dropped a twenty-dollar greenback on the bar.

"That'll cover you having a sign made up telling what happened on this very spot. That hole will draw more business than the whole mirror ever did." Leif jerked his thumb over his shoulder in the direction of the knot of customers. "They're about to bust wide open, telling what they just witnessed."

The bartender snatched the scrip and stuffed it into a pocket before Leif could change his mind. He muttered and then pushed Max hard enough to roll him off the bar onto the floor. He looked over the bar at the prone drunk and snapped, "You get on out of here. I've seen enough of your ugly face for the day."

"Ezra over at the Elephant's Snout will listen when I tell him what Mr. Gu—Mr. Gunn—Trickshot here just done. Ezra might even stand me a drink or two whilst I sp-spin my st-story." Max crawled on his hands and knees and went out the swinging doors.

"See?" Leif saw that the barkeep wasn't going to press the matter any more. He reached out and grabbed the man with the rattlesnake hat before he followed Max out the door. "You lost a bet. Now, tell me what you already told the senorita."

"The Esquivel girl?" The man looked a little sheepish. "I might have been exaggerating a tad with her."

Leif took the man by the elbow and steered him to a table at the rear of the saloon. He pushed hard enough to drop the man into a chair. A quick gesture brought over a half bottle of whiskey and two glasses. Leif had no desire to drink, but his companion did. He knocked back a pair of shots before coming to a decision.

"Well?"

"Well now," the cowboy said, launching into his story. "Don't think nothing's gonna happen to me, what with Harding dead and all." He blinked a couple times as he studied Leif closely.

"Miss Esquivel said Harding mentioned a woman with a scar on her face. Tell me all about it."

"He said it was crawling down her face like a *culebra*. It slithered from her hair down her temple and cheek to her chin." The man traced an S shape on his own face, leaving behind a dirty parody of the scar.

"Which side?"

He shrugged and shook his head. "He didn't say. All he said was that the scar made her undesirable to anyone but Simkins, who claimed it gave him a way to identify her from all other women. I think Harding had a lech for the woman, but she was too attached to Simkins."

Leif's mouth turned to cotton. Petunia had a scar that fit that description. She had been thrown from a horse face-first into a barbed wire fence when she was fourteen and Leif was seven. The accident had happened on his birthday, and she had hidden in her room, her face bandaged. He saw little of his sister after that. She was always riding the range away from home, making their ma anxious and their pa angry.

Every time their pa had erupted and given her a whipping, she rode farther and spent more time away. She was enough older that Leif remembered little about her since he had grown up with his two younger sisters.

Until then. Until that day.

He tried to remember the last time he had seen Petunia. It had been a day or two before Simkins and his cutthroats had slaughtered the rest of the Gunnarson family.

"Did he call her by name?"

"Randy Sally," he said. "Randy Sally Randall. There've been stories about a woman outlaw for years, but nobody ever put much store in them."

"Why not?"

"They're too fantastical, that's why. She's supposed to be the fastest gun in all of Wyoming. And she's as accurate as, well, as you. Who can put any store in that, a woman sharpshooter? All that and a road agent?"

"And she rides with Luther Simkins?"

"Harding made her out to be his bodyguard. Did you ever hear such a tale in all your born days?" The man took another shot and smacked his lips in appreciation. "He said she was Simkins's pet, a delicate flower. Then he laughed like it was some kind of joke. If it was, he didn't bother explaining it, but then he'd as soon stick a knife in your ribs as look at you. Will Harding wasn't in town long, but he made quite an impression—yes, sir, he did. All he did was boast on how he made life for the stationmaster a nightmare." He tentatively reached for the bottle.

Leif grabbed it, considered for a split second that

this man might be one of Simkins's henchmen, and discarded the idea. This was a cowboy, a local, and someone known to everyone else in town. He shoved the bottle toward the man. Without another word, he pushed away from the table and followed Max from the saloon into the street. Leif knew he was creating a house of cards. Nothing said the woman riding with Simkins even existed, much less had a scar that matched what he remembered of his oldest sister.

Leif Gunnarson walked back to the Wild West Show site. Marta Esquivel had tethered his horse there and was nowhere to be seen. He mounted and rode from town, taking the road already traveled by Wyoming Bob's Wild West Show. When he came to a fork in the road, he stopped and stared. One way lay the show that had been his home and family for ten years. He had no idea where the branching road led.

Making his decision, he put his heels to White Lightning's flanks and galloped hard.

CHAPTER TEN

THE WAY STATION looked deserted, but Leif Gunnarson had the feeling of eyes watching him. There were enough horses in the corral for two teams, should a stagecoach drive up and want a fresh yoke. He rode closer, then stopped. A dog barked inside the house. Hardly realizing he did so, he reached down and slid the leather thong off the Peacemaker's hammer, getting ready to swap lead.

"I don't mean you any harm," he called out when he caught a glimpse of a rifle barrel poking through a loophole near the door. Leif rode a little closer and waited for a response. The rifle didn't withdraw, and the dog barked louder. "Do you need help?"

He caught his breath as the door opened a crack. A man peered out, taking a quick look past Leif to be sure he rode alone. Only then did the man step out. The rifle barrel continued to poke through the loophole. The way it bobbed about warned Leif that a nervous finger likely stroked along the trigger.

"I know you," the man said, squinting a mite. "You're that sharpshooter fellow from the Wild West Show."

"Leif Gunnarson. I go by the moniker of Trickshot." He rode a little closer and caught sight of a woman's skirt billowing out the door. She didn't budge from her post, training the rifle on him.

"That's you. You're the one!"

"I reckon so," Leif said, not sure which "the one" he was. But the man then motioned to the woman to draw back on the rifle.

"We rode into town to see you. That's quite a show you put on. You give us, me and my woman, a sample? Just a little bit?" The stationmaster waved his wife out. She clutched the rifle as if her life depended on it. Leif wondered if it had recently.

"Mind if I dismount? This is my horse, White Lightning." He patted the stallion's neck, then slid to the ground when the woman handed the rifle to her husband.

"That's too much of a horse to put in any of our teams. Mostly, we got good horses, strong but old. Older. We get them from the ranches all around after they finish their yearly cattle drives. The cowboys don't need a big remuda anymore."

"Hush up, Bo. This here's a star. He don't care about how you get bilked out of company money by all them swindlers." The woman peered up at him. "You got to excuse us. We're testy after . . . what's happened."

Leif let his horse drink from a watering trough. He took his time asking. The two of them had accepted him as harmless enough, a mere performer, but whatever had set them on edge still burned bright in their minds.

"Don't go getting all upset over what she's saying, Mr. Trickshot, sir. With you here, there's nothing that can happen. We seen how you cut down that owlhoot. From all the gossip about him, he was a bad, bad man."

"We asked Marshal Denny about him, we did," the woman said, elbowing her way in front of her husband. "The marshal, he told us the dead man was one of *them*."

"One of the Simkins gang?" Leif caught his breath. The man in the saloon had given him accurate gossip. And this was finally a trail worth following to find Luther Simkins.

"They been robbing ever single stage what comes by. Got to the point where the company's sending them through at odd times to confuse the gang. A regular schedule only lets them sleep in late, as long as they get out to the road in time to hold us up." The man shuddered, although it was hot in the noonday sun.

"They's worse than that," the woman said. "When they figured out the stages were coming at all times during the day and even through the night, they started putting their gang on as passengers. *She* was the worst." The woman spat. The dark expression on her face matched any Leif had ever seen. Something troubled the woman and made her willing to use that rifle she'd handed over to her husband.

"She? A woman came by?" Leif pulled White Lightning from the trough and led the stallion into the shade cast by the way station. The two joined him.

"She gunned down two passengers, forced the driver and shotgun messenger out of the box, and stole the whole danged coach. The marshal knows all about her but says there's not a wanted poster on her. How's that possible? I asked him, but he didn't have an answer."

"Is this Sally Randall? I've heard the name."

The stationmaster fixed a gimlet eye on Leif. "The marshal said you brung in some of the gang and collected big rewards. You going after Simkins hisself?"

"You turning bounty hunter?" The woman cut through to the heart of the matter.

"Some folks look down on bounty hunters," Leif said, feeling them out. He needed more from them, and saying or doing anything that cut off the flow of information only made tracking the gang that much harder.

"Not us," the man avowed. "Truth is, the stage company's offered a hefty reward for all of them varmints, the woman included."

"Especially the woman," the stationmaster's wife said bitterly. "Whoever heard of a lady murdering two men in cold blood like she done? And one of them was the town's new schoolteacher."

"Graduated from one of them Eastern colleges, I heard," the stationmaster said. He looked glum. "He was the only one to answer the town's call to replace the old schoolmarm. She upped and married Joshua Gardner less 'n a month after his wife died in childbirth. Can't blame Josh none. Raising that brood of his has to be a chore, and with a newborn . . ."

"Do you have a map so you can point out where the gang's held up your stages? I'm especially anxious to see where the woman road agent took over the coach." Leif doubted Sally Randall had driven the stage far by herself. Either the stage was abandoned or driven somewhere near for Simkins or one of his gang to take the reins.

"We got a big ole map on the wall showing the entire route 'tween here and Cheyenne. We're right about halfway between Newell Bluff and Kinney. Come on in," the man invited. Then he glanced at his wife. She nodded approval and lowered the rifle.

They went into the way station. Leif had seen army forts that weren't as heavily barricaded. The gang had spooked these folks something fierce.

"There it is. Finest map I ever did see. I got it from a cavalry captain whose job it was making maps. He said this one started off as something John Frémont did, but it's a good map in spite of that." The station-master chuckled. "General Frémont was always something of a bungler. Even with the likes of Kit Carson showing him around, he never quite got things right. But this map, now, it's an official US government map."

Leif traced the stage routes until he found the northernmost one that curved up like a bow and came down toward Newell Bluff. A greasy spot on the paper showed where someone had pressed a finger repeatedly.

"This is where the stage was held up? The one with the woman robber?"

"That's the exact place." The stationmaster looked suspicious. "How'd you know that?"

"It comes with being Trickshot." Leif knew that wasn't any kind of explanation at all, but it didn't surprise him when it worked. It had many times in the past. People thought he performed miracles because he was so good with a gun. He didn't understand that or have to in order to use it to his advantage.

He studied the map closely and worked out several likely spots where Simkins might hide out. It took him another minute to study the land around Newell Bluff and find the Esquivel home. If the outlaws had been roaming toward the town and encountered that homestead, it eliminated several possible hideouts.

"You promised to show us some of that fancy gun work like you done in the show," the stationmaster said.

"What do you have in mind?"

Leif smiled as the two put their heads together and whispered as if swapping deep, dark secrets. The woman pushed her husband aside and stepped up to tell him, "We got an old tree out back with knotholes in it. Can you shoot them all out?"

Leif nodded. He had to study the matter some before making a promise, but the targets sounded simple enough. They went around back of the cabin, and the old oak tree showed it had been here longer than the way station or the horses or about anything else. The trunk was too large for him to reach around and touch his fingers on the far side. The first limb was a considerable ways up. Near it was a big gnarly knothole the size of his fist.

"Yup, that's one. There's the rest of them." The stationmaster carefully pointed to the knots reaching a full twenty feet up along the trunk.

"This might be dangerous," Leif said. "Wood like that's harder than the trunk around it and can bounce bullets off like rain pelting off a tin roof."

"Does that mean you can't—" The woman's voice was drowned out by the roar from Leif's Peacemaker. He cleared leather and fanned off six shots. The first four slugs hit dead-on. The fifth went ricocheting off into the distance. He settled down and plugged the final knothole with his last slug.

"Glory be," the woman said. "You done hit every last one of them."

The stationmaster let out a whoop and slapped his thigh. "I knowed you could do it, Mr. Trickshot. That's the finest shooting I ever did see. The outlaws won't stand a chance again' you; no sir, they won't have a ghost of a chance."

"Any reason you had a grudge against those knotholes?" he asked as he shucked out the spent cartridges and reloaded. He looked toward the road, through the stand of trees. His six-shooter dropped easily into its holster. He slid the leather thong off the hammer of the Peacemaker at his left side.

"Woodpeckers come down in the morning. They take special glee in hammering at those hard spots. It sounds like a whole danged artillery company's firing off. Can't sleep. With the knots gone, they only have softer wood to peck at for their bugs."

"Makes sense now that you've explained it," Leif said. He continued to study the trees in the direction of the road. As keyed up as he was, he jumped at shadows, but not this time. The way the low-hanging leaves shifted and shook warned him of someone trying to hide. It might have been an animal, but a deer would have no call to move about this long. It could have been someone spying, someone curious as to what went on at the depot, but too timid to come out.

Or was the Simkins gang making the stationmaster's nightmare come true? From what Leif saw inside the cabin, there wasn't anything worth stealing, but to a man like Luther Simkins, that meant nothing. Visions of his ma and pa tied to chairs and barbed wire fastened around their throats flashed. He saw and heard flames and screams. His pa had been a well-off lawyer but wasn't rich. Simkins hadn't even robbed the house before setting it on fire. The torture and killing had been his goal. If he was sneaking up on the way station, Simkins might have in mind more devilment that had nothing to do with robbing a stagecoach.

"Much obliged for everything you told me about the road agents," Leif said. He politely touched the brim of his hat and started around the cabin to fetch his horse before the man or his wife thought up new targets for him.

"You get them scoundrels, Mr. Trickshot," said the woman. "You get them good, and we'll see the stage company's reward is paid. They might try to cheat us out of our pay now and again, but getting rid of those outlaws'd make us beholden to you."

"Us and the company and every passenger coming from Cheyenne." The stationmaster looked up at Leif. "You need anything, you just ask us. It's an honor meeting a great star like you. It is."

"The crowned heads of Europe," Leif muttered.

"How's that, Mr. Trickshot?"

"Performing before the kings and queens of Europe wasn't as good as shooting out those knotholes for you. Sleep tight, now." He touched the brim of his hat, wheeled White Lightning about, and galloped northward, away from the road.

He rode less than ten minutes, enough to be out of sight of the way station. Veering to his left, he found a game trail through the wooded area. The low-hanging limbs forced him to ride bent over until he reached a clearing. He gave White Lightning his head and reached the other side in less than a minute, only to rein in and drop to the ground. If someone followed him, he'd spot them on the far side of the clearing long before they overtook him.

Both hands were filled with his Peacemakers. He took practice sightings across the clearing, then returned the guns to their resting places. Impatiently waiting, he knew he might be jumping at shadows, but he didn't think so. Someone had trailed him. If they came from the direction of the road, his instincts would prove right yet again.

But how long should he wait? He worried that Simkins and his gang would move on soon. There wasn't much for them to steal in this part of Wyoming. From the sound of it, they had reached the point where the stagecoach wouldn't carry enough to make a robbery worthwhile. He made plans and watched across the pasture, coming alert at a small movement.

He dropped into a crouch and drew, twisting as he did so. Both six-shooters were out, cocked and aimed at a bush behind him.

"No, don't shoot! Please, Mr. Gunnarson. I did not mean to frighten you!"

He came out of his crouch and eased his six-guns back into their holsters. Anger flared as he called out, "Get out here where I can see you. What do you mean, sneaking up on me like that?"

"It was a joke. No, that is not so. There was no

joke. It was to see what you were doing." Marta Esquivel pushed through the bush. Her skirt tangled on a thorn. She tugged it free. Leif tensed but did not pull out his pistols again. She only worked to keep from tearing the cloth, not to draw the six-gun belted around her trim waist.

"You're lying," Leif said cruelly. He churned inside at dealing with the young woman.

"You do not need to say such a thing." Marta looked at the ground and shifted uncomfortably, then came to a decision. She straightened, and her eyes fixed on his. Her chin set, and defiance entered her words. "Yes, I lied. I followed you because you hunt down the man responsible for killing my family."

"Let me be. I work better alone." Leif cleared his throat. As righteous as his anger at her was, the way she challenged him now caused him to shift nervously. It was as if her earlier uncertainty had transferred to him. Such feelings dared not slow his hand.

"We make a good team. We should ride together. We should ride for vengeance." She crossed her arms and looked as if this decided everything. For her it might, but not for Leif.

"Get on back to Newell Bluff, and tell the marshal what I'm doing out here at the stage way station," Leif said. If she did as he asked, that would give him several days' head start finding Luther Simkins and his gang. "He'll want to join in." He knew how lame this sounded. He added more incentive for her to return to town. "A posse. He can muster up a posse, tell everyone about the reward, and—"

"I am not so easily duped. I will ride with you. If not at your side, then I will follow your trail. So far, I have done a good job." Marta rested her hand on the six-shooter at her hip. If a man had made such a move, Leif would have drawn, thinking he was being called out.

"If I tie you up, it'd take a day or two to get free. That's all the lead I need."

"The man and woman in the way station," Marta said slowly, thoughtfully. She eyed him like a wolf might a rabbit. "They told you something that set you on the outlaws' trail. Even if it does take a day for me to escape, and I might not—do you want me to die at your hand like that?—those two will tell me what they have said to you."

Leif considered other possibilities to get rid of Marta Esquivel. Short of gunning her down, the result always came out the same. She would dog his steps since he was easier to follow than Simkins was to find.

"Keep up. I won't slow down for you." He spun about, tugged on White Lightning's reins, and mounted. Leif got his bearings and trotted off toward the spot where the stagecoach had been stolen. For a few minutes, he wondered if he had left Marta behind. Then he heard her horse's hoofbeats and resigned himself to having a trail companion.

CHAPTER ELEVEN

WHY ARE WE stopping here? The place you seek is only over that hill." Marta Esquivel pointed to the road and how it entered a rocky patch with steep uphill grades. Any stagecoach entering this tumble of rocks had to slow considerably, the team pulling hard and exhausting itself to reach the top of a hill that marked easier downward grades.

"We camp here and look over the spot the first thing after sunrise," Leif Gunnarson said. "It's twilight. If we blunder in now, we can miss something that'll get us killed."

"There is more. What are you not telling me?" She fixed him with her fiery stare. Even after two days of riding with her, Leif felt a twinge. No matter how he vowed to ignore her, he found it impossible. Not for the first time he regretted allowing her to ride with him. But short of shooting her down, he still didn't see any way to keep her from his side.

The truth was, he enjoyed having such a lovely trail companion. She added to the beauty of the land simply by being in it—until she began pecking away at him for not finding the gang faster.

"I'm not taking any chances of falling into an ambush." He dismounted and scouted around for a suitable spot to build a fire. This was another benefit of having Marta riding with him. He boiled oatmeal and fixed a mess of beans, sometimes with barely edible biscuits, but mostly his trail provender lacked flavor. Too often, chewing on a twig would have been more palatable. Marta worked magic on even the simplest meals, adding herbs and greens growing all around. While some of those meals could hardly be called tasty, they weren't unsavory like his.

He scraped out a firepit and lined it with rocks before gathering kindling and larger hunks of wood more suitable for cooking.

"You said the road agents robbed this stage days ago. More than a week! Do they stay and wait for bounty hunters to come to the scene of their crime?" She made it sound as if he were the stupidest man in the world for believing such nonsense.

"If they robbed the stage here once, they'd do it again. They'll have scouted the area and decided this was the best spot along the road for miles for a holdup." Leif said nothing about blundering around in the twilight and destroying anything that might give a hint to where the highwaymen had gone. The crime having taken place almost a week earlier meant wind and rain had erased much of the trail. He hoped that stealing an entire stagecoach left more of an imprint.

"You just want me to cook another meal," Marta said.

"You don't have to," he said. "It's my turn anyway."

"No, no! I will cook. There is no reason to poison us when we are so close to catching the gang." She began unpacking her saddlebags and taking out this and that to fix dinner.

"I'll fetch some water," Leif said. "I hear a stream not too far downhill." He hefted the coffeepot and set off to find the promised stream. In the gathering dark, he slipped and fell into the water.

Cursing, he backed out of the shallow creek bed and pressed out as much water from his soaked clothing as he could. Leif froze when he heard a soft chuckling. He put down the coffeepot and half turned, his hand going to his Peacemaker. Marta's silhouette cautioned him against throwing down.

"There you go, sneaking up on me again. I told you not to do that."

"Oh, but you said that a day ago. Two. It is such an easy thing to forget." She giggled and came forward with the bottom of a Dutch oven. "I needed more water than you were set to bring. Should I squeeze my water from your clothing? Is there enough in your fine boots to pour out?"

"Very funny," he said. Then Leif had to laugh. "I'm not usually so careless."

"You react quickly," she said. "A striking snake is slow compared to you." She dipped her pot in the stream and filled it to overflowing. With excessive care, she put the water-filled Dutch oven down on a rock. "Teach me." Her voice came soft and serious.

"Teach you what?" The request took him by surprise. Leif expected more joshing and not this.

"How to draw my six-gun as quick as you do. How to shoot and not miss. If we fight the gang, I want every one of my bullets to take a life."

"That's not something you learn overnight."

"Then we should start now. I will practice. I will learn quickly."

There wasn't any doubting her sincerity. What she asked of him was reasonable. Even if she failed to reach a fraction of the skill he had accumulated over a full decade of practice, just not flinching when she fired would make a difference in a heated exchange.

"Come over here."

She hesitated, then came closer with a tentative step.

"What do you want of me?"

"Stand with your feet apart. The width of your shoulders." Leif looked at her critically, then amended, "Make that the width of your hips. Get settled. Keep your balance. Hand resting lightly against your holster."

"Like this?"

He nodded. "As you exhale, slide your hand directly up, no wasted motion; grip your pistol, and keep moving smoothly."

She fumbled. They tried again. This time she drew her pistol without fumbling.

"I should fire then?"

"Not yet, not yet!" Leif scuttled to the side in case

she pulled back on the trigger. "First things first. Baby steps."

"You think me a child?" Her ire rose.

"Not at all," he said in a low voice, then louder, "You'll waste ammo if you fire every time you practice your draw. More than that, you're likely to shoot yourself in the foot." He considered having her unload her six-gun, then decided she would take it as an insult.

"I would never do that." Her words said one thing, but she gingerly replaced the six-gun and squared off again. This time she drew in a single motion.

"That's not the fastest I ever saw, but you won't be facing anyone who wants to fill you with lead."

"What if I do? And what about you?" Marta recrossed her arms. He had aroused her anger again.

"Don't. You want to get your smoke wagon out and ready so you can accurately fire. This time exhale as you draw."

"There is so much to remember," she muttered. But Marta did as she was told. After a dozen more pulls, he signaled for her to stop.

"Let's fix some grub." He looked around. Night had wrapped them fully in darkness. The nocturnal beasts were out, hunting and being hunted. He forestalled her objection by picking up her pot of water along with his filled coffeepot and starting uphill for camp. He heard her behind, tripping now and then on unseen rocks.

The food was simple and went down well. His coffee tasted more like mud, but Marta didn't complain. When he turned in, drawing the blanket up around his chin, he saw her silhouetted from the fire. She was practicing what he had taught her. Leif drifted off to sleep with the soft hiss of gunmetal scraping leather in his ears.

He awoke to the same sound. Coming upright, he reached for his Peacemakers. There was no call for him to get all upset. Marta stood by a cottonwood where she had drawn a crude face on the trunk with a piece of charcoal from the fire, pulling her six-shooter and aiming it between the target's sooty eyes.

"Did you kill him?" Leif stood and stretched, then buckled his gun belt around his middle and settled the six-shooters.

"Every time," she said. "Are you not going to ask whose picture I drew?"

Leif grinned and said, "That's not a good likeness of me."

"I thought it was very good." Marta thrust her six-gun into her holster with a surety that unnerved him a little. She acted as if she were ready to shoot it out this very instant. It had taken him ten years to work up the gumption to kill a man in a gunfight—and he had been forced into it by defending himself.

"I'll fix breakfast. There's not much I can do to ruin a bowl of oatmeal." He waited for her to contradict him. Instead, she turned back to the caricature on the tree trunk and drew. She had cleared leather a half dozen times when he took up the coffeepot and started down to the creek.

They ate in silence. He cast a few sideways glances at her, but Marta was lost in deep thought. Disturbing what dark fantasies raged in her head was the last thing he wanted to do. He let his own mind go as blank as possible, waiting for ideas to come bubbling up from the depths. Leif finally gave up. Whatever decisions Marta had reached trumped anything he had considered.

They packed and led their horses up to the road. Leif signaled her to silence, handed her White Lightning's reins, and advanced slowly until he reached a vantage point overlooking the site of the stagecoach theft. The rocks on either side of the road gave easy cover, but that hadn't been needed. Sally Randall had been inside the coach. Leif walked down the road to a broad U between the higher grades and imagined her drawing a derringer—or did she carry a small-caliber six-gun in a purse?—and cold-bloodedly shooting the two passengers.

"Rest in peace, Reverend," Leif said. He saw a pair of graves not far from the road. The marshal might have come out and buried the dead men, or the stationmaster had done the deed. Or had the driver and shotgun messenger taken the time to do the Christian thing and afford simple funerals? Whoever had buried the men hadn't placed markers on their graves.

Leif circled the area, then cut down a steep incline where wheel marks from a heavy conveyance had left distinct tracks.

He pondered what to do next. Following the stolen stagecoach tracks would lead him somewhere. He just had no idea where. The outlaws had taken the team, but what use did they have for an entire coach? They might have taken it simply because they could. If that was true, he would only waste time following a cold trail to a dead end.

"Mr. Trickshot! Leif! Come back to the road!"

Marta waved frantically to him. Trudging up the

slope took him past the graves again. Any fading resolve hardened. What Simkins and his "pet" had
done here was terrible, but compared to the way his
ma and pa had been killed, this was downright hu-
mane. Leif wiped sweat from his face and kept climbing to where Marta still waved wildly. They were in
this together, and their aim wasn't to stop stagecoach
robberies.

"What is it?" He brushed dust off his hat.

She handed him White Lightning's reins.

"A stage is coming. Do you hear it?" She cupped
one ear with her hand. Instead of listening, Leif
dropped to one knee and pressed his hand into the
roadbed. Vibrations warned that the stage came toward them at breakneck speed.

"They want to get through this stretch of the road
as fast as possible," he guessed. "If the driver keeps up
that pace, he'll have the horses die under his whip."

Even as he spoke, the team crested the hill to the
west. This stage had left Newell Bluff and was heading east toward Cheyenne by way of Kinney. He
started to pull his horse back off the road, then had
a sudden inspiration. Waving along with Marta, he
flagged down the stage. A guard beside the driver
lowered a shotgun and trained it on them.

The coach came to a creaking halt a dozen yards
away.

"You folks in trouble? You're not road agents, are
you?" The shotgun messenger kept the weapon snugged
up to his shoulder.

"No, we're not robbers," Leif called back. "Fact is,
we're tracking them down."

"You're bounty hunters, you and that purty lady?

That don't seem right." The guard lowered his voice and argued with the driver. All the time, he kept the shotgun pointed toward Leif.

"Enough of this," Marta said to Leif. Louder, she called, "This is Leif Johann Gunnarson, the man they call Trickshot. He is the finest marksman in all the West, perhaps in all the world. Of course he hunts road agents! We wish to ride with you and protect you from the road agents."

The guard lowered his shotgun a few inches.

"You're about standing on the graves of two victims of them killers," the guard said.

"Are you the one who buried them? That was a decent thing to do." Leif led his horse closer. Marta trailed. He saw how she kept her right hand resting outside her holster. He hoped she didn't show the guard the skill she had practiced so diligently. Giving him the name Trickshot had made him a tad friendlier, but the driver still held out for the guard to shoot them where they stood. Leif had seen the man's expression before in other dangerous situations.

"Me and Clement here, we done that." The guard rested the shotgun against the front of the driver's box. "You really Trickshot? I seen you at a show in St. Loo a year back."

"Two years," Leif said. "It's been a while since Wyoming Bob's Wild West Show played in St. Louis."

"Reckon that's so." He discussed the matter some more with the driver, then motioned them closer. "Clement says we'd be right happy to have you along, should there be any trouble with road agents. Company rules say you got to pay for a ticket, though."

"Do we get the price back if we kill any outlaws?"

Marta widened her stance and looked the world like a gunfighter. If the wind hadn't whipped around, causing her skirts to swirl, the picture would have been about perfect.

"The company's laid a sizable reward on their heads. If you collect that, the price of a ticket won't matter to you none." The guard pointed to the rear of the stage. "Tie your horses back there and climb aboard."

"After you pay me ten dollars. That's five for each of you."

"I will not pay!" Marta stamped her foot. The guard started to protest, but Leif cut him off.

"How about you let the lady ride for free and charge me double?"

This suited everyone concerned. Leif marveled at how simple some solutions were. All that was needed was calling a dog's tail a leg and everyone was satisfied.

Horses secured, he helped Marta into the compartment, then hopped in and settled down next to a man dressed in a threadbare dull brown suit two sizes too small for him. He wore a starched collar and had a filthy cravat with a stickpin sporting a blue stone. His hands endlessly wove patterns in his lap.

"How do you do?" Leif wondered at the man's nerves when he jumped at such a common greeting.

"Oh, I am doing fine. Why are you getting in out here in the middle of nowhere? Is something wrong? Should the driver have let you in when you didn't board back at the Newell Bluff depot? Or even the way station?"

"Those are nice folks at the way station," Leif said. "You changed teams there?"

The man nodded as if his head were mounted on a spring.

"We stopped and spoke with them. Did they happen to mention me?" Leif saw how surprise spread on the man's hatchet-thin face.

"They said Trickshot from the Wild West Show did some work for them. Are you he? Trickshot?" He looked at the silvered, intricately etched Peacemakers.

"He is," Marta said almost primly. "It is quite an honor to travel under his protection."

"Y-you're guarding this stage?" The man brightened. "I've heard of you. You hit whatever you aim at."

"His fame is worldwide," Marta said. "What of you, sir? What's your business that you brave the road agents to get to Kinney? Or do you travel on to Cheyenne?"

"I'm a peddler. Soaps, fragrances, I have . . ."

Leif stopped listening as the man fell into a familiar spiel, trying to sell his potions and concoctions to Marta, who feigned interest. The stage rattled and clanked up the steep incline and then sailed down the far side. Leif watched the countryside roll past as the driver drove his team mercilessly. Even with the addition of a man reputed to never miss his target, the driver wanted the trip to be over as soon as possible. Leif hoped he didn't kill the horses before they reached the next town.

Then he saw the riders coming up behind the coach, six-shooters drawn and bandannas pulled up over their noses.

The cry burst from his lips at the same instant Marta saw them. "Robbers!"

CHAPTER TWELVE

L EIF GUNNARSON TRIED to draw his pistols, but the
lurching stagecoach threw him around inside the
compartment. He collided with the peddler, and they
crumpled to the floor, arms and legs entangled.

"You pull this here stage over, or I'll kill you dead.
I swear I'll do it, or my name's not Randy Sally!"

The stage hit a rock in the road and threw both
Leif and the peddler into the air. They crashed down
across Marta's lap. The three of them struggled to
keep from being further entangled. Just when Leif
thought he was getting free and coming to his knees
so he could draw, the stage stopped abruptly. He lost
his balance.

Gunfire from outside grew to a deafening level.
The air filled with gun smoke, choking the three of
them inside.

"What're we gonna do? They'll kill us for sure!"

The peddler's voice rose shrilly. He clutched at Leif and kept him from drawing.

"Let go of me," Leif said. He swung around, and his elbow connected with the man's nose. Cartilage broke and blood spurted. The peddler howled like a banshee. The screeching changed tenor when the door was yanked open.

They all stared down the barrel of a six-shooter aimed into the compartment.

Leif blinked and tried to focus. The six-gun's barrel looked big enough for a freight train to come roaring out of, but he stared into the bandit's eyes. Her blue eyes held a violet tint. Just like his sister's. Leif tried to make out any scar on the road agent's face, but the bandanna was pulled up too far and her hat tugged down over her ears, hiding where Petunia Gunnarson's scar had been.

"You folks just get yerselves on out of there. Don't go doing anything dumb, or you'll end up weighing a pound or two more 'cuz you'll be filled with my lead." The woman laughed, and it sounded like a harsh cackle. The sound tore across Leif's nerves.

He shoved the peddler off him. The man tried to jump down, missed the exterior iron rung step, and fell face-first onto the ground, much to the merriment of the woman robber and her three companions.

"We got the strongbox down, and now we got ourselves a right clumsy man down on the ground beside it. Ain't that a sight?"

The peddler tried to stand, but one of the male road agents planted a boot squarely in the middle of his back and held him down. The outlaw reached out a grimy hand for Marta.

"Why don't you let me help you down, missy? I was beginning to think there wasn't any reason we held up the stage. That strongbox can't hold a treasure that comes close to you."

Marta Esquivel skidded along the compartment floor and dropped to the ground. She jerked free of the outlaw's grasp.

"Don't you be like that, missy. Why, I'll show you a real good time." He stomped down hard on the peddler. "It'll be a better time than this worm could ever give you."

The outlaw tugged his mask down and said, "Now, you got to admit I'm a whole sight purtier than this fellow. I—"

The peddler forced himself up to his hands and knees, unbalancing the road agent. This set off a string of explosions. From the driver's box, the guard opened up with his shotgun. The fierce roar drowned the outlaw's outcry as he died. The woman road agent swung around and fanned off three fast shots. From the sounds outside the stage compartment, the guard had taken a tumble to the ground. Leif grabbed for his six-shooters, but Marta stood in the way.

With one hand, he closed on the back of her blouse and yanked her into the stage again, and with the other he cleared his holster and got off a shot. He missed the woman because she had dived to the side, firing as she went, but Leif winged another robber. The slug ripped through the owlhoot's duster and left a strip of canvas dangling that flopped around as he moved. Blood oozed from a shallow wound beneath. Before Leif got off a second shot, the stage lurched and slammed him back into the rear bench seat. The door banged to and fro. Marta kicked at it and wiggled inside.

The countryside flashed past as the driver whipped the team and shouted at the top of his lungs like a mule skinner.

"Get off me," Marta yelped when the speed of the stage caused Leif to fall against her. Leif climbed over her, leaned out the window, and got off another two shots.

"They're not giving up," Leif gasped. He aimed the best he could out the window of the swaying, bucking stagecoach. His marksmanship was better in the Wild West Show when he was blindfolded. Every round went flying far off target. The outlaws' hail of lead drove him back inside.

"I can shoot at them." Marta tried to push past him. He shoved her back.

"The other side. They'll come at us from both sides."

She didn't argue. Scooting about on her knees, she pivoted, ripped away the leather curtain, and let out a cry of surprise. A road agent galloped alongside, not five feet away. She tried to raise her pistol and fire point-blank, but the motion of the stage betrayed her.

Leif hardly looked at the outlaw as he reached back around and fired. It was a trick shot. And Trickshot did not miss.

"You got him! He fell off his horse!"

Leif heaved himself to the front bench seat and tried to get a shot back at the woman road agent. His gut churned as he wondered if she could be his lost sister. The bandanna over her face hid any recognizable scar, and her voice was gravelly and rough, not like he remembered how Petunia spoke. But it had been ten years. Ten years and a passel of miles, if Sally Randall was his sister riding under an assumed name.

"There's no one to shoot," Marta complained. "The stagecoach is bouncing around too much, even if I had a target." She let out a hiss like a striking rattler. "You should have taught me marksmanship instead of how to draw. That did me no good at all."

"You didn't shoot yourself," Leif pointed out. He didn't add that she hadn't accidentally shot him, either. He sent a quick round off to the side of the racing stage. His aim at the mounted robber wasn't any better than before. The outlaw he had winged wasn't even moved to dodge a near miss.

"The horses," Marta said anxiously. "They tire quickly now. We will never outrun those monsters if the horses fail us!"

Leif wasn't jostled about as badly as he had been when the driver tried to escape. He fancied he heard the horses wheezing as air refused to gust into their lungs as they strained along the uneven road.

"We've got no choice but to fight. Rest your six-gun against the coach frame to steady it. When we stop, the outlaws will rush us again." Leif wiped dust and sweat off his face. Why did the road agents persist? The strongbox had been tossed down. Anything of value had to be in it—and it was miles back along the road. All he could think was how the attack was done out of sheer spite. They simply enjoyed torturing and killing.

He swallowed as he remembered too vividly finding his parents, then hiding under the floorboards to escape the fire that ravaged the Gunnarson home. Some men killed because they had to. Luther Simkins and his gang killed and tortured because they got a sick pleasure from others' suffering.

The stagecoach rocked to a halt. The driver screamed and shouted obscenities at the road agents but didn't accompany his words with gunfire. The shotgun must have been the only weapon in the driver's box, and it was on the ground near the strongbox.

"You two come on out. Toss out your guns first; then you follow them out!" Sally Randall sat astride her horse at what she thought was a safe distance.

Leif pushed Marta back. "Watch the other side of the coach. There are at least two robbers besides her."

"But—" Marta quieted when she saw him concentrate on making a long shot using only his sidearm. The outlaw bobbed about on a nervous horse at a range of twenty yards. Worse, the sun was in Leif's eyes.

He sighted in and fired. The instant he drew back on the trigger, he realized he had missed. Sally Randall's horse reared, pawing at the air, then hit on all fours and galloped away. He stuck his head out and fired. The range and target were against him. He emptied one Peacemaker, then the other, and did nothing but make the outlaw's horse run faster.

"They hightailed it. They are afraid of you, Mr. Trickshot!" Marta threw her arms around his neck and hugged him.

He disengaged and sat back, reloading quickly.

"I didn't run them off. They had us dead to rights. Something else scared them." He cocked his head to the side. "Listen. Hooves. Lots of them coming toward us."

Marta thrust half her body out the far window and craned her neck. She popped back inside and said breathlessly, "*Soldados*. Soldiers. Many of them!"

Leif kicked open the door and jumped down. White Lightning was still tied to the rear of the coach, but his flanks were lathered from the frantic run. Leif calmed the horse the best he could, then did the same for Marta's roan gelding. By the time the two horses were settled, the cavalry patrol trotted up.

The young lieutenant at the head of the column barked orders to his sergeant, splitting the patrol into halves. A corporal led one after Sally Randall, and the sergeant motioned for his troopers to head in the opposite direction after other road agents.

"You two survive unscathed?" The officer pushed his braided hat back and rubbed his eyes to clear them of dust. "We heard gunfire and arrived in time to see your driver try to outrun them."

"Is he all right? The guard was hit, maybe killed." Leif looked around and saw the driver climbing down from the box.

The driver limped back and thrust out a grimy finger in the direction of the officer.

"Don't you just sit there astride that scrawny horse and jawing like that. Get after them! They's the ones what stole an entire coach and killed everyone in it, and they gunned down my friends and—"

"Clement, isn't it? Yes," the lieutenant said. "My troopers will catch them. We were sent on patrol specifically to capture them." The whole time the officer spoke, he had his eyes fixed on Marta Esquivel.

"You were too late to keep them from robbing me

again! They shot my friend down in cold blood, and they took the strongbox."

"What was in it?" The lieutenant shifted his eyes back to the driver. "Or do you not know?"

"I never asked, and Bennie Benson at the depot wasn't inclined to let me know, but it had to be something valuable. Otherwise, why put it into an iron box with a big ole lock on it?" The driver threw his hands up in resignation. "I got to get on into Kinney and report this. I lost a passenger, too. Can you have one of your boys bury him?"

"He was a peddler," Leif said. "He died trying to save us."

Marta looked at him and started to contradict him, then fell silent. Leif had no call to bad-mouth the peddler. The man had started the gunfight by fighting against Sally Randall, but he had to have known he was a goner no matter what he did or didn't do. Giving him a moment's glory was a small enough thing.

"He ain't getting no reward, not now that he's dead," the driver said. "The company put up the money for the capture or killing of those mangy . . ." He wandered off, grumbling to himself.

"I know you, don't I?" The lieutenant stared hard at Leif with suspicion. "I can't remember where."

"It's not from a wanted poster," Leif assured him. The officer relaxed.

"I remember now. I saw your face on a poster advertising the Wild West Show that traveled through Newell Bluff. You're the sharpshooter. What's your involvement in all this? Why aren't you with the rest of the show?" He glanced at White Lightning and

Marta's horse. Regular paying passengers wouldn't have their animals tied to the rear of the stage.

"Just victims of chance, being in the wrong place at the wrong time. We . . . we're on our way to rejoin the show. Farther down the road." Leif's discreet look at the woman silenced her. He had no desire to get into a lengthy discussion with the lieutenant about bounty hunters or vigilantes who thought they were above the law. He had seen men like this young officer before. Because they rode at the head of a cavalry column, they thought they were somehow superior to mere civilians.

"Why do I doubt that?" the officer said. He stared hard at Marta and asked her, "Is that true, miss? You're just a victim of chance, too?"

She only nodded. Before the lieutenant had a chance to question her further, the patrol headed by his sergeant returned. Leif saw the grim expression on the noncom's face. The report was terse and to the point. The squad had lost the outlaws. Before the sergeant finished his brief report, the corporal returned with a similar sorry outcome.

"Excuse me, miss." The lieutenant touched the brim of his hat, ordered the sergeant to form up the column again, and led the troopers ahead toward the town of Kinney. By the time the soldiers were out of sight, the driver had tended his horses and climbed into the box.

The driver looked at them. "You going on into town? I won't back your claim for a reward, in spite of you taking potshots at the road agents."

"There is no need to be so disagreeable," Marta said. "It is not your fault you were robbed."

Leif saw this was the wrong thing to say. Clement growled like a stepped-on dog.

"We'll take our leave," Leif called up to the driver. "Go on into town, and we'll be along when we can."

"You got to pay for riding on this here stage," Clement said.

"See you in town," Leif called. He hastily unfastened White Lightning's and Marta's horse's reins before the stage rumbled away. If he had been a second slower, Clement would have driven off with the horse still tied down.

"What an unpleasant man," Marta said, taking the reins of her horse from Leif.

Leif shrugged it off. Driving this section of Wyoming territory had turned into a death sentence. He stepped up into the saddle and wheeled White Lightning about, letting the stallion set the pace as they retraced the path to the spot where the outlaws had held up the stage.

"Why have we come back? There's nothing to see here." Marta looked around.

"There's the strongbox," Leif said. He dismounted and went to the box. The lock had been broken off with a rock. He kicked open the lid. "Empty. Either the road agents took whatever was inside, or the depot master sent this along with Clement as a decoy."

"Why?"

"The real money or letters or whatever was supposed to be in the strongbox might be hidden in the stage."

"If the robbers took the box," Marta said thoughtfully, "then the real shipment would be overlooked. Do you think they are that clever?"

Leif had no idea. For all he knew, the strongbox had been stuffed with greenbacks or a pound of gold. He hiked back to the road and stared at the peddler's body. Swarms of flies and gnats rose from the corpse as he neared. A coyote or another scavenger had already sampled the fresh meat. He turned away with a grimace when he saw the man's face. Crows had feasted, too.

"I'll bury him. There's no call taking him back to Newell Bluff or on to Kinney. Not in this condition." Leif held down his gorge as he found a spot where the earth was soft enough to dig. Using a stick and a flat stone, he scraped away a foot of dirt before he hit solid rock. He dragged the man's body to the shallow grave and laid him to rest. It took longer to pile rocks on top to keep the ever-hungry scavengers away than it had to dig the hole.

When he finished, he took a step back.

Marta came over and stood beside him. She laid her hand on his arm.

"Should we pray?"

"Go on, if you want to say a few words."

Whatever she said came out in Spanish and sounded appropriate to the task. She finished quickly, crossing herself.

"Let's get on into Kinney. There might be someone there willing to give us a hint where to find Simkins."

"Leif," she said. She gripped his arm more firmly. "I do not know if this is important, but I found it near the spot where he was killed." She held out a handkerchief.

He took it. Leif ran his fingers over the fine linen

and turned it around to stare at the frayed corner. Part of a monogram remained. *D? R? P?*

"Do you think Sally Randall dropped it in the fight?"

Leif had no idea what to answer. His sister Petunia had had a set of such handkerchiefs given to her by their parents to celebrate her twentieth birthday. At least, this looked like the handkerchief he remembered with the distinctive lace pattern. Their mother had ordered them sent all the way from Sweden.

He tucked it into his coat pocket and ignored Marta's questions. Whether or not he found answers in Kinney, he was not giving up the hunt. The partial monogram haunted him.

CHAPTER THIRTEEN

LEIF GUNNARSON DREW rein and stared down the town's main street. For an instant, he thought he had doubled back and gone to Newell Bluff. Then details sorted out in his head. The names were different, and the placement of a few stores varied. Kinney was simply close to looking like Newell Bluff, but it was different in ways he found immediately.

The town marshal came striding over to him, jaw jutting out and looking mean. A deputy flanked him, carrying a rifle in the crook of his arm. For two cents, Leif thought, this lawman would swing the weapon around and open fire on him, on Marta, on anyone who looked cross-eyed at him.

Kinney wasn't an inviting town.

"You the people who were on the stage when it got held up?" The marshal rested his hand on the butt of his six-gun. Leif sized him up. The man tried to look tough, but there was something about him that hinted it was all a bluff. Calling him out would send the lawman running.

Leif had the feeling the marshal would fetch a rifle and shoot him in the back from as far away as he could. The man was a bully and a coward, trying to put up a front of false bravado.

"Clement told you what happened out on the road," Leif said. "There's not much we can add."

Marta started to speak up, but Leif lightly tapped her arm to shush her, unnoticed by the marshal. Explaining how they had found the strongbox broken open and empty only complicated the story. He was even loath to mention that they had buried the peddler, though the man might have family who would want to know he had been treated right.

"You shot it out with the road agents. You looking to collect a reward for that?" Again the marshal showed some belligerence, as if daring Leif to try to claim a bounty.

"We did. And we were lucky not to get ourselves filled with lead. They're a dangerous crew. You have any notion who their leader is?" Leif closely watched the lawman's reaction.

"Heard rumors, nothing more. The army thinks they're chasing a gent by the name of Simkins. That name mean anything to you?"

"I've heard it mentioned. Marshal Denny over in Newell Bluff is of the opinion he's responsible for the stage robberies. Do you think he's right?"

"You two passing through? If you got other ideas, forget them."

"Much obliged for the advice, Marshal. We'll stay the night and move on tomorrow."

"See that you do. I don't like your kind in my town. We don't cotton to show people coming to town, wrecking our general order, then moving on, not caring what trouble you leave behind." He jerked his head in the direction of a nearby saloon, and he and his deputy stalked off. The marshal hesitated before going in to look back and glare at Leif.

"I am not accustomed to such a greeting," Marta said. "I had heard people in Kinney were not inclined to be pleasant toward strangers. I did not know it started with their marshal."

"He's got some reason for being so disagreeable." Leif walked his horse on toward the livery. "If he's in cahoots with the outlaws, that might explain it."

"Or he sees us as going after the same reward he seeks," Marta said. "We need to assure him we are not rivals but friends."

"I wouldn't go as far as friends," Leif said. "But we might convince him we're allies."

He dismounted and handed over his and Marta's horses to the stable boy. He slung his saddlebags over his shoulder and stepped outside to look around.

"Must we sleep in the stable with our horses?" She eyed the three-story wood-frame hotel down the street. In spite of a rickety look, it was more inviting than anywhere he had seen since leaving Fargo in such a hurry.

"We have a few dollars to spare," he said. Leif rummaged through his pockets, counting the coins and the few greenbacks stashed there. He hardly wanted to mention to her that the "few dollars" were truly very few. Wyoming Bob had left before paying him his due for the performances in Newell Bluff.

He never thought to ask Marta if she had any money. That wasn't a proper thing to ask of a lady.

"We can get rooms," he said, "but it might be a little hungry until we get back on the trail. I can hunt for small game then." As they passed a restaurant, both he and Marta inhaled deeply. His mouth watered at the savory aromas coming from inside. His stomach growled and made him reconsider staying in the hotel.

As inviting as a soft mattress was, his stomach told him a decent meal was a better choice.

"You have only a little money," Marta said. "How much?"

It made him a tad uneasy to confess his lack of wealth to her.

"We need more," she said when he told her he had only three dollars and a few small coins.

"How are we going to get it?"

"Let's eat first, then think about ways to get money without running afoul of the law." The marshal was cantankerous because of whatever mess Wyoming Bob had made as the show passed through town. Leif was lucky he didn't find himself sleeping in a jail cell. A slow smile crossed his lips. That might be the way. Give Marta what money he had, then get locked up for a couple days. That would give him a bunk to sleep on and a meal or two. All he had to do was put up with the choleric lawman.

"Hey, that there's the sharpshooter from the Wild West Show," someone called, pointing at Leif. "I recognize his picture! It was on the side of the big wagon that rumbled through yesterday." The man stepped into the street and waved his arms around to attract attention to them.

To Leif's chagrin, the ploy worked. He tried to steer Marta away, but she dug in her heels and refused to budge.

"He is the greatest shot in the world!" Her voice carried along the main street. Whoever wasn't drawn by the man's identification was by Marta's. "There is no one who can outshoot him."

"What are you doing?" He tried again to steer her away from being the center of attention. She yanked free and stepped up onto the boardwalk in front of the feedstore.

"Who will bet against Trickshot?"

"Well now, I reckon I might." A bearded man with an eye patch stepped up. "You looking to make a bet, little lady?"

"How much will you bet?"

"For any amount. I got me a whole pouch of gold dust here. The assayer says it's worth nigh on one hundred dollars."

"Even odds?" Marta tried to sound sure of herself, but a small tremor in her voice betrayed her lack of confidence.

The man scratched himself, then lifted the eye patch and scratched there, too. "That hardly seems fair, what with him being the best shot in the whole danged world and all. Five to one."

Marta looked uneasily at Leif. If he lost, they'd owe five hundred dollars. With a poke of only three, losing and not paying meant getting strung up from the nearest tree.

"Ten to one," Leif called out. "That's how sure I am I can outshoot you."

A murmur went through the crowd.

The one-eyed man hitched up his pants and drew his six-shooter. He fired into the post holding up the awning in front of the feedstore. The bullet dug deep in the dried wood and sent splinters flying. Before anyone said a thing, the man walked over, spat tobacco juice onto his finger, and drew a circle around it.

"There. I done hit smack-dab in the middle of the target." He laughed in delight. The crowd joined in at the joke.

Leif went and peered at the hole. "Let's double the bet. Can you put up two hundred dollars?"

"I was joshing. Are you serious?" The man craned his head around and turned his good eye toward Leif.

"Can you make it or not? I am the best shot in the world, after all."

"You can't bet that. I cheated! I drew the target after I fired."

Leif spun and addressed the crowd. "Miss Esquivel will take bets from any of the rest of you. At five to one."

The rush forward almost bowled Leif over. He lost count of how much was being laid that he couldn't top the shot already made.

"I ain't got two hundred dollars, but I'll put up my gold dust and the claim to my mine," the one-eyed man said. "It's worth a danged sight more than one hundred dollars."

When the furor settled down, Leif studied the hole again. The tobacco juice around it dripped a little, making the target look as if it were melting in the sun.

"From back here. Here!" Someone in the crowd drew a line in the middle of the street. "That's twenty feet."

Leif went to the line, shrugged his shoulders, and drew one six-gun. He cocked it amid great expectation in the crowd, aimed, and then lowered it, shaking his head.

"It's not right. This is the finest pistol in existence, and I'm the best shot. I'd be stealing from you unless I make it harder."

"Harder? What do you mean?" The noise of the crowd grew. The miner squinted at Leif and shushed everyone. "You saying you won't take the shot? You lose, then."

"Who's got a black powder rifle? A musket. The older the better." Leif looked around. A man in front of the gunsmith's shop ducked in and returned in a flash with an old Brown Bess rifle.

"I got one for you, Mr. Trickshot. This here Long Land Pattern musket's old but accurate." The gunsmith handed the musket to Leif, who took it and bounced it in his hands a few times.

"You have powder and shot for it?"

"Right here. And I want to put down a ten-dollar bet, if you're still giving odds." The gunsmith grinned. "The musket's a fine weapon, but you'll never beat Ole Cooper. He's a sneaky one, making sure he hit the bull's-eye like he did."

Leif examined the musket balls, then handed the pouch back to the gunsmith. "Do me the honor of loading it for me, will you?"

This set off a new round of excitement in the crowd. They watched the gunsmith methodically load. Leif saw how pale Marta had turned. More in the crowd wanted to put down bets. He nodded for her to take them. Her hands shook as she recorded the bets on a scrap of paper.

"Here it is, Mr. Trickshot." The gunsmith handed it back. "Can I up my wager to fifty dollars?"

"Covered," Leif said. He toed the line and raised the musket, taking careful aim. The crowd fell silent; then a low buzz started when Leif didn't fire. Protest rose when he lowered the musket, unfired. He shook his head again.

"What's wrong, Trickshot? Getting cold feet?" The miner Cooper came over and thrust his face forward, his one eye peering at him with glee. "You don't shoot, you lose the bet. Right? Right?" The crowd roared in response.

"It's still not fair," Leif asserted. "It's too easy a shot. Somebody fetch me a frying pan and a nail."

"What are you up to? You're not weaseling your way out of the bet," Cooper said.

"I'm serious. It's stealing if I don't make it harder. That's only fair."

"Here, here!" A cook from a restaurant ran up with a frying pan still dripping grease. Someone else in the crowd handed over a nail. Leif handed the musket to the gunsmith, then held up both the frying pan and nail for the crowd to see.

He made a big show of pointing at the target, then doing a smart about-face and marching away. He stopped in front of another wood support, this one for a saloon. A quick move placed the nail just above eye level. He twisted it back and forth until it sank halfway into the post. With great fanfare, he hung the pan on the nail and worked it around until it banged against the post in just the right way.

Leif strode back to the line drawn in the dusty street, made a production out of determining angles and distances, then asked the gunsmith, "Would you load even more powder into the musket? And be sure to tamp it down real good with wadding."

The gunsmith looked at the crowd for approval. A silence had fallen over the entire town. The man quickly added another charge to the barrel and rammed down a large piece of wadding before handing the weapon back to Leif.

Leif faced his target, rested the musket on his left shoulder, shifted it a bit to properly position it, then yelled at the top of his lungs, "Look out!"

The musket belched an immense cloud of smoke. The skillet spun off the nail as the musket ball struck it, and Leif immediately raised the weapon in both hands high above his head. He kicked up another cloud of dirt as he spun and shouted, "A direct hit!"

The agitated crowd choked on the gun smoke and milled about for a few seconds, recovering from the suddenness of the discharge.

"Wait a goldanged second," Cooper cried. "He didn't even hit the post, much less land his bullet inside the target." The miner got closer and stared at the bullet hole he'd put in the post, then backed away when Leif shouldered past.

Those in the crowd began to respond, but Leif silenced them. He went to the post and pressed his thumb down and stepped back.

"You got a knife?" He looked at the gunsmith,

who nodded. "You come over here and dig out Cooper's bullet and tell everyone what you find."

Scowling, the man drew a short-bladed knife and began carving away at the dried wood. Something dropped into his hand. He looked up, startled. Leif silently urged him to keep digging. A second bullet popped out of the post.

"What'd you find? Tell everyone. Tell them!" Leif leaned on the Brown Bess.

"There was a musket ball smack-dab on top of Cooper's bullet."

"You mean he fired blind over his shoulder, bounced the musket ball off that there skillet, and followed my bullet perzactly into the target?" Cooper's good eye widened in shock. His jaw dropped.

"That's exactly what happened," Leif called, "because I am Trickshot, the world's finest marksman. Now pay the lady!"

Marta began taking money as fast as possible. Many in the crowd slipped away, not paying their due. Leif didn't care. He had won the bet. The gunsmith took the musket and rested it over his shoulder.

"Tell me, Mr. Trickshot, how you made that shot. The musket ball's not even scratched. Not a bit deformed from getting fired into a skillet. Tell me how you made that shot."

"It's a fair question since you never loaded a musket ball in. You wanted me to fire, and no matter what happened, it'd look like I missed."

The gunsmith scratched his chin, then grinned crookedly.

"I think I got it. You stole one of the balls when

you examined the pouch. Hid it somewhere, then fired. It was the wadding that hit the skillet, not a musket ball. With all the commotion and the air filled with smoke from all the extra powder you had me stuff down the barrel, you pressed the musket ball you'd hid out into the hole Cooper had already shot into the post. That about it?"

"We're a pair of thieves, aren't we?" Leif thrust out his hand. The gunsmith hesitated, then shook.

"It seems we are, but I'm not paying you a dime."

"Most of them in the crowd aren't paying, either, but I have a way to take care of that," Leif said.

"The marshal'll never serve process on any of his neighbors," the gunsmith said.

"Here you are, Mr. Trickshot, sir," Cooper said. He handed over the bag of gold dust and a crumpled piece of paper. "That there's the deed to my mine. It's a good one, proved and full of blue dirt just waiting to be clawed out." He heaved a deep sigh and squared his shoulders. "Don't ever let it be said that I welsh on my debts, no matter what it costs me."

Leif bounced the pouch of dust, then handed it to Marta. She hadn't heard any of the conversation with the gunsmith and looked at him with awe.

"Thank you kindly for the gold, but as to this deed, Mr. Cooper, you keep it. I want you to get more gold from the ground and tithe a church or help any of the urchins in town who don't have folks to help them. If the mood moves you, give some gold to the school to buy books."

"That's mighty kind of you." Cooper looked at the bag of gold dust. "I can start with that hundred dollars' worth of dust." The miner looked at him with some anticipation.

"No, Mr. Cooper, I've got a better use for this." Leif held it out to the miner. "Take it into that saloon and buy drinks for anyone who lost money to my skilled marksmanship."

"All of it? At a nickel a beer, you'd see the entire town stumbling drunk 'fore midnight."

"Then get everyone in Kinney stumbling drunk. You lead the way!" Leif slapped the miner on the back.

"You're more 'n the best shot in the whole danged world. You're the finest man what ever lived!" Cooper grabbed the gold-dust pouch and ran to the saloon, bellowing for anyone with a thirst to come wet their whistle.

"If your boss had half your sense, he wouldn't have been run out of town the way he was," the gunsmith said. Musket on his shoulder like he was a Union soldier trudging off to war, he marched back to his store, whistling "Battle Hymn of the Republic."

"Wyoming Bob must have locked horns with the marshal and been sent on his way," Leif said. He stared at Marta for a moment. She positively glowed as she held a double handful of greenbacks. "How much is left?"

"Enough to outfit us for months!" She handed over the money with some reluctance.

Leif divided it in half and gave her a share of the money. She looked up in surprise.

"Mine?"

"You earned it. You set up the crowd so they wanted to give us whatever jingled in their pockets."

They started down the street toward the general store. Marta walked especially close, bumping into him more than was necessary. He didn't mind at all. Then she whispered, "Where'd the real bullet go?"

The question surprised him; then he laughed and said, "I don't know. I'm glad the wadding didn't break a window, though that wouldn't have mattered. With the roar of the shot, the smoke, and the ding on the skillet, nobody would have noticed. I hope it went flying off harmlessly." The wadding might have stuck to the skillet, though as greasy as it had been, he doubted it. Nobody was going to check the skillet bottom to see that it wasn't dented from a ricocheting musket ball.

"And you bellyached about Wyoming Bob being a confidence man. You cheated them all!"

"Not before that Cooper fellow tried to cheat me, but nobody has any gripes. They all came out ahead. They got a show for a few dollars, and a hundred dollars will stand most of the town to drinks while we stock up and ride on."

Leif stopped dead in the middle of the street when he spotted the general store and a customer on the boardwalk in front. He swallowed hard.

The woman waved to a man who trotted up, leading her horse. She mounted, and the pair rode off together. Leif's heart almost exploded. The man wore a duster with a tear in the sleeve. And if he had to bet, Leif would have laid all his hard-earned money on the woman being Sally Randall.

And maybe his sister Petunia Gunnarson.

CHAPTER FOURTEEN

WAIT—DO NOT run away!" Marta Esquivel strained to catch up with Leif. He skidded to a halt in the dust and stared after the two riders. They vanished from sight just as the woman came to him and grabbed his arm. "Where are you going in such a hurry?"

He considered telling her his suspicion, then realized the futility. He had no proof the woman he had just seen was Sally Randall, much less his long-lost sister. There was no reason to make Marta doubt his good sense.

"Nothing. Let's get our supplies and hit the trail." Even as the words left his mouth, he knew what he had to do. This was his responsibility. Marta would only be in danger if she rode farther with him. Kinney wasn't the friendliest town, but it was a whole lot friendlier than the reception he'd get if he was right about the man in the duster being the outlaw he'd winged during the robbery and the woman being Randy Sally Randall.

In the store, he piled up what he needed for a solitary ride. Adding cartridges enough for a full-fledged war made him feel better. Not that he wanted to kill anyone—except Luther Simkins—but running out of ammo wasn't in the cards. He could concentrate on other things, such as never missing with a single round.

"Why are you tapping your fingers on your six-shooters?" Marta dropped the last of the goods she had selected onto the counter. "You are anxious?"

"Nervous. Tired. I need rest. Let's stash the supplies in the livery and see what the hotel has to offer in the way of rooms."

She simply looked at him. Her expression defied any attempt to figure out what thoughts ran through her head behind those dark eyes. Marta finally nodded, then counted out the money when the clerk tallied their purchases. Leif mechanically added his share.

"This is good. We have many dollars left over. Have you ever shown off your skills like you did?"

"It's something I heard about being done in another Wild West Show. Not all their performers are as good as I am."

"Could you have actually shot a bullet into the same hole?" Marta scooped up their supplies. Leif hefted what she didn't carry in a bulging gunnysack.

"I've never tried, but I don't see why not. Maybe not from twenty feet away, though that's not too big a distance."

Silence fell between them as they returned to the livery and stashed their supplies. The silence became

uneasy as they went to the hotel. The clerk looked up
and started to speak. Leif cut him off.

"Two rooms. For the night."

"Two?" The clerk looked pleasantly surprised.
"That's four dollars."

Leif counted out the four dollars from change in
his pocket. It removed a lump and made movement
easier, leaving him mostly with paper money. He suspected reaching for his six-shooters would soon require all the speed and access possible.

"The rooms are at opposite ends of the hallway
upstairs. Is that a problem?"

"No," Leif said. Marta sighed deeply. He wondered
anew at what ran through her mind. Without looking
at her, he slid the key along the counter to her.

She took it. They went up the steps and stopped at
the upper landing.

"You take the room at the rear of the hotel," he
said. "It's quieter back there, and nothing will disturb
your sleep."

"We . . . I . . ." She gripped the key fiercely and
looked up at him.

"Go on. Grab some sleep while you can. It'll be a
hard trail in the morning."

"In the morning, yes," she said. Marta half turned
and whirled back, threw her arms around his neck,
and pulled him down to deliver a passionate kiss.
When he didn't respond, she released him and backed
away. Anger flared in her eyes, and her cheeks red-
dened with embarrassment. "In the morning," she
said with more than a touch of bitterness. Her foot-
falls echoed loudly down the hallway.

Leif waited until she went into her room, then

opened his door and hesitated to see if she would sneak a peek out. When she didn't, he closed the door behind him and took the steps down to the lobby two at a time. The clerk looked up as Leif dropped the key on the counter. Not bothering to explain, he left the hotel and went straight to the livery.

White Lightning protested when he saddled the stallion and secured his supplies. He used the last of his money to pay the stable boy for both his and Marta's horses, then hit the trail. It took all his willpower not to set White Lightning into a gallop to go after the two he had seen outside the general store, but he knew tiring the animal would only make it more difficult to overtake the pair.

Within an hour on the trail, he regretted not having eaten, not getting some sleep, and . . . Marta. She perplexed him. He wished she had stayed in Newell Bluff, or even better, had accompanied her sister back East to a safer life. As much as he understood her need for vengeance against Luther Simkins and his gang for what they had done to her family, he wanted the same revenge. And he deserved it more since Simkins had murdered his family ten years earlier.

Leif snorted in wonder at his own convoluted thinking. Cold revenge for a ten-year-old crime or hot revenge for one committed just weeks earlier?

He snapped alert when he came to a fork. If he rode straight ahead, he'd return to Newell Bluff eventually. Seeing the couple at the way station would be useful. They gathered gossip of all kinds from the stagecoach drivers. Seeing if they were still hale and hearty wasn't amiss, either. They had barricaded themselves against a threat that could snatch away their lives in an instant.

Leif pondered a knotty question. Even though they were married, would Simkins bother torturing them, given that they didn't have any children? That entered into Simkins's twisted crimes. Killing children, whether in front of their tormented parents or not, spoke to something in the man's evil personality.

Again Leif shook himself. His tired mind drifted. If he found the duster-wearing rider and the woman, he had to be completely alert. Even a fraction of a second too slow on the draw spelled his death.

"My death," he whispered. Before tracking down the others in Simkins's gang, he had never shot another man. Now his pistol would fall apart from so many notches, if he chose to keep track of his killings. "Only Simkins matters."

Bending low, he studied the tracks in the dry, dusty road. While the fitful wind had erased some of the hoofprints, he saw that two riders had recently taken the fork. The paucity of travelers gave him an edge. Tracking was easy.

He studied the terrain ahead. The road lifted upward into a hilly area with trees cresting summits and the road winding away into a forest. He had to be careful, or he'd ride straight into an ambush—if the two thought anyone trailed them. But why should they? They had gone to Kinney without a hint of anxiety at being identified.

Leif sagged a little as he realized this might be a wild-goose chase. He only guessed that the man wearing the duster was injured from the stagecoach robbery, and that the woman had led the attack. With some reluctance and a touch of nostalgia, he pulled the partially monogrammed handkerchief from his pocket and stared at it. If the woman road agent wasn't his sister, how had she come by the simple cloth square? The lace was so distinctive. If only more of the letter remained.

He had questions to ask, and he intended to hear the answers.

The road took a sharp bend into the woods. The sudden change from the warmth of the afternoon sun to a touch of forest cool made him shiver. His horse tried to crow-hop.

"There, there, old boy. It's only a bit chillier." White Lightning reared, almost throwing him. Leif clung to the saddle horn but still slid backward.

That saved his life. A bullet ripped through the air where his head had been an instant before. He released his hold and slid to the ground. His feet hit fresh pine needles, and he sat heavily while his horse reared again, then landed and bolted away.

A second bullet added to the horse's gallop.

Leif tried to get his feet under him but slipped again. Giving up on that, he flopped out flat and rolled through the undergrowth until he was hidden from the sniper trying to plug him. He sat up and drew both his Peacemakers. Using the one in his left hand to push away the brush, he peered out. His hunt for the unseen gunman failed. Nothing moved ahead of him. Even the light wind had died, dropping on the forest a deathly still worthy of a cemetery.

Strain as he might, he heard nothing moving. Leif finally got his feet under him, crouched low, and began duckwalking to get behind a more substantial shield. A few feet from a tamarack, he straightened. Bullets filled the air around him, driving him back down. He crossed the few yards from the tree, wiggling along on his belly. Only when he had the tree between him and the hidden gunman did he edge up again. He leaned against the trunk, panting.

Leif closed his eyes and remembered what he could of the terrain ahead. The road curved again to the right. That had to be where the sniper took his potshots. Both six-shooters cocked, he braced himself.

"Don't shoot! I don't have any quarrel with you. I'm coming out. Don't shoot!"

He stepped out, six-guns raised. The instant he saw movement, he fired using both pistols. Nobody was a finer marksman, but even Trickshot needed a target. His flying lead chewed through the greenery, but he had no sense that he hit anyone.

He had only driven his opponent back. Taking advantage of his enemy's momentary retreat, he plunged through the scrubby brush, kicking thornbushes and low-growing silver buffaloberry aside. Like a charging bull, he rushed forward and burst out onto the road. His quick eyes took in the scene.

The man wearing the duster sprawled on the ground. Even from a distance, Leif saw that the man's open eyes stared upward into the forest canopy—and saw nothing. He was dead. Leif looked at the gun in his hand in surprise. He was a great shot, but this one bordered on the miraculous. In any gunfight, he'd accept that.

Darting from tree to tree, Leif hunted for the woman who had ridden with the man in the duster.

Haunting stillness smothered the forest. She hadn't come back past him, so she'd ridden farther along the road. As far as he could see, the road was empty. If she had ridden to one side or the other, she had completely camouflaged herself. Keeping his guns trained on the empty road, he stepped closer to the fallen man.

When he didn't draw fire, he dashed to the man's side and dropped to his knees. Leif poked the man. His instincts had proved true. The man was deader than a doornail. Tugging on the man's duster revealed his left shoulder where a flap of canvas hung down. The threads had been cut by a bullet. Blood had oozed from a shallow wound and stained the duster. Leif pulled the man's hat down low and blocked his lower face with a hand. He couldn't be sure, but his gut told him this was the owlhoot who had held up the stagecoach.

He rocked back and looked around. The forest remained still, but vibrations caused the ground to rumble. From the intensity, he could sense many horses approaching.

Leif started to duck back into the forest and find his own stallion when the guidon bearer for the cavalry troop trotted into view. Immediately behind him rode the lieutenant at the head of his patrol.

The officer motioned for the sergeant to scatter soldiers throughout the woods while a few remained on the road to block any retreat.

"Drop those six-shooters," the lieutenant called out. Beside him, his corporal had a carbine hiked to his shoulder, aimed at Leif. "Drop the weapons and raise your hands!"

"It's all right, Lieutenant," Leif answered. He rolled the Peacemakers around on their trigger guards and settled them in his holsters. "It's me, Leif Gunnarson. You saved me from the road agents." Seeing his identification did nothing, he added, "The stagecoach that was being held up. You and your men ran off the road agents."

Leif half turned as soldiers rode from the woods. One private led White Lightning.

"Thanks for fetching my horse for me," he said. Leif took a step and jumped back when the corporal fired. The carbine slug tore up the grass a few inches in front of his boots.

He spun angrily.

"What are you doing, shooting at me? I'm Leif Gunnarson. Trickshot! From the Wild West Show."

"Drop the gun belt, or my corporal will put a bullet through your heart." The officer's voice came brittle and cold. As he spoke, he drew his sidearm and trained it on Leif, too.

"I don't know what you think happened here, but I haven't done anything wrong." In spite of his rising anger at the foolish lieutenant jumping to conclusions, he unbuckled his gun belt and let it slide gently to the ground. He valued the twin six-shooters above about anything else in the world, other than White Lightning. Carelessly dropping them invited damage.

"I rode into the woods, and somebody opened fire on me. I shot back and found him like that." Leif pointed to the dead man. "I think he's one of the outlaws from the robbery."

"You say it was self-defense and that he shot at you?" The lieutenant dropped to the ground and kneeled beside the fallen outlaw.

"It's more than me saying it, Lieutenant. It's the

truth." Leif started to add that the outlaw's traveling companion had hightailed it, but he clamped his mouth shut when the officer rolled the corpse over.

"Shot smack in the middle of the back."

"I couldn't see who was shooting at me. I—" Leif's mouth dropped open when the lieutenant pulled back the duster.

"He's not wearing a gun belt. Where's his gun?" The officer stood and motioned to his soldiers to come into a circle around Leif. "It looks like you shot an unarmed man in the back. You're under arrest for murder, Mr. Gunnarson. Put shackles on him, Sergeant."

Leif stared in disbelief at the dead outlaw. All Leif knew was that he had fired toward the source of the attack as he entered the forest. The man might not have been armed. He wasn't able to say, but that meant the woman had shot her own partner in the back. Whether the incident was accidental or intentional didn't matter.

He was the one being arrested for a hanging crime.

CHAPTER FIFTEEN

"Y OU'VE GOT THIS wrong," Leif Gunnarson protested. He tried to lift his hands and gesture, but
the shackles kept him from moving too far. Shifting
in the saddle, he looked to the front of the column.
Between him and the lieutenant rode a dozen soldiers. The sergeant trotted alongside his superior
while Leif had the corporal who had all too willingly
been anxious to plug him as a companion.

"They all say that," the noncom said tiredly. "Shut
up."

"The woman who led the stage holdup. She must've
been the one who shot him. I was too far away, and he
was off to the side, anyway, when I returned fire."

"Keep up a story like that, and the jury'll find you
guilty in a flash." The corporal chuckled. "Considering the way the people are in Kinney, they won't take

more 'n a minute anyway. The jury'll want their free booze. I've heard tell they get more if they convict."

Leif knew the soldier only poked him out of boredom.

"Why not take me back to your post for trial?"

The corporal snorted in disgust.

"You've never seen it. Even the rats left. The major's a drunk, and the captain's more interested in the major's wife than in keeping discipline. I was with the Third Indiana. That was a good outfit. Better than anything out here in Wyoming."

Leif turned a deaf ear to the soldier's reminiscences about earlier days and better commanders. At least he wasn't going on and on about seeing his prisoner swinging at the end of a noose. Without a chance to convince the corporal or the lieutenant of his innocence, Leif settled down and stared hard at the shackles on his wrists. As he bounced along, he noticed the link going into the left cuff was rusted.

The corporal never noticed when his prisoner began rubbing the link against the shackle. To Leif's delight, the ancient link parted quickly. If the cavalry post was a calamity because of lax discipline, it certainly carried over to the equipment. He had freed himself with almost no effort, at least enough so he could use his hands. The iron cuffs still chaffed, and the length of chain dangling from the right one slowed him, but he wasn't held captive in fetters anymore.

The column slowly pulled ahead as Leif held White Lightning back. The corporal never noticed as they eventually separated from the others.

As the soldier some distance ahead vanished around

a curve in the road, leaving corporal and prisoner on their own, Leif acted. He twisted around in the saddle, then uncoiled, using all the strength he had to swing the chain on his right wrist around like a scythe. The end link hit the corporal on the cheek and left a bloody, rusty mark. The soldier's eyes went wide, and his mouth opened. Then he toppled off his horse.

Leif bent over and made a frantic grab. He snared the reins on the corporal's horse before it bolted. Pulling back hard, he brought the horse to a halt. The soldier lay on the ground, moaning. Leif grabbed and caught the saddlebags dangling over the horse's rump. Fumbling, he opened the canvas bag and found his prized Peacemakers inside, beckoning him with their highly polished gleams.

Knowing he had little time, he dismounted and kneeled by the fallen soldier. In a jacket pocket, he found the keys to his shackles. The locks were half-rusted but yielded to hard twists. He dropped the chains and stared at the corporal. The man was coming around, moaning louder now. It would be easy to silence him—forever. But that wasn't the kind of man Leif Gunnarson was. He measured his punch and clipped an outjutting chin. There wasn't time to tie him up or gag him. Other soldiers soon enough would notice they were running a couple riders shy in the column.

"Come on," Leif said, jerking on the soldier's horse. "We're going on a ride." He stepped up into the saddle and winced. The McClellan saddle hurt as he sank down onto it. The horse might have appreciated its design, but the rider suffered.

Leif caught White Lightning's reins and secured them to the rear of the saddle, then put his heels into the horse's flanks. He galloped until lather formed. He pushed the horse even harder. When the stallion began faltering, he slowed and got as much additional distance from it as possible. Only then did he jump over into his own saddle with some relief.

"You're rested enough, old boy," he told White Lightning, patting the horse's neck. "Let's put even more distance between us and the soldiers." He rode away, varying the gait to keep the stallion fresh. The lieutenant's command had been in the saddle all day, and their horses weren't rested. Leif intended to out-run them.

Over his years with the Wild West Show, he had spoken to more than his share of wranglers. Their stories had been laced with boasts and outright lies about their own prowess, but enough truth had come through that he had learned a thing or two about horses and being on the run. Never in all his born days had he thought he would be dodging the law, but listening instead of topping the lies now paid off.

He rode back into the hills where the gunfight had occurred and trotted past the bloody patch of grass where the outlaw had been cut down. A mound of dirt without a marker told of how the soldiers had taken care of the body. Leif walked White Lightning beyond the spot and deeper into the forest. Before, the woods had been as silent as a grave. Now birds chirped, and small animals rustled in the under-growth. Insects whirred, and he heard the sounds of life everywhere.

It was past sundown, the time of day when hunters

and the hunted came out. He knew which he was, not only from being ambushed but also realizing the lieutenant wasn't likely to simply ride away. An escaped prisoner reflected poorly on him. The corporal might get his stripes yanked off. Leif felt little sympathy for him. He remembered the expression on the soldier's face when he drew a bead with his carbine. The man was disappointed when he was ordered to stand down. He wanted blood.

Leif slowed and finally saw a place along the road to camp for the night. He wanted a fire and a hot meal, but the vision of soldiers riding down on him, howling and demanding his blood, convinced him a cold camp and a piece of jerky were more prudent. After tending White Lightning, he settled down and wrapped the blanket around his shoulders. Riding into Kinney and the scam there, leaving Marta behind, and dealing with the ambush and arrest had all tuckered him out. He either fell asleep or dropped into a stupor, thus letting the soldier creep up on him unawares.

A hard poke in the ribs brought him around. He moaned, rubbed his eyes, and looked up into a frightened face partially lit by the dawn sunlight filtering through the trees. Immediately, he was wide awake and alert at the sight before him.

"Don't you go doin' nothing sneaky now, mister. I got the drop on you. I ain't afeared of you like the others."

The private wasn't a day over seventeen. How much younger was a question Leif wanted to answer. Weathered veterans like the sergeant or world-weary men like the corporal were different. And their lieutenant had a military reputation to earn. But a youngster like this might never have been in a gunfight and be worried about his own unproved courage.

"You've got good reason to be afraid of me," Leif said. "I've got both my six-guns aimed at you." He lifted both hands under his blanket and moved them around just a tad, mimicking the moves he'd make if he held his deadly six-guns.

"I got the drop on you." His voice quavered. The soldier lifted his rifle and snugged it into his shoulder to steady it. His hands shook so hard, he risked pulling the trigger by accident.

"You can't see through this blanket. You've heard how accurate a shot I am. I never miss."

"But I got you in my sights." In spite of the truth that he did, the boy sounded unsure. That was all Leif needed.

"Two bullets in your heart against your one. Who's likely to walk away?"

"I was ordered to find you. The lieutenant'd be furious if I let you go."

"He doesn't know you caught me. You ever see a man all shot up?"

"Not 'fore yesterday. The fellow you gunned down was the first dead man I ever saw. Well, not the first dead man but the first one that died from a gunshot. My pa lost his hand when a wagon wheel broke and he bled to death, but that's nothing like what you done."

"I didn't shoot him."

"Did, too!" The private began trembling as if he had the ague.

"I'm on the trail of the real killer. Why would I lie to you? I've got you dead to rights. Two of my guns against your carbine." Leif was beginning to cramp up but dared not move for fear of revealing that his hands were empty and both his six-shooters were still in his holster.

"If you shoot me, the rest of my squad will be here in a trice."

"No, they won't," Leif said, gambling that the boy lied. "You came here on your own. You've got good instincts. Use them now. I'm innocent. I never shot anyone in the back."

"You're threatenin' to shoot me!"

"Not in the back. Never. Why should I do that when I'm the fastest gun that ever lived—and the most accurate shot?"

"I don't know. What are you tellin' me?"

"Lower the carbine, and we'll talk this out. I'll put away my guns if you lower your rifle."

"Well, all right." The private lowered the rifle. As he did, Leif pushed away the blanket and came to his knees. From this position, he could draw, if necessary. The soldier's eyes went wide. "You didn't have me covered. You lied!"

"That just shows how fast I really am. I put the guns back in their holsters so quick, you'd have seen only a blur."

"I don't believe you." As the soldier started to raise his rifle, Leif went for his guns. Both slid from his hips. Before the private had the rifle half on target, he realized Leif had him dead to rights.

"I'm an even better shot," Leif said softly.

"Please don't kill me." The private dropped his carbine and raised his shaking hands. "What are you going to do with me?"

"Make you a hero in your sergeant's eyes, I reckon." Leif got to his feet, picked up the carbine, and examined it. "You're going to take me on and get outshot."

"I don't understand." The private backed off a pace.

"Get on your horse, ride back to the column, and tell them you shot it out with me. Don't say any more than that. Let them come to their own conclusions."

"But—"

"Then lead them straight back here," Leif said. "Shoo!"

The young soldier lit out, running. Leif looked around and decided how to stage what would become a major battle rivaling anything during the Civil War. He hefted the carbine. A story began to unfold, a fantasy that would stand up to a first impression but not much more.

He put his tall-crowned hat on a stump, backed off, and began firing. The first shot ripped through the crown and whined off into the woods. He continued shooting into the trees, blowing splinters everywhere. When the magazine came up empty, he placed the rifle on a stump, judged angles, and fired so his bullet smashed along the length of the stock and hit the trigger. The impact tore away metal and left a shiny, sharp metallic spike.

"There," he said. "Almost complete." He cut his finger on a splinter and found his hat with the fancy silver conchas. Leaving it behind was a pity, but he needed evidence that the private hadn't turned tail and run like a craven. A large bead of blood formed on the tip of his finger. He turned the hat over so he could smear the blood around inside the exit hole.

When enough blood soaked into the felt to make it look like a serious, but not fatal, head wound, he sent the hat spinning away. He had done all he could to set the scene.

Leif had no time to waste now. If the other soldiers hadn't heard the gunfire and already set out to investigate, the private would report in any second. He mounted White Lightning and sent the horse galloping down the road. When he found a likely spot, he cut away from the road, splashed along a small stream to cover his tracks, and kept riding.

He wasn't inclined to kill any of the soldiers, much less a wet-behind-the-ears boy, but he wasn't going to let them take him to town for trial, either. The sergeant, or whoever was the patrol's tracker, had a simple enough scene to decipher. The private had fired on the escaped prisoner, then had his rifle disabled by a return shot. He had then done the proper thing, reporting back to his superiors, because staying meant death, no chance of recapturing the prisoner.

Leif had given them his tracks. Now it was up to him to evade discovery—and to find Sally Randall. It sounded easy, but he knew how close to impossible it could be.

It was time for him to prove he was as good as Wyoming Bob claimed, only he had to do so much more than shoot the center of a target.

CHAPTER SIXTEEN

T HEY WERE ABOUT to catch him. Leif Gunnarson
felt it rather than saw it. He tried riding while
keeping an eye in front and on the trail behind him,
where the lieutenant and his soldiers would have to
appear. He expected them to pop up suddenly in
spite of his efforts at hiding his tracks. Leif wasn't any
frontiersman, and this was the longest he had been in
the saddle for years. Traveling with the Wild West
Show was usually easier because the larger animals
had to be fed and watered more often than horses or
men. That always provided frequent rest stops and
the chance for him to climb down from the saddle
and stretch muscles tired from the road.

But no rest for the wicked now. As he rode, anxiety high, he wondered if he would ever see Wyoming
Bob and the others again. If he gave up on his chase

after the woman outlaw, he could overtake the Wild West Show in a few days. The owner wasn't likely to say anything about his star's absence. Wyoming Bob would be happy to see Trickshot return, even if he never said a word about it. He might never even ask where Leif had been, just relieved that his prime moneymaker had returned.

Rejoining the show posed a new problem. The cavalry might suspect he'd try to hide among his old friends. That put everyone in danger. All the lieutenant needed was to find a telegraph station and send the alert all the way east.

Leif's resolve steeled. Riding with the Wild West Show again wasn't in the cards until he had settled the questions raised by the woman road agent. If she was his sister, why had she chosen to ride with Luther Simkins all these years? And the biggest problem to settle was Simkins himself. Somehow he had evaded the law over the years. Leif intended to bring him to justice. He had stewed and boiled for ten years about the murderer. Revenge—justice!—was finally within his reach.

"Whoa." He drew back on the reins and lifted his head. His thoughts of the future and Simkins and avoiding the cavalry disappeared in an instant. The whiff of smoke dilated his nostrils. The stench on the smoke turned his stomach. He had smelled it before. Not only was a fire raging; it was burning human flesh.

He traced a double-rutted road from across the plains to the mouth of the valley. Leif tensed when he saw a rider skulking behind a cottonwood, glancing nervously at the trail leading into the canyon, as if waiting for another wagon. Or was that what he scouted for?

Leif looked at his own back trail. The lieutenant's patrol came hot on his heels. The sentry below might be worried about the same hunters after him. He touched a pistol at his hip, then drew back. The choking clouds of smoke warned of something more going on. The lookout had been posted to prevent anyone—the cavalry or anyone else—from sneaking up on the cause of that vile smoke. Taking the sentry out silently wasn't possible. Leif would be spotted no matter how he tried to come on the man. Any gunfire alerted not only anyone deeper in the canyon but also the cavalry. If he wanted to keep out of the lieutenant's shackles and see if he could lend assistance farther up the canyon, he had to avoid the lookout.

White Lightning balked, but Leif set his horse onto a new trail, cutting up and across a ridge that better suited the stallion and hid him from the sentry. When he reached the crest, he found the source of the stench. A wagon burned on the floor of a U-shaped valley.

Two men wearing bandannas against the smoke tried to pull the contents away from the raging fire. They gave up and called to others in the party. Leif reached instinctively for his six-shooter when he saw that two others standing away from the fire held captives. Two small children struggled to escape, but their captors were too strong. Getting involved put him at risk. There was a good reason for the children to struggle. No adults were to be seen. Their bodies probably fed the sickening odor from the fire. The four men might be Good Samaritans rescuing the children and trying to save their parents.

That didn't explain the furtive sentry at the canyon mouth.

Then the matter was settled. Loud cries echoed up from the burning wagon as the four men argued. Distance and the roar of the fire consuming the wagon muffled their words, but from the tone, he knew the gist of the disputation. Two wanted to kill the children. The others insisted on taking them as prisoners. That caused his resolve to harden. Before he galloped down, six-shooters blazing, two more men joined the others. He watched sides in the argument form. The newcomers joined those wanting to take the children prisoner. Shouts and undoubted insults were exchanged. Leif wasn't sure if he felt relief that the side wanting to kidnap the children prevailed.

What contents that remained unburned from the wagon were taken. Two men poked through the rubble and held up trinkets hardly scorched. Whether they were jewelry or something else, Leif couldn't tell. It didn't matter compared to the children's welfare. Their captors hoisted them onto a horse and rode away through the trees dotting the canyon floor, leaving the scavengers to their ghoulish hunt. Before Leif convinced himself he could quietly take the two lingering behind, the sentry from the canyon mouth joined them. A new argument resulted. The men gave in to the sentry, mounted, and rode up the canyon in the direction the wagon had traveled. It was bad fortune that the settlers had come this way. Leif waited for them to disappear before making his way down the steep hill to the valley floor. If he had any sense, he'd ride away, let the men keep the children, and continue his own quest.

He circled the smoldering wagon and saw the charred bodies. Two, a man and a woman, lay close together. Another, a smaller body, was almost entirely consumed by the fire that had ravaged the wagon. Leif rode White Lightning some distance away and tethered the stallion. He returned to the wagon and began the distasteful chore of digging graves for the deceased settlers. It took the better part of an hour, and the result wasn't as satisfactory as it should have been. The rocky ground prevented him from digging a deep grave—he buried all three in the same one.

Their bodies cracked and broke as he rolled them onto a large piece of canvas from the wagon. He had to sweep some body parts into the shallow grave. The only consolation he found was that scavengers were unlikely to dig up the bodies. Coyotes and wolves preferred fresh kill, not cooked meat.

Exhausted from too many things, Leif sat and stared up the valley. The kidnappers were probably camped not far away. The hills protected them from occasional storms, and the stream running down the center of the valley provided sweet water. Not for the first time he pondered what to do.

"First things first," he said, climbing to his feet. Rather than ride, he walked along the stream to hide his tracks, should the cavalry chance upon the settlers. Tangling with the men who had plundered the wagon by himself was foolish, even suicidal, but letting the children remain with the men who might have killed their parents and set fire to the wagon was worse. While the cavalry had a better chance of fighting the outlaws and winning, he sized up the lieutenant as being a stickler for duty. Rescue the little children, capture the fugitive wanted for murder, then get back on the trail of Luther Simkins. The officer's priorities were almost good enough. Leif simply didn't like being on the list, especially ahead of Simkins.

"Unless those are Simkins's men." This set off a new train of thought. Riding away and letting the cavalry find Simkins and his cutthroats solved all his problems. The lieutenant would stop hunting him if he had the outlaws in custody. That also freed the children.

Leif sucked in his breath and held it. The cavalry officer didn't strike him as a particularly caring man. A full-out assault would be the attack of choice for the troopers with trumpet blaring, hooves pounding, medals in the offing. Simkins was the kind of low-life no-account to use the children as human shields. Or he'd use them to barter for his own freedom. Putting them at risk after all they'd endured chewed at Leif.

Leaving the gang for the lieutenant to capture was a good idea. It was an even better one if the two kids were spirited away before any gunfire.

The only satisfaction Leif took from that was freeing the two kids.

He walked along the stream; then cut off at an angle to get him on the trail taken by the outlaws. Wary of any sentries who might spot him, he stayed in the sparse stands of cottonwood trees to reduce his chance of being seen. But he wasn't kidding himself. The gang of owlhoots would be keyed up and on edge. The way the sentry at the canyon mouth had acted showed they weren't going to be easily taken by surprise.

Thin curls of white smoke from several campfires rose in the still late-afternoon air, warning him of the encampment long before he heard voices and the sounds of horses. He led White Lightning from the stream deeper into a stand of trees and tethered him there. Leif made certain both six-shooters were loaded, then began a slow creep forward, alert to sentries or anyone casually wandering about in the gathering dusk. When he spotted the fires, he dropped to his belly to reconnoiter. More than a half hour passed before he figured out where the children were being kept, how the horses were staked out, and that he faced almost a dozen outlaws. Spying on them failed to reveal if any was Luther Simkins.

And none was a woman. Sally Randall was not in the camp. This made him worry that more road agents than the Simkins gang prowled these hills and he had found one.

There wasn't any way to fight off so many. Even if he walked into camp, drew, and started firing, there were too many for even his sharpshooting skills. Chances were excellent that he would miss after the first few shots alerted them. This wasn't a bunch of cowboys out to round up strays. He might startle them, but he had no chance of scaring them.

Moving slowly, he circled to a spot where he had a better look at the children. Two little girls were fastened to stakes driven into the ground. Their tethers let them move a foot or two, but no farther. One cried softly. The other, a few years older and perhaps all of six, sat with her arms tightly wrapped around her drawn-up knees. Both of them faced away from Leif, looking toward the campfires and their captors.

The men ate noisily. Leif thought the best time for a rescue was after they fell asleep, but the sorry plight of the children made him reckless. He started to them flat on his belly, wiggling about like a snake. He sank down, still as death when a guard came over. The man threw a piece of partially cooked meat on the ground between the children, slurred something to betray he'd been hitting the bottle, turned, and strutted back.

Food. He had dropped scraps for them. Just as Leif started forward again, the guard stopped, cocked his head to one side, listening hard, then whirled about. His knife came free of a sheath at his waist.

Leif watched helplessly from the ground. Both his six-guns were securely holstered.

The outlaw roared as he reared up over the children. Both began crying as he slashed the air above their heads. He began yelling threats and making scary faces. Leif wanted to close his eyes, as if that made him invisible, but he forced himself to watch. The darkness hid him. Partially.

The owlhoot stopped his bullying, laughed, and started to return to camp. Something gave Leif away because, in spite of being half-drunk, the guard deftly flipped the knife about in his hand, gripping it for a downward stroke and rearing up for the killing stroke. Leif got his knees under him and lunged forward. His arms circled the man's knees. A quick jerk upward brought his foe down hard to the ground. For an instant, air knocked from his lungs, the outlaw was vulnerable.

Old reflexes came into play. Left-handed, Leif drew and swung his pistol about hard. He connected with an exposed temple. The guard jerked once and lay still. Leif collapsed on top of the body until he regained his senses. With another quick, practiced move, he snatched up the fallen knife, rolled away, and sat in front of the two little girls.

"I'm here to rescue you. Don't be scared." He hacked at the tough rawhide bonds. It wasn't much of a surprise that the slovenly, drunken outlaw hadn't bothered to sharpen his knife. Leif started sawing frantically at the sturdy fastenings. First one and then the other came free.

"I want my mama," sobbed the younger girl.

"Where is she? Mama? And Papa?" the older girl cried, but was aware of what a stranger rescuing them meant.

"First, we get away. Then we can talk." Leif pushed them back toward the deep shadows. They reluctantly moved, still crying, but he lingered. He held the captured knife in his hand as he stared at the fallen guard. He stirred now, moaning softly.

Leif glanced toward the camp and the other outlaws. Outnumbered. No way to fight his way free, not with the children in such a sorry condition. He lifted the knife and brought it down hard into the recovering man's chest. The blade deflected from a rib and went into a still-beating heart.

He felt sick at such a killing, but not only his life but those of the two little girls depended on being ruthless. The outlaws probably had slaughtered their parents without remorse. If they weren't responsible for the fire, they did nothing to put out the fire. Plundering the dead settlers' belongings was a new low. Leif was sure they had burned the wagon. Burned it. Like his own house. Parents. Dead. Burned.

Tears welled in his eyes, not only for the girls but for himself. The same story played out again and again. It was up to him to bring the murderous tale to an end.

"Come on. We can go to my horse and get away."

"I want my mama." The younger girl started to whine. Her shrill voice cut through the still night air.

Leif clamped his hand over her mouth and said to her sister, "We're all dead if she makes any more noise. Keep her quiet, for all our sakes."

The six-year-old held her sister close like she might a doll, rocking her back and forth. Leif wanted to get away but knew this moment had to be settled.

"Eliza will stay quiet. She promised me."

"Good. It means your life," Leif said.

"I'm Susan. Susan Habermann. Me and my family—"

Leif put his hand over her mouth, then released it to press his forefinger to his own lips. Having Susan ramble on nervously was as bad as letting Eliza cry.

"Faster," he whispered. "Run." Even with the children running, he felt as if they were moving through molasses. He waited for the sound of discovery back in the camp. As vigilant as he was, he still failed to see the sentinel in the darkened forest in time.

The huge hulk of a man appeared suddenly. With

a single smooth action, he drew back his arm and lunged. Leif heard it whistling through the air, saw the bright flash of steel. The dull thunk was instantly followed by a tiny gasp. But he was already moving. His hand went to the pistol in his left holster. Before the sentry drew back his knife for a second lunge, Leif drew and fired. His instincts were good. His bullet flew true and caught their attacker in the middle of the chest. The hulking man took a half step back, then simply collapsed.

"Come on," he urged, tugging on Susan's hand. She jerked free.

"Eliza's hurt. The knife stuck in her."

Leif moved the girl out of the way and saw she wasn't exaggerating. The hilt protruded from Eliza's tiny chest. He started to yank it free, then remembered what one of the former soldiers riding with the Wild West Show had said. That was a sure way to bleed to death. Leif left the hilt sticking out from the girl's quivering body. With a heave, he lifted her in his arms and started running.

The commotion from back in the camp warned him they had even less time than he'd hoped to slip away. They reached White Lightning. The stallion nervously pawed at the dirt.

"Up you go." Leif hauled Susan into the saddle. "Hold her for me." He let her sister hang on to the wounded girl as he mounted.

He wheeled about and let the horse have its head. The stallion had a better sense picking an escape route in the dark than he did. Leif tried to soothe Susan, but she openly cried again. Her sister had gone limp. If he hadn't felt her tiny heart beating, he would have declared her dead.

All he could do now was keep riding into the night and hope the outlaws gave up. With two of their gang dead, he doubted they would give up chasing him down anywhere this side of the Mississippi River.

CHAPTER SEVENTEEN

BOTH GIRLS HAD stopped crying. He heard Susan gently snoring. Moving about, he put his finger under Eliza's nose and felt soft, hot air gusting out. Somehow, she clung to life in spite of a knife in her small body.

Leif looked around the countryside, wondering what to do. He had ridden directly from the valley without the outlaws overtaking him. They might have balked at tracking him in the dark. The two he had killed might not be worth revenge. If they were Simkins's henchmen, doing anything without their boss's permission would be met with his notorious towering anger. And if they were a different gang, sitting around the campfire, drinking and bragging about what they'd do if they ever caught whoever stole away the two children might be the extent of their wrath.

Ahead of him, darkened plains stretched all the

way to Nebraska. To either side rose hilly terrain—and he knew what lay directly behind.

From the map he'd seen, somewhere to the north must be the answers he sought to the identity of the woman road agent. Luther Simkins probably camped there, too, if those weren't his men in the canyon. But heading in that direction was as dangerous as confronting the outlaws he had tangled with. The only choice for Leif lay in riding south.

Directly into the arms of the cavalry patrol.

He'd be lucky this time if the lieutenant simply didn't string him up from the nearest tree. Worse than the crime of murder, he had made the officer look foolish by escaping. The corporal had probably lost his stripes, but from everything Leif had seen of the gullible man, it wouldn't be the first time. The newly demoted private, depending on his skill at spinning a tall tale, had likely received no additional punishment other than being chewed out. The sergeant might make him pay for the destroyed carbine, but the noncom and the rest of the patrol had to admire his shooting it out with a sharpshooter named Trickshot.

Leif thought the private was clever enough to realize the simpler the story, the more likely everyone would believe it.

He considered finding a secluded spot to leave the girls, but they were so young that they would never survive. Eliza's wound was serious, and she wasn't going to hang on much longer without a doctor. Even then, her survival was going to be dicey.

Worse, the cavalry might ride past and never see them. Or the road agents could follow the trail directly to wherever Leif thought they'd be safe. And if the cavalry found them, it might be a day or two. He wasn't certain Eliza could survive much longer on the trail.

He looked south. To ride that way would cut the time between the cavalry finding him and getting the girls to Kinney. Whether any doctor could save Eliza gnawed at him, but his conscience won. Letting her die through his own attempt to escape the army patrol wasn't right. He had an obligation.

Turning White Lightning back in the direction he had ridden from Kinney, he urged the stallion into a canter. The girls' extra weight was nothing to the powerful horse.

The outlaws caught up with him within the hour.

"Susan, can you ride? Can you stay in the saddle and hold your sister, too?"

"I suppose." She rubbed sleepy eyes. "I'm hungry."

"You and Eliza ride on. White Lightning will carry you faster without my weight on him. You ride as fast as you can without falling off, and you'll find soldiers who will feed you."

"Soldiers? I want to stay with you." She threw her arms around his middle and hugged him tight. He gently pulled her from him.

"You find the soldiers and tell them I'm here waiting for them. Can you do that?"

"You won't run off?"

Leif saw the outlaws spread out. One or two already let out whoops and brandished rifles. They were preparing for their attack, and no quarter would be given.

"I won't run off. Go on. Ride. Hold tight to Eliza."

Leif jumped to the ground, made sure Susan clung to the reins and saddle horn and had a secure grip on her sister, then gave White Lightning a swat on the rump. The horse rocketed away. For a heart-stopping instant, he thought the girls would tumble from the saddle, but Susan clung on for dear life.

Leif drew his six-shooters and found a waist-high tumble of rocks that would slow an attack.

Two outlaws saw Eliza making her escape. In the midst of a hail of bullets, Leif stood and fired with expert precision. His first shot took the closest road agent from horseback. Four rounds were spent before he hit another attacker's horse and sent its rider somersaulting to the ground. Then he ducked back down as a renewed assault on his small fortress began.

He winced as hot lead creased his right biceps. Two other rounds cut long tears in his duster. A quick peek over the rock almost cost him his life. The outlaws with rifles rushed forward, firing as they came. Leif ducked back, slid around the edge, and emptied both six-guns into the leading rider.

This drove the others back, giving him a chance to reload. His right arm began to ache. Holding his Peacemaker made his hand cramp.

He slid the Peacemaker back into his holster and concentrated on using the pistol in his left hand. He winged another outlaw and drove the pack of them back just beyond the range of even a crack shot. Leif settled down and prepared for what he knew was a final attack. An all-out rush in the dark would overwhelm him. He vowed to go down fighting. Letting them capture him meant hours or even days of torture. He had seen how they acted at the burning wagon. Somehow, he blamed Simkins, and he wasn't even sure these were his men.

A deep breath settled him when he heard a volley. He popped up like a prairie dog and hunted for a target. To his surprise, there wasn't one. The gunfire continued. He saw a pair of riders retreating, then heard the thunder of hooves. He rested his Peacemaker on the rock and hunted for a single last target.

Nothing.

Then he returned the six-gun to its holster and raised his hands. The corporal had him squarely in his sights. The grim set to the man's chin warned that the slightest move would send a carbine round through his head. Even if Leif didn't move, the soldier was likely to fire.

"Stand down, Corporal," came the sharp command. "This miscreant is surrendering. Aren't you, Mr. Gunnarson?"

"I am, Lieutenant." Leif moved from around the rock, hands above his head. "Thanks for saving my bacon. In another minute, those desperadoes would have had me."

"If I didn't consider returning you for trial as my bounden duty, which I always do, I would have let them take you."

Leif looked past the lieutenant and his sergeant. Immediately behind them, the private he had let go sat astride his horse, looking uneasy. The position might have been one of honor because riders at the front of the column didn't eat the others' dust, or maybe the lieutenant wanted to keep his eyes on the private. Leif hoped it was an honor rather than a punishment that let the youngster ride forward in the column.

The officer motioned for the sergeant to once more take Leif's sidearms. The noncom muttered, "No shackles for you this time. You broke the only pair we had."

"The corporal wasn't too badly hurt," Leif said. The corporal still fingered his rifle, itching to use it.

"I ought to put you back under his thumb." The sergeant shoved Leif forward to stand in front of the lieutenant. The officer glared at him.

"I can't figure out if you're a hero or a clumsy fool. The little girls said you saved them, but that's not the way I read you, Mr. Gunnarson. You are a killer, sir, and it will be my pleasure to see you hanged."

"The girls are on their way to a doctor?"

"You somehow did the right thing, not removing the knife from the younger one. She would have bled to death. The broad blade proved to be a decent plug that kept her alive." The lieutenant looked around and bellowed, "Are there any spare mounts?"

When no answer came, he said to Leif, "You have quite a walk ahead of you back to Kinney."

"Any chance you could go after the gang that was attacking me and bring a little justice to them for killing the girls' parents and . . . sibling?" Leif fought to keep the image of the three charred bodies from making him gag.

"So that's what happened?" The lieutenant shook his head. "They might have killed them, as you say, but my orders are to bring the road agents to heel." With that, he wheeled about, issued curt orders, and led the column back toward the plains.

Leif started to call out that those owlhoots might be Simkins and his gang, but he held his tongue. He stood stock-still, hoping to be ignored. His luck didn't run that way. The private inched closer and said, "I'm s'pposed to look after you. You better get to walkin', or I'll have to rope and drag you. I wouldn't want to do that."

Leif began slogging along, his legs like lead and his feet hurting. He had been through too much recently. Being the headliner for the Wild West Show had been both glamorous and tedious. He missed both the glamour and the tedium now as he walked toward a noose.

The column pulled away, traveling faster than Leif could walk. Squads of five or six occasionally cut off from the main troop and galloped away, returning an hour or two later. The lieutenant was serious about scouting for the road agents. They just never patrolled toward the canyon. That the woman outlaw and the man Leif was accused of murdering had ridden in this direction convinced him Simkins was holed up somewhere near. It pleased him that the officer took his orders seriously and still tracked the outlaws, but nothing deterred him from getting his sole prisoner into a civilian jail.

"Why'd you do it?" the private unexpectedly spoke up. "There wasn't any call for you to do it."

"I didn't shoot the owlhoot in the back." Leif looked up at the private, who was obviously wrestling with the question.

"Not that. Why'd you go and give me such a fine story? You coulda kilt me dead, right then and there when you had the drop on me."

Leif wasn't going to tell the youngster that he had been bluffing since he had already convinced himself that Trickshot had the upper hand. Both his six-shooters had still been in their holsters while the soldier had the drop on him.

"I'm not a killer," Leif said, images of all the men he had killed in the past weeks racing in front of his eyes. The worst had been the outlaw back in camp guarding the children. That was murder pure and simple, yet it had been necessary. There wasn't any way he could have escaped with the captive girls without silencing the guard permanently.

"There was other things, but you didn't tie me up or knock me out."

"Any of those would have landed you in the stockade," Leif said. "It wasn't your fault you found me before any of the others." He considered the matter a few paces and added, "If your corporal had found me, he'd have shot me while I slept."

"He'd have done that very thing," the private said, nodding in agreement. "He's got a mean streak. All you done to him's made it a sight worse, too. If the cut on his face doesn't heal right, he'll have a scar from the chaining you gave him."

Leif vowed to watch his back around the corporal.

"That was a mighty fancy hat you left behind," the private said. "The silver must be worth a fortune."

"Traveling with Wyoming Bob's Wild West Show pays well. And since I was the star attraction, I needed something flashy to draw attention. I got those conchas when we put on a show down Sonora way."

The private turned around and fumbled in his saddlebags. The first rays of morning sun flashed off silver.

"Here. You ought to get your belongings back.

The hat, well, the corporal was so mad, he shot even more holes in it and then had his horse stomp on it. I picked up the silver after he was done."

Leif took the battered conchas and stared at them. They represented better days, less deadly ones in spite of using his six-guns to make his living.

"You won't get into trouble giving them back to me?" He stared up at the grinning youngster.

"Sayin' things like that makes me wonder if you did shoot down that fellow back in the woods. Always thinkin' of others. Naw, they don't even know I took 'em."

Leif trudged along in silence a few minutes, then looked up and saw the private shake his head vehemently. "No, sir, I ain't gonna look the other way whilst you sneak off."

"Do you have a carbine? To replace the one I shot up?"

"Don't," came the reluctant answer.

Leif sagged.

"Losing both your rifle and your prisoner means you'll be in a world of trouble. I can't let you take blame for something that's my doing and not yours. If you'd lied about your carbine, I would have tried to escape. You're honest as the day is long," Leif said. "I have to respect that."

The private nodded and pointed to the horizon.

"It's a good thing. We'll be in Kinney 'fore you know it. That's smoke risin' from all the chimneys in town."

Leif shielded his eyes with his hand against the sunlight and saw the smoke spotted by the soldier from his higher vantage point. Even if he had figured a way of slipping away, being this close to Kinney dashed his hopes of even trying to escape. The marshal need only snap his fingers to form a posse. Hunting for an escaped prisoner this close to town would draw willing vigilantes by the score. They wouldn't have far to ride to earn their shot of whiskey for their service.

By moonrise, Leif Gunnarson was securely locked up in the town jailhouse.

CHAPTER EIGHTEEN

"I BROUGHT DINNER FOR the prisoner."

Leif Gunnarson stirred, then sat up on the hard cot in his jail cell. Peering around a partially open door leading to the marshal's office, he caught sight of the woman belonging to the soft, lilting voice.

"Let me look. I want to make sure you're not smuggling in a gun."

"Put that down," came Marta Esquivel's scolding words. "The food's for him, not you."

"Elsie never fixes anything near this good when I go eat at the restaurant. How's it that she does chicken and dumplings for the likes of *him*?"

Leif cringed. He imagined the marshal jerking his thumb over his shoulder in the direction of the cells and scowling to show his disdain. For two cents, the lawman would let him starve to death. This was only the second meal he'd had in the two days since the cavalry patrol had turned him over.

"Does he get it, or do I take it back?" Marta demanded. "I am not letting you eat it."

"Be like that." Keys jangled. The light coming through the partly open door dimmed as the marshal's bulk filled it. Then he came back and shoved the key into the cell door lock. "Get back and set yourself down on the bed, or I'll make sure you never see another crumb."

Leif did as he was told. Even with his swift reflexes, there wasn't any chance for him to leap off the cot, cross the cell, and bowl over the marshal. The lawman stepped away to let Marta into the cell. He held the keys in his left hand and rested his right on the butt of his six-shooter. He wasn't taking any chances with his slippery prisoner.

"I'll stay while he eats," Marta said.

"Set down the tray and get out of the cell." The marshal locked the iron-barred door and grabbed a chair. He put it as far away as possible. "You set yourself there and don't stand up without letting me know. Otherwise, I might come in with my gun blazing."

"I'm sure you'd enjoy that, Marshal," Leif said. He moved the tray to the end of the cot and inhaled deeply. The aroma made his mouth water and his stomach growl. A sample here and there further whetted his appetite.

"No whispering, either," the marshal said. "I don't want you two conspiring to break the law even more." He gave Marta a final once-over look and returned to the front office. After settling into his chair, he hiked his feet up onto the desktop.

Leif looked at Marta, who gestured at the tray. He pushed back the napkin over the food. Pinned to the cloth was a note. Carefully removing it, he scanned the sheet, then looked up in surprise. He shook his head.

She had laid out a scheme to break him out of jail. He crumpled the paper and stuffed it into his vest pocket. If the marshal saw it, Marta would be tossed into the cell next to him.

"I can do it, Leif," she said.

"I don't want you to even try." He picked his words carefully to keep the eavesdropping lawman from getting suspicious.

"The circuit judge comes to town tomorrow."

He nodded. "I heard. Rather, the marshal made sure I heard. I want to stand trial. The judge has the reputation of being an honest man. When he hears my side of it, he'll have to see that I'm innocent."

Marta made a face. She fumbled in her skirts and found another piece of paper. Using a stub of a pencil, she began writing as she talked.

"The judge might be fair, but the jury gets more whiskey if they convict." She scribbled the rest of her note, then crumpled it into a ball and tossed it into his cell.

He picked it up. Again she outlined her plan to break him out.

"This is too dangerous," he said. "I won't do it."

"After the trial," she said. "Will you do this thing then when they convict you?"

"If," he corrected. "If they convict me."

"You put too much faith in your powers to convince. You will not sweet-talk your way out of this."

Leif grinned broadly and said, "It's worked on you so far." He enjoyed her shocked expression. She started to argue, then fell silent. As she watched intently, he finished the meal. "Those were mighty good victuals. Pass along my appreciation to the cook."

"Leif, I—" Marta was halfway out of the chair. The marshal burst in and shoved her back down.

"I told you not to budge."

"There's no need to be so rough with her," Leif said. "She was only coming over to pick up the tray."

The marshal unlocked the cell door and stepped back, hand on his six-shooter again. Marta took the tray and the licked-clean plate.

"I will thank her for you, Mr. Gunnarson."

"You might send in your request for a last meal," the marshal said. "There's no way you won't get a suspended sentence." He made a choking noise, then laughed. Seeing his mockery, Leif almost called to Marta that she should try to spring him from jail. The marshal herded her away before he made such a mistake.

The door to the outer office slammed shut, leaving him alone with his desolate thoughts. He fell asleep with the belief that he had done the right thing denying her plan. The slightest mistake would get her killed. And doing the right thing would get him hanged.

THE SALOON WAS packed to overflowing with spectators. Six chairs, still empty, stretched along the bar, as much to show where the jurors would sit as to keep the horde from trying to order booze. The judge's table sat at the rear of the saloon, with a large sign stating that no one would be served until the case was tried. Leif wasn't sure if that made him feel better. If the jurors were knee-walking drunk, maybe they would ignore the prosecutor's case. The man was dressed all in black and had a serious demeanor. Spring-held glasses perched on the end of his nose, giving him a learned look. Learned and mean.

The lawyer beside Leif reeked of liquor and had eyes of indeterminate color because they were so bloodshot. If he had been dragged behind the stagecoach, his clothes couldn't have been in more dirty disarray. A couple books open on the table in front of them revealed legal cases that had no bearing on the crime for which Leif was charged. A shaky hand reached out and pointed. The lawyer cleared his throat and spat, missing a cuspidor by a foot. He never noticed.

"This here's how I'm gonna get you off." The defense attorney half turned to Leif. "You got money to pay me, right?"

Leif touched the silver conchas in his pocket. Those ought to be more than enough, but he found himself wanting the prosecutor on his side rather than the counsel he had. Marta had asked around town, and these two were the only lawyers. He had a suspicion they took turns prosecuting, and, if so, he had the bad luck to get the drunk while the competent lawyer intended to send him to the gallows.

He jumped when a gunshot rumbled through the packed room.

"Hear ye, hear ye, and all that," bellowed a short, sturdily built man sporting a walrus mustache and bushy sideburns. "This here court's in session. The real honorable Justice Horatio Hansen presiding. All you gents climb to your feet. Now!" The bailiff fired a second round to motivate the crowd.

Leif watched as the black-robed judge came from the back room. If he had to guess occupations, Judge Hansen looked better suited to bottom-dealing at a poker table. Sharp features, eyes black as night that darted about nervously, a thin mustache, and hair slicked back with sweet smellum that made him seem to glow with an inner light, although only the gas lamp high above lit the room.

"Don't you worry none," Leif's attorney whispered. "I've argued dozens of cases 'fore this judge."

"How many have you won?" Leif felt as if he had stepped off a cliff when he saw his lawyer try to remember even one.

"Set yourselves down," the bailiff called. "Let's get on with the trial, Judge. You got another case tomorrow early over in Newell Bluff that'll pay us half again what this one will."

"Very well," the judge said. He shuffled a stack of papers and took one from the top. A quick glance at whatever was written caused him to look dyspeptic. Horatio Hansen leaned back, crossed his hands in front of him, and declared, "I do not like murder trials. They are always sad, and there's never a happy ending no matter the verdict. You, Prosecutor, get on with presenting your case."

Leif listened hard and made mental notes of all the points to attack the story. His lawyer's chin dropped to his chest, and he fell asleep as the prosecutor droned on.

"All that's well and good," Judge Hansen said after a few minutes, "but listening to you tell me's no substitute for hearing from witnesses who were there and saw the murder. Call your first witness."

The prosecutor cleared his throat, then chewed on his lower lip for a moment before saying, "What we've got, Your Honor, is the body of an unarmed man shot in the back. The only other one present at the time of the murder is the defendant."

"No one saw the crime? Then call a lawman who arrested the defendant." Hansen ran his finger down the sheet. "That'd be a military officer. A lieutenant. Let's hear his testimony."

"Lieutenant Ballinger is with his company tracking down a ruthless gang of robbers and is unable to show up today."

"No eyewitness, no arresting officer. Do you have a skunk or marmot or a wood nymph present to accuse the defendant?"

"No, Your Honor, but he was the only one there when Lieutenant Ballinger arrived, so he had to be the killer."

"That's your case?" Hansen harumphed. Then he pointed at Leif. "You. Take the stand. You're the only one here today who survived to talk about it."

Leif stood, wondering if his lawyer would object. He'd give his version, but unless he had agreed, this would count as testifying against himself. The defense attorney softly snored, oblivious to the proceedings. He came to a sudden decision and marched to the chair where the bailiff swore him in.

"You'll find yourself in a world of trouble if you lie under oath," the bailiff said, as if being convicted of murder were a mere bagatelle.

"So, Mr. Gunnarson, let's hear your version," demanded the judge.

"It's the truth, Your Honor, not just 'my version.'" Leif laid out the chase from town, the gunfight, and how he had found the dead man. He tried to figure out what the judge was thinking, but the six jurors were more important to believing him. They talked among themselves and mostly ignored him. That couldn't be a good thing, he decided.

"Let me get this right," Hansen said. "This cavalry lieutenant arrested you because you might have shot a man no one's identified in the back at a distance of a hundred yards. That's pretty remarkable shooting, I'd say."

"Your Honor, if anyone can make a shot like that, it's this man," the prosecutor piped up. "He goes by the name of Trickshot and claims to be the world's greatest marksman."

"Do tell." Judge Hansen leaned forward and fixed a gimlet eye on Leif. "Is that so? You claim to be Trickshot? I saw a gun handler of some ability at a traveling show. Wyoming Bob's Wild West Show, it was. That was a passel of years ago, however."

"That was me." The words slipped from Leif's lips before he realized this was evidence against him. He as much as admitted that the cavalry officer was right about his ability to shoot the dead man from a great distance.

"Your Honor, this *is* the man who appears in such a show. He admits it!" The prosecutor struck a pose as if he intended to launch into a long oratory. The judge gaveled him to silence.

"I have one further question, Mr. Gunnarson," the

judge said. "Were any of those fancy shots you made during the show faked? Somebody with a rifle shooting the targets you missed? Anything like that?"

Leif again had a chance to worm out of the charges. If he convinced the judge his marksmanship was all rigged, he could claim inability to shoot a man at such a range.

"No, Your Honor."

"I didn't think so." He turned and faced the jury. "You gents can come to a decision now. What is it? Guilty or not guilty?"

One whispered to the jury foreman, who shook his head emphatically. Two more half climbed over each other to get into the argument. The foreman rubbed his lips and cast a covetous look toward the barkeep, who stood with arms folded across his chest. This set off a new discussion among the jury, causing the juror at the rear to cock his fist and prepare to unload.

The judge rapped his gavel and sternly looked at the jurymen. This settled the building fistfight.

The foreman got to his feet, a bit shaky, and said, "We find the varmint guilty."

"That's what I thought you'd say, not guilty. You're free to go, Mr. Gunnarson." The judge pounded the gavel a couple times, then tossed it to his bailiff, who deftly caught it.

Leif sat in the witness chair, as stunned as the jury by the reversed verdict.

"No man who tells the truth like you did can commit such a heinous crime. Without any witnesses to the contrary, I can only let you go on your way, a free man."

"Thank you, Your Honor." Leif stood, but the bailiff blocked his way. He poked the gavel into Leif's chest.

"There's the matter of court costs," the bailiff said.

Leif touched the silver conchas and knew parting with them would be hard, but if they assured his freedom, the loss was worth it.

"One thousand dollars, payable before the judge and me make our way to the next town on the circuit."

"Drinks are on the house," Judge Hansen cried. The cheer that went up woke Leif's defense attorney. He jerked forward and pointed to a page in the book and started spouting something legal.

"You've got about an hour to pay the court fees or be held in contempt," the bailiff said. "You don't want to be held in contempt in Judge Horatio Hansen's court." He puffed himself up and went to get a drink.

Leif wondered how far he could ride in an hour to escape town, then saw the marshal and his deputy watching him like hawks. Sneaking out of Kinney wasn't in the cards. But finding a thousand dollars in an hour wasn't, either.

CHAPTER NINETEEN

D ON'T JUST STAND there, Mr. Gunnarson. Go get
yourself a drink. The barkeep is a friend of
mine." Judge Horatio Hansen slapped Leif on the
back in a comradely fashion, then leaned closer to
whisper, "Don't get so soused you can't pony up your
fine. It'd be a real shame to clap you into the clink
again."

"For how long?" Leif thought this might be a way
around paying. Even a few days in jail would be worth
it, in spite of Luther Simkins's riding free around the
countryside and robbing at will.

"'Til the next time I swing by Kinney, of course.
That might be months. If there's no other case on the
docket, a year's not out of the question." Hansen
laughed when he saw Leif's expression. "But you're
an honest man. You'll pay your due." With that, Judge

Hansen went to the bar and worked his way around the saloon, sharing drinks with every man.

Leif edged out of the saloon and stood in the hot late-summer sun. Sweat beaded his forehead as he considered his options. He had no choice now. Getting on his horse and riding like the wind was the obvious solution to his woes. That meant Lieutenant Ballinger and his soldiers would be hunting for him when word came of his nonpayment of the court costs. Hunting for the Simkins gang had added danger attached to it. Not only the outlaw but the law would want his scalp.

He walked down the street to the doctor's office. A sign with fading letters and several holes shot in it proclaimed this to be the surgery. Leif opened the door a fraction and chanced a quick look in. The doctor sat at his desk, reference book open in front of him as he took notes. The hot air gusting through the door made him look up.

"Get inside or close the door. Your choice," the sawbones said irritably.

Leif slipped in and looked around. A curtain into a back room swayed in the breeze. Seeing his interest, the doctor closed his book and pointed to a chair.

"You look healthy enough, so you must be the fellow who saved the girls come to check on them. You surely do match the description the girls gave me." The doctor rocked back in his chair and laced his fingers behind his head. Leif had expected an older man. The doctor was hardly out of his twenties, if that. He had watery eyes and a nose that ought to put any bloodhound to shame in a sniffing contest. His white lab coat showed a few bloodstains.

"How is she? Eliza?"

"Young children show remarkable ability to survive such disasters. The knife missed anything vital, and by keeping the blade in place, you kept her from bleeding to death. That was real smart on your part."

"Glad to hear she'll be all right."

"I don't know about that. Seeing her parents murdered and burned to death in the wagon might take a lifetime to get over, especially because she won't remember much of it. Their deaths will always be a goblin haunting her. The older girl might learn to live with it."

"What'll happen to them?"

The doctor shrugged.

"Wish I could say there was a list I could run down, checking off this and that so everything'd be right. There's not. Now, is there anything you want? It's not a good idea to disturb Eliza. She finally got to sleep." The doctor glanced toward the curtain.

"I've got no call seeing her. I just happened to be in the right place to lend a hand. Let's leave it at that." Leif went to the door, hesitated when he tried to think of something more to say, then left without speaking. He might have doomed the little girl to a lifetime of jumping at shadows, but at least she had a life.

He went back to the street in front of the saloon. The boisterous cries and clinking of glasses as the men inside toasted one another wore him down. As much as he hated the idea, running away was his smartest course of action.

"Maybe that's what the judge wanted," he said to himself.

"I have seen men like him before. He just wants money."

Startled, Leif jumped and looked over his shoulder. Marta had crept up on him because he was too absorbed in his thoughts.

"You may be right, but there's no way to collect that much money in an hour."

"How many six-shooters do you have?" She came around and faced him.

"Two. You see that."

"Five hundred dollars each. You can earn that much with your skill. You have done it before, from what I hear." She smiled.

"I milked the people of Newell Bluff for every dime they had. You're telling me to do the same here in Kinney?"

"New town, new . . . money."

The sounds of drunken revelry poured out from the saloon. He had long since learned that men with too much booze in them had lubricated their good sense. They seldom knew when to stop betting—or what to bet on. His entire career with the Wild West Show had been learning to make the challenges so absurd that even a sober man would bet against him. Those with a little too much whiskey under the belt would pony up their money against what they thought were sure odds.

All he had to do was sell the notion they couldn't lose.

"Fifty targets, a twenty-dollar gold piece won on each," he said. Put that way, it sounded easy. But there had to be a gimmick to loosen the purse strings.

"What do you tell them?"

"Find fifty Mason jars." Leif paced around to find the right spot for his spiel. He overturned a crate and stood on it. He shooed Marta off on her quest, stood a moment on the crate to gather his thoughts, then drew a Peacemaker and began firing it in the air. By the time it came up empty, he had attracted enough attention for a crowd ten deep all around him. With methodical movements, he reloaded and slid the six-gun into his holster.

"I'm Trickshot, the best marksman west of the Mississippi." He let the murmur die before he said, "Wait. That's wrong. I'm not the best on this side of the Big Muddy." Nervous chuckles and a few hoots of derision rippled through the increasingly large crowd. "I'm the best shot in the entire country!"

"Those are mighty bold words, sir." Judge Hansen and his bailiff stood on the saloon steps, working on drinks.

He appreciated the judge's part. The man realized the way to get his "court fees" was to encourage the crowd and see how Leif played them.

"It's not bragging if I can prove it," Leif said. "There's my assistant. She has fifty glass jars. Show them, Miss Esquivel."

Marta began taking the jars from their crates.

"What're you gonna do, Trickshot? Can your brags?" This caused laughter in the crowd. Leif let it build and then start to fade before he spoke.

"I'll give odds that I can break all fifty of those jars with fifty bullets. Ten to one. Who'll take those odds?"

"Any kid can do that," the judge called. "Even at such odds, that's not much of a feat."

"Thrown into the air. By any of you gents in the crowd. If you have strong enough arms, that is."

This produced a raft of activity. Marta began taking bets.

"Hand out twelve jars to twelve men who can heave those jars up high in the air."

Marta continued to take bets as she gave one jar after another to members of the crowd until she had passed out a dozen.

"One at a time or all at once," Leif said. "It's up to—"

All twelve men jumped the gun and threw their Mason jars sky-high. Leif hit leather with both hands, filled his grip with the butts of the Peacemakers, and fired as fast as he could. Shards cascaded down all around them.

"He got all twelve," muttered a man in front of Leif's podium. "Bet he can't do it again."

Leif reloaded and easily demolished another dozen. And once more. The crowd grew restive. Everyone had seen his quickness and straight shooting. They weren't going to bet he could do it to a fourth set of a dozen jars.

"Twenty-to-one odds," Leif said. "But even that's cheating you—unless I do it blindfolded."

The crowd fell silent.

"A moment, sir," Judge Hansen said. "You are offering such odds that you can break another dozen *blindfolded*?"

"I am."

Leif was almost bowled over as the crowd surged forward, greenbacks and coins thrust toward Marta, who had become quite expert at taking and recording the bets. When the rush died down, the judge stepped down and came over.

"I have been known to make a bet or two in my day. But, sir, I don't gamble. I don't think you can do it. I bet one hundred dollars."

Marta hurriedly took the bet, then nodded to Leif, letting him know they would cross the thousand-dollar threshold—if he delivered on such a wild bet.

"All I ask is that a few pebbles be placed in each jar so they rattle. That and the jars be tossed one by one."

"Give me a jar," the judge said. "For the size of my bet, I've earned the right."

"Give the judge two jars," Leif said. He checked the loads in both Peacemakers. He started to blindfold himself, but the judge stopped him.

"My bailiff will do the honors." The judge snapped his fingers. The bailiff took a large handkerchief from his pocket, rolled it up, and then secured it around Leif's head.

From the sound the crowd made, Leif figured the judge made a punching motion toward his bound eyes. Unable to see the movement, Leif did not flinch.

"I am ready. One jar at a time, please."

A tiny clink. Leif drew and fired. The gasp from the crowd drowned out the crack of shattering glass. Then he had to concentrate. The jars flew fast. Listening for the stones' rattle took all his concentration.

"Ten down, two to go," he said.

He heard the judge suck in his breath. That told him all he needed to know. A six-gun in each hand, one shot remaining in each, Leif spun and fired. The judge had tossed both jars at the same instant, but Leif had been prepared for such trickery.

For an instant, he stood, smoke curling from the barrels of his guns. He spun them both back into their holsters, then yanked off the blindfold. The crowd stood and stared, stunned at such leaden virtuosity. Then a cheer went up that rattled windows across town.

"That there's the finest shooting I ever did witness," Judge Hansen said. "You mind if I look at your six-shooters?"

Leif silently handed them over. The judge bounced them in his hand, shook his head, and handed them back. "Fine pieces of iron, but they're not the reason you hit all those jars." The judge looked over a field of broken glass. "You've quite a talent, sir. Now, you owe the court one thousand dollars. From the look of it, you'll have no trouble paying."

"Extortion is beneath you, Judge. If you wanted the money, you should have asked for it," Leif said.

"This works for me, and it's all legal. And there's no need to be beholden or to pay back a loan." The judge smiled like a hungry wolf and beckoned Marta over.

"Nine hundred dollars," Leif said. "That's minus the hundred you bet, Your Honor."

"So it is." Hansen spun and walked away, letting his bailiff handle the money. The small man counted it twice, wrote a receipt, and started to hand it to Leif.

"She takes care of money matters," Leif said. The bailiff scowled but handed the receipt to Marta. He followed the judge into the saloon. They had another hour before the stagecoach would arrive to take them to Newell Bluff.

Marta held her hands cupped in front of her. Bills and coins threatened to tumble to the ground. She squeezed tight and clutched them to her bosom.

"We made many hundreds more than that thief asked."

"How much do we need for supplies? A hundred? Let me have the rest."

Marta reluctantly handed over almost four hundred dollars. Leif counted it, then folded the bills together and said, "I'll be back in a few minutes."

"Where are you going?"

"Come along, if you like." Leif retraced his footsteps to the doctor's office. The man was still poring over his book.

This time he looked up and said, "Can't I ever get rid of you?" He peered around Leif and asked Marta, "You needing a doctor, ma'am?"

"She's with me." Leif dropped the money onto the doctor's desk.

"What's this?"

"Your fee for patching up Eliza."

"Too much. Twenty dollars." The doctor started to push it back, but Leif stopped him.

"The rest is for the girls. They'll need it, being without a ma and pa."

"You continue to surprise me," the doctor said. "I'll be sure they get it." Before Leif turned to leave, the doctor added, "You ever hear of the Drake family?"

"Can't say that I have. What about them?"

"Well now, they lost six children last year to cholera. The missus isn't likely to have more children since she was laid up sick, too. It might just be they'd be willing to take in a pair of children like Susan and Eliza. I can ask."

"You don't need my permission," Leif said.

"I wasn't asking for it. I was letting you know since you seemed so concerned about them." The doctor looked back at his book and started taking notes again.

Leif herded Marta from the surgery.

"That takes care of a couple problems. Now I need to send you back to Newell Bluff while I track down the Simkins gang."

"You ran out on me," she said hotly. "I do not know why I stayed." She mumbled something, then said, "I thought you would come back. You did. But you need me in order to stay out of trouble. And I owe Simkins just as you do! I have been practicing with my gun. I can hold my own in a fight!"

"Go back to Newell Bluff with the judge. I intend to—"

He cut off his orders when the marshal and his deputy came up, glaring daggers at him.

"I been looking all over for you, Gunnarson. You're going back to jail," the marshal said. The deputy lowered his rifle to cover Leif.

"Because I left glass in the main street? I'll get it all cleaned up. Or do you want a cut of the money I earned?" The thought of handing him money made Leif angry, but it was the only reason he could think of to explain why he was going back to jail.

"Do you think I'm stupid? I'm arresting you for robbing the bank!"

CHAPTER TWENTY

"I DIDN'T ROB THE bank," Leif Gunnarson protested. "Everyone saw me—I was in front of a whole crowd. Before that, I was standing trial. Judge Hansen can give me an alibi for both times."

"Yes," Marta cut in. "The judge lost money in a bet. He will not forget that."

"I'm not saying you robbed the bank, but you created a diversion so it could be robbed while everyone else was gathered around watching your tomfoolery outside the saloon."

"Where were you, Marshal?" Leif had endured all he could take from the lawman. The deputy had the drop on him, but none of them knew how fast Leif was. He could clear leather and shoot before the deputy's trigger finger curled back to fire.

"You blame Mr. Gunnarson because you failed. That is what happened, was it not? You let the bank get robbed under your nose." Marta moved to one side, anticipating Leif going for his Peacemakers.

"I was watching you," the marshal admitted reluctantly, "but that's all the more proof you had something to do with the robbery."

"Was it the Simkins gang?" Leif's ire rose. "You're letting them escape while you're trying to pin a bogus charge on me. Do you think it'll be that easy convincing the bank president you caught the robber when a judge speaks up for me?"

"And the townspeople who put their money in the bank," added Marta. "They know Mr. Gunnarson had nothing to do with the robbery. They all watched his marksmanship." She smiled just a little. "They all watched and lost money betting against him."

"I'll send a messenger out to find the army patrol and let them know what's happened," the lawman said.

"That's all you're going to do? Then let me get on the robbers' trail while you sit around your office with your feet hiked up on your desk." Leif saw the marshal's anger rising to match his own. There'd be a shoot-out any instant between him and the law.

"Come on over to the bank with us. I want the tellers to look you over. If they say you were there casing the bank, I swear I will clap you in jail again."

Leif nodded curtly. This suited him fine. He wanted to hear from the tellers directly every detail of the theft. He had a gut feeling Simkins was responsible. It was the kind of audacious robbery the outlaw delighted in. But most of all, he wanted to know how Simkins had taken advantage of the distraction he gave with his shooting demonstration. Leif hardly thought the gang hung around Kinney waiting for such a chance.

The deputy reached to take Leif's guns. He found how snake-fast Trickshot was. Leif grabbed his wrist and twisted, forcing the deputy to his knees. His eyes locked with the marshal's, but neither said a word. Leif released the deputy and started back down the street. He didn't even know where the bank was, but in a town this size, it wouldn't be hard to find.

The marshal hurried to catch up, grumbling about how crime had soared since Leif had ridden into his town. Leif ignored the man. Marta walked close, her hip occasionally brushing against his. In other circumstances, this would have been distracting, but now all he thought about was finding Luther Simkins. For once, the outlaw might have made a big mistake. His trail was fresh enough for even a novice trailsman like Leif to follow.

They went into the bank lobby. Two tellers looked up, frightened. One reached for a six-gun on the counter beside him. Behind a low wood rail, a man palmed a derringer, then relaxed a mite when he saw the marshal and his deputy.

"You caught the criminal already, Marshal? Good work!" The man pushed through a creaky gate and thrust out his hand for the lawman to shake.

"Mr. Underwood, you ever see this fellow before?"

Leif looked Underwood over from head to toe. The distraught man was obviously someone important—an officer of the bank or even the owner.

"Why, no, I can't say I have. The outlaws wore masks." Underwood looked at Marta, who gave him a bright smile. "Are these two helping you?"

"They're not the robbers?"

"The woman certainly is not. That woman was

taller, thicker set. And she wore trail clothes. I can't imagine what the world's coming to. A woman bank robber." Underwood shook his head in wonder. He stepped closer and myopically stared at Leif. He blinked and shook his head even faster. "This gentleman's not one of them. He's, I don't know, different. His clothing is nothing like theirs, either. His bearing is different, too. He's confident. They were . . . arrogant, scornful of anyone not in their gang."

"I'm a bounty hunter after the Simkins gang," Leif said, trying to gauge whether the banker recognized the name.

"His voice is different, too." Underwood glanced at his tellers. Neither reacted to Leif as they would to a robbery suspect.

"We're wasting time, Marshal. I need to get on the trail." Leif saw the huge Regulator clock dutifully ticking off the seconds on the back wall. "If that schedule on the wall is right, it's almost time for the stage to leave."

"Get out of here," the lawman said, his anger bubbling up again. "I need to get a few more details and then form a posse to get after the robbers."

Leif and Marta left and stood outside the bank. Down the street, the stage depot drew a small crowd. Leif steered the woman in that direction.

"You think they will take the stage out of town?" She laughed. "That is crazy."

"There's the judge and his bailiff, already in the stage. You get in, too, and go back to Newell Bluff."

"I will not! I want to ride with you. Those monsters killed my family. This is the best chance yet to find them."

She yelped as he curled an arm around her waist and lifted her into the coach. He slammed the door and said to the judge, "See that she gets back to Newell Bluff, will you, Judge?"

"Having such a lovely traveling companion will brighten the trip. Of course, I will do so, Mr. Gunnarson." The judge patted his bulging breast pocket. The trial in Kinney had proved very lucrative for him.

"Stay," Leif said sternly. "I'll pay for your ticket." He circled the coach and waved to the driver.

"You lookin' fer a free ride, Mr. Trickshot? Step on up here and ride shotgun fer me. I'll square it with the company."

"I have other business. Thanks for the offer, Clement." Leif went into the office and pushed through another knot of people to reach the depot master. It took a few minutes to pay for Marta's ticket. Before he finished, the driver snapped the reins and got the stage rolling. Leif caught sight of the bailiff and waved, not sure whether Marta saw him.

He went to the livery and found White Lightning groomed, fed, and raring to hit the trail. To his surprise, his saddlebags and the contents were intact and stored safely in a grain bin. The stable owner got him on his way in less time than it had taken to buy Marta's stagecoach ticket. Leif rode out, then drew rein in front of the saloon, where the marshal had assembled a dozen men.

"A dollar a day and a hundred-dollar reward if we get the bank's money back," the marshal declared. "And the usual shot of whiskey when we get back to town, whether we catch the crooks or not." A murmur passed through the crowd. A few peeled off and sidled away. The marshal worked to keep a decent number of men interested in forming the posse. "And the sharpshooter'll join us. Trickshot, he calls himself. Isn't that right, Trickshot?"

Leif started to laugh and tell the marshal what he could do with his offer, then decided having deputies on his side increased his chance of bringing down Luther Simkins. While his proof that Simkins was responsible was thin, the banker's identification of one robber as a woman upped those odds.

"Let's hit the trail," Leif called. "You don't want those varmints to get too much of a head start." He was feeling his oats. The judge had gotten paid off after a successful shooting demonstration, Marta was on her way safely to Newell Bluff, and Simkins couldn't be more than an hour ahead of a posse.

"You heard him. Mount up!" The marshal exchanged a few words with his young deputy, who was left behind in town to keep the peace. Leif wanted the deputy to ride with them. Even a poorly trained lawman on the trail was better than a bunch of trigger-happy drunks, but he knew that beggars couldn't be choosers.

He saw that the marshal was expert enough to find hoofprints just outside town. This caused a new tension among the posse. Leif wondered why Simkins and his gang had taken the road toward Newell Bluff, and then found the reason less than a mile farther on. The tracks vanished as if a giant broom had swept them away. The marshal circled the area, hunting for spoor, to no avail. He finally gathered the posse.

"We'll split up. Half with me will go north. The other half with Trickshot will go south." The marshal glared at Leif, as if daring him to argue. "If you haven't found the trail by this time tomorrow, get on back to town. Good luck!" He pulled on his reins and trotted off. It took overcoming a bit of indecision, but more than half the posse went with the marshal.

The four left, including Leif, looked southward. They exchanged worried expressions. Leif hadn't been named as their leader but took charge. "This way, gents." He let White Lightning set a brisk trot, not caring if the other three came along or not. By the time he crested a low hill a mile off the road, he saw he had kept his small posse intact.

"Where're we going?" asked one. "We might camp for the night and—"

"We've got three or four more hours of sun," Leif said sharply. "We spread out and hunt for tracks. This far off the road, any we find are likely to be left by the robbers."

As they started to obey, Leif yelled for them to halt.

"Quiet. Listen up. What do you hear?" He swiveled about like a prairie dog on its hill hunting for trouble. Gunshots echoed from off to his right. He didn't ask the others to come with him. He lit out at a gallop.

Within a couple miles, Leif realized he was heading back toward the main road. It had curved around south. As much as he hated to do so, he brought White Lightning to a fast walk to preserve the horse's energy. Running the stallion into the ground before he found out what happened was foolish—and deadly.

The terrain turned rockier as he crossed the main track between Newell Bluff and Kinney. The road dipped down and then wandered through a rougher area. The shooting had stopped, giving him some hope. He waited for the other three to catch up. Their horses were lathered and ready to drop under the riders.

"We approach together, slow-like, keeping an eye peeled for trouble." He drew his Peacemaker to set an example. They followed suit without any real enthusiasm.

Leif saw how they hung back, but when he reached a rise in the road, he knew their reluctance didn't matter. The stagecoach stood alone and lonesome, its team missing. Leif's mouth turned into a bale of cotton as he slowly rode to look into the coach compartment. Both the bailiff and the judge were filled with more bullet holes than he could count.

"Driver's done for," came the report from above. "Clement never had a chance. His gun's still in its holster."

"The judge and bailiff were gunned down, too," he said. Leif reached through the window and saw that the judge's wallet had been taken. He backed away and called to the man balanced on the roof, "Do you see any trace of a woman? There was another passenger with them."

Leif wasn't sure how to react to the murders. Marta wasn't in the stagecoach, which gave him a sliver of hope, but he also had no clue what had happened to her. He knew what Simkins did to women after a killing.

"There's nothing in any direction. I don't even see dust settling down, Trickshot. What are we gonna do?"

Another of the posse wanted to return to town and report what they'd found. Leif almost sent the man off. He wouldn't be any good in a gunfight, but Leif needed scouts more than he did peace of mind.

"Circle the area. They stole a team of horses. They left tracks, lots of them."

Leif held down his panic when the men failed to find the tracks in the rocky ground. He tried to think things through, but one of the men said, "We're heading on back to town. The marshal's got to know about this."

Another chimed in, "And the depot master. There might be a reward for findin' out the stage was all shot up."

"Go on back to town," Leif said, "after you bury these three. I'm going to find the cutthroats who did this."

He started his own circuit of the area, as much to avoid the two men's grumbling, when the third called out, "Over here. I got what looks to be a track."

Leif rode to the spot and saw the hoofprints. If the two men working to dig graves had been blind, they couldn't have missed such a trail. He shrugged it off. He didn't want to tangle with an entire gang of killers and robbers, either, but he had a good reason to do so. The quicker he found them, the better chance he had of freeing Marta before she came to harm.

"Good work. You going on back to town with them?" Leif looked over his shoulder at the men near the stagecoach. Digging in the rocky ground was difficult. He suspected they'd settle for piling rocks on top of the bodies rather than scraping away any decent grave. If the depot master cared, he could retrieve the bodies and give them a decent burial in the town cemetery.

"Naw, I'll ride with you, if you let me. I want a share of the reward money." The man grinned broadly, showing a broken front tooth. "Divvying it up two ways is better than four."

Leif only nodded assent as he set off along the trail. When the ground turned softer, he had no trouble seeing where the road agents had made their escape. They never tried to hide their tracks.

He looked to the horizon for any trace of the fleeing outlaws and saw nothing. White Lightning kept a steady pace, which meant they'd cover a greater distance than a pell-mell, headlong run, but the gait caused Leif to increasingly worry about Marta's safety. The outlaws had the horses from the stagecoach team to swap over to when their mounts flagged. That let them make their escape far faster than Leif could follow on a single horse, even a stallion as powerful as White Lightning.

"You lived in Kinney very long?"

The man riding alongside turned and looked sharply at him.

"Why are you asking?"

"Just passing the time," Leif said, slightly taken aback at the harsh reply.

"Been there a week or two. Just passing through."

"Where are you heading?" Leif saw this question rankled, too. This put him on guard. "I hear the ranches to the south are hiring cowboys for the fall cattle drives."

"You think I have the look of a cowboy?" This amused the man. If he hadn't spoken the way he did, Leif doubted he would have noticed the small details. But he did now. The man's holster was hard leather and well worn. The ebony butt of his Colt was polished, well used, ready for action. His clothing was something between that of a cowboy and a tinhorn gambler.

"I'm not sure what you look like," Leif said.

"What's that ahead? Riders!"

Leif went for his Peacemaker in the left holster, cleared leather, and aimed across his body before the other man squeezed off a round.

"Drop it," Leif said, and then he fired. The hesitation on the other's part was only a fraction of a second. He fired across his body, too, but Leif's aim was on target. His bullet drove through the man's left arm and into his body, exploding his heart.

The rider toppled from his horse and lay still, his pistol still clutched in his right hand.

It had been clever having one of the gang ride with the posse. Leif had to make the most of the shooting now to rescue Marta. Luther Simkins wouldn't expect anyone but his henchman to show up at their hideout, wherever that was ahead.

Leif dismounted, took the dead man's gun and ammo. The fight ahead was going to be long and lethal. He wanted as much of an edge as possible . . . if only it was enough.

CHAPTER TWENTY-ONE

LEIF GUNNARSON WORRIED that he should have buried the dead outlaw. At least a few rocks piled on the body would have kept the buzzards from wheeling about in the sky. A few looks up made him ride faster before the gang spotted the distinctive sign that something had died nearby.

The low hills turned into small mountains as he made his way directly into the rocky patch. The horses' tracks became indistinct and forced him to watch the ground more closely. Broken twigs and occasional piles of horse droppings were his primary clues to where the road agents had ridden. By now they had a good-sized remuda. Other than their being outright horse thieves, intending to sell whatever they stole, the best reason for their gathering so many head had to be a big theft. Tethering fresh horses every few miles from the robbery let the road agents switch from tired mounts and outride a posse. Three or four stations of such horses insured a clean getaway.

But what could Simkins be after? He had kicked up such a fuss in the region already that every lawman slept with his hand resting on his six-gun. The stagecoach company had to be ready to call in the Pinkertons to track down the gang preying so viciously on their drivers, passengers, and cargo. Even the cavalry had fielded a patrol to find him. With so many eyes scanning the horizon, they had to come across Simkins eventually.

"Trains? Some big army payroll?"

Leif realized he might be crediting Luther Simkins with too much forethought. It might give him a sense of power, having so many posses hunting for him. In the past, his vicious, cruel murders had never been for gain. They satisfied some deep, festering darkness—or fed it. Leif recoiled as he smelled burning flesh. His parents. Marta's ma and pa. Those kin of the two little girls.

He sat straighter when he realized it wasn't burned human flesh that made his nostrils flare. It was only woodsmoke from a campfire. He slowed and then stopped to study the terrain around him. It had turned steeper and rockier. The game trail he followed wound in and out through large boulders with heavily wooded areas just beyond. Ahead a fair distance rose a thin twisting column of white smoke. He had to be downwind to have caught even a tiny scent of it. That made approaching whoever built the fire easier.

Easier and harder. If he stuck to the trail, there

had to be a sentry. The outlaws wouldn't camp without watching their back trail.

He cut off the narrow dirt track and rode through the rocky field until he reached the edge of a forest. Dismounting, he tethered White Lightning. He estimated the campfire was a good half mile ahead through the wooded area. If his horse made any noise tied here, it wasn't likely to alert anyone.

Leif checked his Peacemakers, then the pistol he had taken from the outlaw. Ammo filled his pockets. He patted White Lightning, then made his way through the forest. The farther he went, the more carefully he picked his footing to keep from breaking twigs or rustling bushes. Even if the gang hadn't put out guards where he approached, they might think he was dinner waiting to be shot if he made too much noise.

He caught his breath when he saw the blazing fire through the trees. Falling onto his belly, he watched for several minutes to be sure they hadn't spotted him. He counted men moving about. Three. Four. His heart almost exploded when the woman riding with the gang stood between him and the fire. Her face was hidden in the shadow for a moment until she turned, and he finally got a good look at her profile— the profile of Petunia Gunnarson.

The woman spun and bellowed, "Where'd you get off to, Luther Simkins? We've got plans to make."

Leif drew a six-gun and rested it on the ground, bracing it. The shot would be at least twenty yards in shadow, with dancing firelight complicating his aim, but whoever she was, she had identified Luther Simkins as being in the camp.

"Over here, Sally. I got the map all laid out."

"It's dark over there."

"When have you ever been scared of the dark, my pet?" A boisterous laugh sounded. The woman whirled about and drew her six-shooter. Leif blinked at her speed. She moved faster than about any man he'd ever seen.

"I'll shoot your eyes out if you keep calling me that."

"Why, Sally? Is that sharpshooter fellow getting under your skin?" A dark figure came up on the far side of the fire. The woman's body shielded him and prevented Leif from getting a good look.

From his hiding place, that hardly mattered. He hadn't seen anything but wanted posters for Luther Simkins. His eyes welled with tears. It had been ten years since he had seen his sister, since his family had been slaughtered. Until now, he had thought it a little bit crazy that he carried such hatred for Simkins over such a long time. If the Wild West Show hadn't returned to Wyoming, he'd never have crossed trails with the outlaw again.

He came to a decision. He couldn't recognize Simkins, but the woman had called him by name. That was good enough for him. Leif took careful aim, then caught his breath. Something moved in the forest behind him. Every muscle trembled when he realized someone walked through the underbrush, not trying to be quiet.

The movement stopped. Then he knew why someone from the camp had come out like this. The man relieved himself against a tree trunk. Leif willed himself to be invisible and for the outlaw to return to the campfire.

"Hey, what're you doin' out here? You're all sprawled out and—"

The outlaw realized Leif wasn't one of his partners. The familiar hiss of metal against leather sounded. A hammer came back. Leif rolled onto his back and fired blindly. His instincts saved him. His bullet hit the man high in the right shoulder and spun him around, forcing his gun off target. Lead dug a pit in the dirt next to Leif's head. A second round exploded from his Peacemaker. This removed all threat from behind.

The camp erupted in action, shouts and orders and questions that went unanswered. For a moment, Leif thought luck rode with him. Then the woman shouted, "Out there. In the woods. I saw a flash."

She showed the others where she had seen the muzzle fire by opening up with her six-shooter. Lead tore through the air above him. Leif tried to dig down into a hole to avoid it. The gunfire went above his head, but Simkins snapped out, "He'll be on the ground. Shoot lower, men."

Dead leaves and twigs and dirt danced all around Leif. He scooted back, and when he did, he drew more accurate fire.

"Get him. Don't let him get away. It's got to be that marshal from where we robbed the bank!" Simkins led the way, walking steadily and firing as he came. To his side, the woman provided an even more deadly barrage.

The rest of the gang filled the woods with death, but those two were coming ever closer to Leif with their outpouring of lead. One emptied a gun while the other reloaded. Leif thought he faced an entire army.

He stopped retreating and took careful aim at the dark figures. In the night, he missed his intended target but hit another. The outlaw gasped and dropped to his knees off to Simkins's left.

"He hit me in the leg, Luther. Help me."

"Shut up. Either join us or quit!"

Simkins fired again, finishing Leif's work. He had shot down his own henchman. If only taking care of the others would be that easy.

Leif emptied one gun, grabbed the one taken from the outlaw he had killed on the way, and emptied it. This drove back the advancing wave long enough for him to get to his feet and press his back against a thick tree trunk. Bullets spanged into the far side but couldn't reach him. That would change fast as the outlaws spread out on either side of the tree. While Simkins pinned him in place, the rest would catch him in a cross fire.

He reloaded his Peacemakers and judged distances. To both sides he saw movement. Firing first left, then right, he ducked and dashed away into the night, using the tree to protect his back.

The forest lit up with gunfire.

"Stop, stop shooting, you fools. He's got you firing at each other!" The woman understood right away what he had tried to do. Let the outlaws kill one another. "He's running away from me and Luther. After him!"

She added a few shots in Leif's direction. They came close enough to make him duck involuntarily, though they were wild and away from where he crouched.

Sally Randall had figured out his ploy. Leif changed direction and tried to sneak off by crossing past the outlaw on his left. It almost worked, but something gave him away.

"Here. He's here!" The owlhoot began shooting with such accuracy that Leif winced as a piece of lead creased his shoulder.

He dropped to his knees and aimed both six-shooters. Movement guided his pistols. He fired three times from each gun—six slugs headed for the outlaw. Leif had no idea which one hit its target, but at least one did. The man grunted and collapsed. The death caused a flurry of firing from the gang.

Leif retreated farther and reloaded, but this let them creep closer to him. He was a crack shot, but being unable to see his targets clearly put him at a disadvantage. Once more he tried to count his opponents. The only two he knew for sure were Simkins and Sally Randall. They called out instructions to the others on how to circle him. Their voices located them, but they remained sheltered by trees, letting the rest of the gang risk their necks.

With some trepidation, he changed tactics. Instead of trying to retreat ahead of the gang, he slipped around the tree and hoped the gang on either flank kept hunting where he wasn't. Leif worked his way toward the tree where Luther Simkins remained hidden. If he was going to die, he'd take the killer down with him.

"Where is he? What's happening?" Sally Randall bellowed out her questions from off to Leif's left. He strained to hear Simkins's reply so he could take him out. Leif's heart hammered louder in his ears. Nothing but silence ahead of him warned that Simkins either was staying quiet or had moved.

"Don't know where he got off to, Sally. He's a slippery one. I think he's a mile away by now."

"No, he's not. He's still here. I feel it in my gut." She moved, making a considerable noise as she crashed through dried brush.

Leif suspected a trap. She was trying to draw him out so he'd fire at her. He kept his attention focused toward the last spot where Simkins had taken refuge. Leif raised his six-shooter when he saw a shadow move from a tree to his right. A hundred things raced through his mind. Before he consciously came to a decision, he fired. He hit the shadow—it jerked back, then dropped and lumbered away.

He caught his breath. He had fired on a bear and wounded it. Worse, the flash from his gun revealed his location to not only Sally Randall but another of the outlaws behind him. Ducking and running got him away from where they had spotted him, but the crunch of his boots on dried leaves made it obvious where he fled. Bullets tore through the forest around him. He flinched when one passed close enough to an ear to deafen him momentarily.

The near miss still whistling in his head, he fired again in the direction of the wounded bear, but the animal had more sense than he had. The bear had hightailed it away from the gunfight.

"He's there. Boys, he's there!" Sally Randall spotted him and opened up with a furious barrage of lead. Only her gun's coming up empty saved him from being hit. Leif pushed forward and burst around the tree where Simkins had been.

Leif heard slugs tearing splinters from the tree behind him. A quick shot to his left drove the woman to cover. This was his only chance. Leif sprinted forward, hot on Luther Simkins's heels. He burst into the clearing where the outlaws had camped. He scanned the entire area. Instinct caused him to fire across the campfire into the night. For an instant, he thought he had failed. Then he heard a low moan followed by a curse.

"That you, Simkins? Come out and face me like a man, or can you? You're a woman-killing, children-stealing coward." Leif leaped over the fire and landed hard, going to one knee. This saved him from a bullet coming from his right side.

A quick turn and he loosed three rounds. The dull thuds of bullets hitting a body told him more than the sound of a falling body.

"Simkins. You killed my family. You're going to pay for that."

"I don't even know who you are, boy. But chances are good I did kill your kin. I've killed more people's kin than I can remember." He let out a laugh.

Leif got to his feet. He held his six-shooters, one in each hand. He returned them to their holsters.

"You can draw anytime you want, Simkins."

"Tell me who you are. It's always good to know who I'm killing." The man stepped up. The guttering fire behind lit Simkins's face.

Seeing how he outlined himself, Leif edged to the side. This gave him a better look. He had only glimpsed Luther Simkins from a distance before, and those times he had only guessed this was the man he sought. Simkins, who was about his height, had a weathered face and was thin, very thin. His clothes hung from his frame. His hat had been pushed up on his forehead, giving Leif a clear look at the face of the man who had murdered his family.

"Draw, old man," Leif said. It startled him how old Luther Simkins was. The folk saying "Rode hard and put away wet" came to mind. The years had not been good to him. Living on the edge, dodging the law, had taken its toll. Now Leif intended to collect the final coin in the man's life.

"You'd deprive me of spending all the money I been accumulating?" Simkins laughed hoarsely, then coughed and spat. "You got to admit I've been on a tear. I got me enough horses to start a breeding ranch, and that bank back in town filled my pockets."

"The stagecoach robbery," Leif said, his nerves settling. He felt the calm usually reserved for a complicated shooting sequence. "You killed the judge."

"He surely did have a wallet packed with greenbacks." Simkins lifted a hand and waved. Leif thought he was waving off his men so he could gun down this upstart on his own.

"What happened to Marta Esquivel? Did you kill her? She's not anywhere I've seen in camp."

"Don't know what you're talking about, boy. The judge and his toady were all of them in the coach. And the driver, but he didn't count; I shot him before he went for his iron."

Leif felt like a raw nerve. He absorbed information from all directions and reacted to it. He fired to his right again, hit one of Simkins's henchmen, whipped to his left and fired several times. Another of the gang screamed as Leif's bullet ripped into him. Jerking back around, Leif fired twice at Luther Simkins.

The gang leader shot back. The flash from his pistol showed that Leif had been off by a couple feet. He corrected and prepared to end the man's life. His parents. Marta's ma and pa. Marta! And so many others had been slaughtered by the outlaw. Justice was at hand.

The hammer on Leif's right Peacemaker fell on a spent round. He dropped the gun, fanned off the gun in his left hand—and its hammer fell on an empty chamber, too.

Leif Gunnarson jerked erect when a sledgehammer smashed into his back. He staggered forward a step. Another powerful blow hit him. Pain shattered his world. He toppled forward onto the ground, not moving.

CHAPTER TWENTY-TWO

"Y OU FINALLY GOT the range, my pet. It was about time." Luther Simkins walked over and kicked Leif in the ribs.

The shock caused Leif to regain consciousness. He tried to lift his six-shooters, but they had fallen away from where he lay. The memory of pulling the triggers and the hammers falling on spent cartridges seeped upward into his brain. His guns would do him no good. The pain in his back spread and numbed him when Simkins kicked him again.

Pretend. He had to play possum. The outlaw couldn't know he was still alive. Shot in the back. By Sally Randall, "my pet."

"Luther, we gotta ride," came a distant call. "I think those soldiers have found us."

Simkins swore.

"Too much gunfire, and all because of this one."

He kicked Leif again, but this time the toe of his boot hardly affected his victim. "You ever see him before?"

A garbled voice became clearer as the woman came up from where she'd backshot him.

"From those fancy hoglegs, he's the gunslick that traveled with the Wild West Show. Name of Trickshot. Never heard his real name. And I never got a good look at him since I was always casing a bank or asking around at the stage depot about their schedules. Let me take a better look."

Leif was bent backward as strong fingers laced through his long hair and pulled his face upward, as if she intended to slit his throat.

"Can't tell. Too much blood and dirt. I might have seen him, but I don't much care. What's it matter? I did him in good and proper. You owe me, Luther. I saved your worthless life again." She dropped Leif facedown into the ground. His weakness kept him from reacting. His act worked. She stepped away. From half-closed eyes, he saw her boots next to Simkins's.

"You'll never pay off your debt to me, Sal. Look what I took you away from."

"Away from," the woman outlaw said slowly. "That reminds me of—"

"Of a life that kept you in slavery. Let's clear out. Taking a risk that the cavalry isn't coming and jumping at shadows isn't one I want to take."

"We're close to the brass ring, Luther. We have to grab it now. The Russians won't be in the territory much longer."

"Get the horses ready. All of them, enough to pack away a ton of gold when we nab it. We're clearing out of here right now." Simkins took a step away, out of Leif's limited field of vision, then came back. He nudged Leif again. "You had a grouse with me. I don't know what it was, but it mattered to you, so it matters to me."

Leif kept his eyes closed as Simkins rolled him over and sat him up. It was easy enough to flop around as if he were dead. He was closer now than ever before. Life trickled away every second, and he could feel the warm blood seeping through his clothes.

His eyes widened slightly in shock when he felt something cold and sharp around his neck. Though he hardly breathed, the barbed wire noose cut off his air entirely now. Simkins flung him back to the ground after tightening the wire.

"That's my signature, gunslick. Maybe somebody'll find you and bury you like that."

Leif fought to stay alert and awake as he lay on his side. Eyes open, he saw nothing. Distant noises told him the members of the gang gathered their tack and trooped off into the forest, where they'd corralled their horses. Pounding hoofbeats told him they had gone.

And he was dying.

With a barbed wire noose like Simkins had used on his parents.

That penetrated his benumbed brain and sparked old memories, old hatreds. He had come here to get even with Simkins. Never would he give up. Never would he let the outlaw win!

Energy surged through his body even as his lungs burned from lack of air. Leif touched the barbed wire necklace. Devil's rope. Joe Glidden's revenge. What Luther Simkins used as a brand on his victims.

Leif Johann Gunnarson would not be a victim. He was Trickshot. His fingers turned bloody as he worked on the double twist that held the fang wire around his throat. Leif turned and struggled, and air suddenly filled his lungs. The pain of returning breath gave him new determination. He flopped onto his back and stared at the stars overhead. His vision was still blurred, but finding a single star and wishing vengeance on it kept him alive.

"Wounded," he gasped out. Leif rolled over and over until he dropped flat into a low fire. The pain from the searing flesh guided him to the double bullet wounds in his back. The flames cauterized his injuries. He jerked around and rolled over and over in the dirt to put out his duster and burning shirt underneath.

Exhausted from the fight and his injuries, he finally closed his eyes to darkness.

Leif cried out in pain when he reached up to brush away a fly on his nose and his shoulder protested mightily. He blew upward to shoo the fly away. It worked for a moment. When the fly returned as obnoxious as ever, Leif forced his eyes open. The sun blazed down from directly overhead. He finally made sense of his predicament. Lifting his left shoulder caused less pain than lifting his right. After sitting up and getting his blurred eyes to focus, Leif saw the deserted camp all around, mocking him with glinting brass scattered all around on the ground.

Luther Simkins and his henchmen had reloaded,

leaving behind their debris. The campfires had died down, but some still had coffeepots sitting in the embers.

"They hightailed it fast." His attempt to speak aloud prodded him into remembering Simkins had feared the cavalry finding him. Leif smiled grimly. He had done his part. The fierce gunfire had alerted the army patrol. His smile died when he realized the lieutenant and his troopers had never arrived. If they had, the soldiers would have tended him and his wounds.

Leif got to his feet and took a shaky step before collapsing. His right shoulder still carried two bullets.

"Sally Randall," he muttered. "You shot me in the back. Simkins trained you well." A coldness settled over him. "Shot by my own sister."

The Petunia he had known and loved would never have shot her own brother in the back. Simkins had totally corrupted her.

"Peacemakers," he whispered. "They took my six-shooters!" Outrage brought him back to his feet. He hardly wobbled now as fury burned brightly. Leif looked around and found both his six-guns half-covered in the dirt. The outlaws had ignored them or overlooked them entirely in their rush to run.

They'd said something about Russians. What did they mean? Or had he misheard?

Leif picked up one six-gun with his left hand. His right refused to work. Those fingers half curled and froze in place. He fumbled as he reloaded, then holstered the gun and went to work on the other. Putting it into his right holster required some twisting that brought new pain. He made a few practice draws with his left hand. Then he tried with his right and failed. Every move felt like bones ground together in his shoulder.

He dropped to the grass and sat cross-legged beside a burned-out fire where a coffeepot still sat among the charred twigs. Leif swirled coffee around. He tipped the coffeepot back and sampled the contents. Cold coffee. But he didn't have to make it. He choked, tried again, and drained more, trying not to splash more on his chin than he got into his mouth. The bitter brew brought even more energy to his limbs.

"Still not working," he said, trying to move his right hand. A doctor could fix him up in nothing flat. That was what he told himself.

Finished with the coffee, he poked around and found scraps from the outlaws' last meal. As many bugs as actual food went down his gullet. He swallowed, choked, and kept eating until every morsel was gone. Then he curled up on his left side and passed out again.

When he woke, a chilly night wind whipped through the trees. He heard a horse neighing far away.

"White Lightning," he choked out. "They didn't take you." He felt stronger and got to his feet. One step at a time carried him in a wide sweep of the camp. The reflection of moonlight off a scrap of paper diverted him from going to his horse.

He kicked away a stone to reveal the upper corner of a map. Leif stamped down to keep the paper from blowing away. Carefully bending, he picked up the map and held it so the moon illuminated the page. He turned it over to get a better sense of direction.

The camp the gang had vacated so quickly was some-where off in the part ripped away. A railroad from Cheyenne ran north, looping around above the towns of Newell Bluff and Kinney. Someone had marked several spots along the tracks with small pencil marks, but one area with a faint X gave Leif hope he knew where the gang intended to hold up a train. Simkins had committed every other kind of robbery around the region. Stagecoach and bank and horse thieving.

Leif counted on the big robbery being marked off with the X. So much gold to be stolen, it needed a dozen packhorses to carry it? Leif had no idea what Simkins intended, but something valuable was being shipped on a train following this route.

If Luther Simkins was going to be there, so was Leif Gunnarson.

Moving slowly, feeling his way in the darkness to be sure he didn't step into a hole or trip over a tangle of roots, he worked his way through the forest more by feel than sight. Occasionally, he'd whistle, and White Lightning would respond. Leif was almost ex-hausted by the time he saw the white stallion rearing and trying to pull free of its tether. Leif untied the horse and led it to a stream. There had been enough grass for White Lightning to crop, but water was an-other matter. Weakened, he almost failed to pull the stallion back to keep the animal from bloating.

Leif clung to the saddle, then pulled himself up slowly. The anguish radiating from his shoulder made him feel like a pane of glass ready to shatter. He sat astride the horse until he recovered. Returning to the outlaws' camp, he got his bearings once more.

The horse willingly followed the road agents and their remuda. Leif nodded on and off but felt better by the time the sun poked its fiery disk above the horizon. As slow as he rode, he had no chance to overtake the outlaws. They had feared the cavalry had discovered them, but seeing no sign of the troopers made Leif wary. They might have gone off in a completely different direction. And a quick scan of the terrain from a ridge similarly failed to reveal the marshal or his posse.

Simkins had bamboozled both Lieutenant Ballinger and the marshal.

Leif ate what he could from his supplies, not wanting to stop to fix a decent meal. He worried that if he stepped down from the saddle, he'd never be able to mount again. His hands shook, and his right side was a dull, aching mass. Every time the horse jolted him with a misstep, new agony blossomed in his shoulder. Using that to focus, he rode on with grim determination until just after noon.

He rubbed his eyes to be sure what he saw wasn't a mirage. A man on foot trudged along not a quarter mile ahead.

"Let's find out who that is and why he's taking shank's mare." He patted White Lightning on the neck. The horse shied for the first time, as if warning him away from such foolish behavior. The only hope he had in a fight was to surprise the man—Leif refused to believe the man was anything but one of Simkins's gang. But as weak as he was, any fight had to go against him.

Leif hunted for a way to circle the man and get ahead of him to lay a trap. That didn't seem possible from the rocky terrain. The man hadn't spotted him. Saddle balanced on his shoulder, the man put all his effort into simply hiking.

The decision was made for Leif when he man dropped his saddle to take a rest. He half turned and spotted the horse and rider on his back trail. Leif had two options: press on or retreat.

He hadn't come this far and suffered this much to turn tail and run. Tapping his heels gently against the horse's flanks, he approached the man. Leif didn't recognize him as one of the gang, but then he had only seen poor likenesses of them on wanted posters ten years earlier. He had instinctively identified Luther Simkins. The rest of the gang were strangers, even the woman riding with them.

The man took off his hat and waved. He beat it a couple times against his leg, causing a small dust cloud to rise, then settled it on his head once more. Leif saw how he pulled the brim down to shield his eyes. The man was ready for a fight. Leif wished he still had his hat, but it had been stomped into tatters by the cavalry corporal.

"Hello there," the man called. "Am I glad to see you come along. I thought I'd have to walk the rest of the way."

"Where's your horse?" Leif drew rein ten feet away. He shifted the reins into his right hand and rested his left hand on his holster. "This isn't any kind of territory to be walking."

"Stepped into a prairie dog hole and broke a leg. I had to shoot it." The man squared off. "It's real kind of you to offer me your horse. I got to make a rendezvous, and I'm going to be plenty late if I have to keep walking."

"A rendezvous? With Luther Simkins?"

The man went for his six-shooter, but Leif was already in motion. He gripped his Peacemaker and dragged it out. The iron weighed a hundred times more than usual. With White Lightning sidestepping under him and his finger slower than usual, Leif fired a split second after the man on the ground.

His reaction time was slower, but his aim was as accurate as ever. His bullet sent the man's hat flying. For an eternity, the man stared at Leif, his smoking gun thrust out at arm's length. Leif started to fire a second time, but the man slid to the ground as if every bone in his body had turned to water.

Leif circled him, six-shooter pointed at him. As he rode closer, he saw the small bullet hole in the middle of the man's forehead. He was glad his victim had fallen on his back. The bullet had passed clean through his skull. The exit wound would be the size of a silver dollar. He returned his six-gun to its holster, then held on to the saddle horn to slide from the saddle. The horse supported him; his knees would have buckled otherwise.

"Who are you, mister? You wanted to steal my horse, that much is for sure." He dropped to his knees and searched the man's pockets. Two silver dollars and five dollars in greenbacks, along with a cheap pocket watch, were all he carried.

Leif stared hard at the man, as if willing him back to life. Dead, the man offered no answers. Try as he might, Leif wasn't able to identify the dead man as part of Luther Simkins's posse. Why he hadn't been with Simkins and the rest of the gang was a poser. As much as he hated to admit it, the man might not have been one of the gang but a drifter with loose morals and no inhibition against horse stealing.

Turning to the saddlebags gave Leif some small relief. A half dozen wanted posters, each with the man's likeness, had been wadded up and stuffed in the bottom of one bag.

"So your vanity made you save your own posters." That eased his conscience but did nothing to get him on Simkins's trail.

He sat, drained of all energy. He dozed and came awake when the sun dipped under the mountains to the west. Leif considered all the things he could do, all the trails to ride. He had been lucky facing this man. If the outlaw had a partner, Leif Gunnarson would be laid out on the ground, a bullet in his head.

The way his shoulder felt, how he was feeling feverish and shaky, warned him the bullets in his shoulder had to come out soon. Again using his horse as a crutch, he climbed to his feet. He hung from the saddle horn, sweating. He spun wild fantasies about hoisting the dead man over White Lightning's rump, riding back to Kinney, and claiming a stack of rewards.

He tried several times and failed to mount. Leif climbed onto the dead man's saddle and used this as a boost to flop belly down. Some twisting and turning got him properly astride the stallion.

"Back to town, old boy. Let's head back." Leif slumped forward and gave the horse his head. He had no idea where Kinney lay, but White Lightning must have because he trotted off so confidently.

CHAPTER TWENTY-THREE

H E CHOKED. LEIF grabbed for his throat where the barbed wire garrote had squeezed the life from him. His fingers found only bare skin and raw punctures.

"Calm down. You are safe again. Do not struggle so."

A cool hand pressed into his forehead. He remembered being feverish and letting his horse go where the trail led. But what trail? He lifted eyelids that weighed a ton. The world blurred around him, and then dim movement turned into a heavenly vision.

"Am I dead?"

A sweet laugh answered. A cold compress replaced the fingers on his forehead. He blinked rapidly to get his vision back.

"Marta! Where'd you come from? I made it back to town?" Luck had been astounding, if true, but unless the fever possessed him completely, this was Marta Esquivel, and she put cool, damp cloths on his forehead.

"No, you did not return to Kinney. You crept away like a thief in the night. You tried to put me on the stagecoach, but I got out as it left town."

Her words tumbled around in his head as he tried to make sense of them.

"We're not back in town?" Leif forced himself to sit up and look around. Grassy plains stretched in front of him. Twisting about, he looked over his shoulder and saw forested hills. His intention to get to town and find a doctor had been smart, but he hadn't made it very far.

"Stop turning about like that. You will open your wounds."

"My shoulder? My back?" He tried to lift his right arm. It refused to budge. Clenching his fingers into a fist worked better, but not much. There was no way he could hold a six-gun in his right hand, much less lift a three-pound piece of iron and fire accurately. "What happened?"

"You left me." A tinge of anger made her dark eyes flash. "I have as much claim on shooting down Luther Simkins as you, but you abandoned me."

"For your own good. Look what they did to me." He reached across his body with his left hand and ran it up and down his right arm. Tingles in his biceps and forearm buoyed his spirits. His right arm wasn't entirely useless. Given time, he'd once again use his six-shooters in both hands and be Trickshot.

"If I had been there, they could not have shot you in the back. Twice." Marta stood so he saw that she had her gun belt strapped around her waist. "I have been practicing every day." She grabbed for her six-gun. It slid smoothly from her holster, and she held it securely. All she had to do was squeeze back on the trigger to send an ounce of lead sailing into Luther Simkins's worthless black heart. "Is that not good?"

"Better 'n me right now." He arched his back and did a quick inventory of all the pain he felt. "I need to get the bullets out of my shoulder, or lead poisoning will do me in."

Marta's musical laugh put him on edge.

"You think it's funny that I can die from the bullets? I've never seen a man die that way, but enough stories from others in the Wild West Show ring true."

"I am not laughing at you dying. I laughed at the idea that you would think I'd let you die. I dug out both bullets." She reached into her skirt, fumbled about, and then drew two bullets from a pocket. The bullets shined like tiny stars in the palm of her hand.

"Had you ever done that before? My pa was a lawyer and never had occasion to tend anyone wounded. My ma set my sister's leg once when she broke it, after falling out of an apple tree." Leif tried to put a name to which sister. The name eluded him. So much of his life seemed as if it belonged to someone else. Or that he made it up as he spoke, and now the words refused to come. Tears of frustration ran down his cheeks.

"There, there, Leif. Sleep. Rest. You need to regain your strength. I cannot tell how much blood you lost, but it was a great deal. Your shirt was matted to your back."

He closed his eyes and whispered, "I can't remember. I can't remember."

With that fear haunting him, he drifted off to sleep. When he awoke, confusion shook him up again. The sun hung on the wrong horizon, the bright ball sneaking up from the far eastern horizon.

"It is dawn," Marta said. "You have slept another eighteen hours. How do you feel?"

"Hungry," he said, surprising himself. To emphasize this, his stomach growled. "And thirsty."

"I must fetch water. Drink this." Marta handed him a silvered flask.

He tipped it back. Whiskey burned his lips, mouth, and all the way down his gullet. His throat clenched, and he choked. Leif stroked over his neck, and his fingers came away wet with blood where he scraped away scabs. Simkins hadn't finished the job with his barbed wire. Leif almost hoped the punctured spots would scar into a pink necklace to remind him of what Simkins had done until the day he died.

"I have no beef. That builds the blood," Marta said. She put down a coffeepot brimming with water from a nearby stream. "But any food will give you strength at this point." She started a fire and began fixing breakfast.

"Let me help. I feel useless just sitting and watching."

"You *are* helpless. Do not even think about trying to help," she said with mock sternness. She worked with quiet efficiency and soon had a plate of beans, a tortilla, and shredded meat ready for him.

He ate slowly to keep from gagging. Simkins had bruised the muscles in his neck when he tried to strangle him. The whole time, he watched Marta over the edge of his plate. She was right. He felt stronger as he ate, and the food built his energy. His mind worked better, too. The big question rose. What was he going to do about Marta? Having her ride with him as he hunted down the gang was loco. She pretended to be adept with his six-shooter, but it took years of practice to perfect it. He doubted she had practiced firing it, even at a paper target. For all the years he had worked on his skills, he had never killed a man until a few weeks ago.

Leif smiled ruefully. He had never even shot a man, much less killed one. It had been gut-wrenching and still kept him awake, but better that than face nightmares. He doubted Marta had the anger in her to pull the trigger with another human being in her sights. If Sally Randall hadn't shot him in the back and Simkins kicked him when he was down—his hand traced the barbed wire pattern on his neck—he might have flagged in his determination.

Not now.

He fought to get to his feet. It took a few seconds to regain his balance.

"Draw against me." The words hardly left his lips when Marta drew. He was still quick, but not as quick. She outdrew him. Leif sagged.

"Let's get on back to town so you can rest up. You need decent food and a bed to sleep in." She supported him as he experienced a wave of weakness. "This time you actually use the bed you pay for and not sneak away."

"But Simkins . . ."

"Whatever he's up to, he's not likely to leave the territory until he finishes."

"A train," Leif said, frowning. "I found a map he left behind. And Russians. One of them mentioned Russians. I think. It's all so confusing." He tried pulling it from his coat pocket. Marta caught his wrist.

"Later. In town when you can be sure it means something and is not just a scrap of paper."

Leif gave in. She was right. They packed their gear. It embarrassed Leif that she had to help him mount. White Lightning was as frisky as ever. Leif concentrated to keep control of the horse, though Marta riding ahead of him on the trail seemed to give the stallion direction independent of whatever Leif wanted.

That suited him just fine. He and Marta exchanged a few words, but they eventually fell silent, giving him time to think through all he knew. Simkins had robbed and killed aplenty up until now, but his big robbery lay ahead. A train? That made sense since his constant predations of the stagecoach must have turned the company wary of sending anything of value that way. He shuddered, remembering how Clement, the judge, and his bailiff had been killed.

"Marta!" he called to get her attention. "Why weren't you on the stage? The one Simkins robbed?"

"The robbery where he killed everyone? I am sorry to hear of how the judge died. He was a good man."

"He was an honest crook. He stayed bought. But you were supposed to be on the stage. What happened? Why did you leave?"

"I wanted to join you in hunting the gang." She looked sheepish. "After I snuck off the stage, I got my horse and sought you. I tried to follow the posse but became lost."

"A good thing," Leif said. "Otherwise you'd never have found me." He rode in silence for another few minutes. "But you will get yourself killed not doing as I tell you."

She snorted derisively.

"You can do better, Mr. Trickshot? Who caught two bullets in the back?"

He had to admit she was right. His luck had turned on him, but with careful planning, he would face Luther Simkins again. The two of them would shoot it out. The outlaw would pay for killing the Gunnarson family the way he had.

Leif half drew his six-shooter, then let it drop back. Marta had matched his speed. That wasn't good. He needed to recuperate more, but Simkins wasn't going to stick around forever. It was surprising he hadn't moved on already, with the cavalry hunting him, the marshal leading a posse, and the stagecoach company offering a huge reward for his capture or death. Word of that alone spread like wildfire. Every bounty hunter in Wyoming had to be coming to Kinney for that payoff.

Whether he dozed or passed out, the next thing he knew was the sound of people all around. He rubbed his bleary eyes and sat straighter in the saddle.

"First I see you to the hotel; then I will put the horses into the livery." Marta took control and left him no room to argue. He half fell from the saddle, but his feet were steady under him when he hit the ground. "In. Get a room."

"A room? Not two?" He looked at her.

"You need someone to watch over you. One room." She locked eyes with him, challenging him to contradict her. He saw more there than desire to be sure he didn't kick the bucket in the middle of the night. He approached exhaustion and wasn't inclined to argue.

He climbed the steps onto the porch and watched her ride away with White Lightning. She was a handsome woman. Immediately after her family had been killed, she had acted hesitant and unsure. He wondered if time had given her back confidence and courage, or if learning to draw the six-gun at her hip was responsible. Whichever it was, she was more attractive now than before. But she was getting too headstrong. There wasn't any way he woiuld dare allow her to join him when he ran down the Simkins gang. It was too dangerous.

Shuffling slowly, he went into the lobby. The clerk looked up and smiled in recognition.

"Mr. Trickshot! You're back. Last time you lit out like a scalded dog. You want a couple rooms?" The clerk pushed the ledger around and held out a pen for him to sign.

"One room," he said. Leif tried to hold the nibbed pen. It slipped and rolled strangely, and after he dropped it a second time, he switched to his left hand. Signing his name this way wasn't something he had ever practiced. He scrawled an *X* with a flourish.

The clerk's mouth opened, then snapped shut. He finally grinned.

"You don't want fans to know you're here. I understand. My lips are sealed, Mr. Trickshot." The clerk snagged a key and put it on the counter. "Upstairs, toward the back."

Leif remembered the stairs going to the second floor. Climbing a sheer mountain cliff would have been easier.

"Do you have a room on the ground floor?"

"Sorry, sir. Them's all taken for the night. The upstairs room's all I got that's fit for you."

Leif started to ask for a ground floor that wasn't fit for man nor beast, then bit off the request. It wasn't worth explaining.

"I'll sit in the parlor for a spell." When Marta returned, she could help him up the stairs.

"You want a drink? I can fetch one for you. There's a bottle in the manager's office, saved for special occasions. Having a guest like you's as special as it gets, I'd say."

Leif fished through his vest pocket. All the money he had was what he had taken off the dead outlaw. He put the scrip on the counter, saving the silver for when he needed it more.

"Very good, Mr. Trickshot," the clerk said, disappointed his guest hadn't parted with the silver cartwheels. The clerk hurried away, letting Leif make his way into the sitting room without drawing questions about his condition.

He sank into a love seat and looked at the empty side. Marta would be here soon. She could sit there, and they—

Boisterous laughter tore him out of his reverie. His left hand went for his Peacemaker when he saw Luther Simkins strutting along, on his way out of the hotel. In the light from the gas lamp, Leif saw details missed before when he had shot it out with the murderous outlaw. Again he was struck by how old Simkins appeared. The man was in his fifties, with a craggy face and sharp nose. He wore black and had pushed his hat back on his forehead, showing a receding hairline. The shock of hair that poked out was a mixture of black and gray. Simkins needed a shave, but his scraggly growth of salt-and-pepper beard hid a weak chin.

Leif fixed his eyes on the six-shooter hanging at the man's side. The Colt was well used but had been taken care of. He expected to see notches cut in the handle, but at least Simkins had more class than that. Leif snorted. Simkins probably realized doing such destruction to a well-balanced handgun made it more likely to fumble or fail to aim properly. When that gun filled his fist, Simkins wanted to shoot straight and fast.

"Here you go, Mr.—" The clerk came from the back room, a glass sloshing full of an amber liquid.

Leif cut him off before he used his stage name and drew Simkins's attention.

"Thanks." Leif tried to stand, but his legs gave out. The clerk stepped forward and put the tray on an end table to steady his guest. Leif gripped the clerk's arms the best he could and steered him around as a shield.

He need not have worried. Luther Simkins had something else to draw his attention.

A woman made a grand entrance, skirts swirling. She was dressed to kill, flashing expensive jewelry and hair all done up with sparkly pinpoints of light— diamonds woven into her coiffure. She threw her arms around the outlaw's neck and planted a big wet kiss on his lips.

"You clean up pretty good, Luther."

"And you're the loveliest woman in all of Wyo-

ming, my pet." He offered her his arm. She looped
hers through it, and they left, laughing gaily.

"You look like you've seen a ghost, Mr. Trickshot,
sir. Is there anything I can do for you?" The clerk
moved enough for Leif to clearly see the woman's face.

He gestured the clerk away, took the drink, and
downed it in a single gulp. The burn and pooling in
his belly went unnoticed. He had found his sister, and
she rode with the most notorious outlaw in all of Wyoming.

The same man who had murdered their parents.

CHAPTER TWENTY-FOUR

"Leif! you are so pale. You are trembling. Has the fever returned?" Marta Esquivel dropped into the seat next to him and half turned to him. She laid her cool hand on his forehead. "You are not hot."

"It's her," he said in a low voice that barely escaped his lips. "The woman riding with Simkins is my sister. I know it for sure now."

"Oh, Leif, you are not in your right mind. They are not here. You are seeing mirages."

Leif wasn't going to argue. That had been Luther Simkins, and the woman with him was Petunia Gunnarson. If he hadn't seen the distinctive scar, he might have convinced himself he was jumping to conclusions, that he was, indeed, seeing a mirage. Sure that the ghost of his sister had left with Simkins, he tried to stand and follow them. His legs gave way, and he sank back into the love seat.

"You tire yourself for no reason." Marta held him down.

Leif saw the curious look the clerk gave them. It wouldn't do if the man started to gossip. Simkins had to keep his ear to the ground for such chin-wagging. That was how a clever outlaw stayed alive—and how he overheard of shipments worthy of robbing and banks laden with money itching to be stolen.

"Go ask. Ask the clerk who the two that just left are." Leif knew Simkins wasn't foolish enough to register under his own name, but the woman might be. She wasn't infamous, even if she was a cold-blooded killer like the gang leader. She had shot him in the back. Twice.

She had shot her own brother and left him for dead.

"Very well. Stay here." Marta crossed the lobby and spoke quietly with the clerk. At first, he shook his head, but her bright smile and a little sweet talk got him to spin the ledger around and point to it. Marta returned, her expression unreadable.

"Well? How did he register?"

"He did not sign. She did. As . . . Petunia Gunnarson."

Leif had known she was his sister, but hearing that confirmation still took his breath away again. All strength drained from him, and he walked like a drunk. Marta helped him to his feet and steadied him as they climbed the steep stairs to their room on the second floor.

He sank onto the bed and took a few deep breaths. His mind raced.

"They're in town for a reason. Gussied up like that means they aren't expecting trouble."

"There is so little to do in Kinney, other than the saloons. Unless the town is holding a social."

"The only reason Simkins would dare to come into town without a six-shooter in his hand is to find out something he needs to know for the big robbery he's planning." Leif bent forward, hands on knees. He ached all over, but the pain was gone. A few tries to flex his right hand showed he was regaining the use of it, but too slowly if he had to act immediately.

"The only reason?" Marta scoffed. "If there is a social tonight, he might want to enjoy it with his woman."

Leif jerked as if she had cut his heart out with a dull knife. He refused to believe his sister rode willingly with the gang, with Luther Simkins, but the evidence spoke against him. His head convicted her while his heart demanded her innocence.

"The marshal has wanted posters on Simkins. He can arrest him."

"Is he back with his posse? If he believes he is on the trail of such desperadoes, only a deputy or two will be in town."

"Let's find out." Leif heaved himself to his feet. Determination powered him now. Still, letting Marta support him, just a little, helped.

They left the hotel arm in arm, and he couldn't help but remember Simkins and Petunia leaving in the same fashion. The outlaws were happy, whereas his mood was black and lower than a snake's belly. They stepped onto the porch and immediately knew where to find Simkins and Leif's sister. The music bellowed and boiled, mixing with sounds of merriment.

Marta looked at him, her question unspoken. He shook his head.

"The marshal's office first. He's got to be back. He's just got to be."

Leif knew disappointment the instant they rounded the corner near the lawman's office. The jailhouse door stood open to let the air circulate. At the desk sat a deputy, hardly more than seventeen, if that, working to clean his pistol on the marshal's desk. While maintaining his six-gun was a noble pursuit, it told Leif that there wasn't much happening in town that warranted a lawman's attention.

He stood in the doorway until the deputy—the boy—looked up in surprise.

"You spooked me some," the deputy said. "I shouldn't get so intent on what I'm doing, but remembering the parts is a chore. What can I do for you?"

"Where's the marshal?"

"You must be new to town. Him and a dozen others are out scouring the countryside for a notable road agent and his gang."

"You the only deputy left?" Leif sagged. Marta supported him until he regained his composure.

"Naw, Franco got left behind, but he's takin' the night off. He's been workin' close to every hour of the day since the marshal rode out. Franco kinda recruited me to look after the office while he went to the social with Miss Wilson. He's sweet on her and—"

"You do not recognize this man?" Marta looked significantly at Leif.

"Should I?" The youngster scowled as he studied Leif.

"You didn't hear about the marksmanship contest after the trial?" She gripped Leif's arm a little tighter.

"Well, ma'am, I heard about it, but I was out on the family ranch. It seems like I miss all the notable things that happen in town. I'm not used to wearing a badge, but the marshal told me there wasn't going to be any trouble, not with all the lawbreakers on the lam. And Franco's really the lawman, anyway."

"Have you even worn a badge before?" Leif knew the answer didn't matter. Pitting this wet-behind-the-ears youngster against Luther Simkins was premeditated murder.

"No, sir, first time, and I'm just returning my uncle a favor. He helped us out a lot last year during the drought. You around here then? The crops all dried up and—"

Leif slid his arm around Marta's waist and herded her from the office.

"You folks have a problem I can help with? Don't hesitate to call on me. I'm the town's law right now."

Leif kept walking, not bothering to respond. The marshal hadn't done anyone a favor leaving a greenhorn like his nephew in charge, but then, what was there to lose? The bank had been robbed of everything in its vault. The stagecoach wasn't running, not until a new coach came in from Cheyenne. The amount in the till of stores along the main street wasn't near enough to excite an outlaw like Simkins. All the boy had to deal with was a drunk or a fistfight, and if Deputy Franco was on duty, he wasn't likely to do that much.

"You cannot tangle with him, Leif. Please. Don't

even think about that!" Marta gripped his arm tighter to communicate her fear. He knew the risks. Letting Simkins escape now that they had him in town was unthinkable.

"I want to go to the town social."

"No gunplay. You will only cause the deaths of the townsfolk." In a quieter, huskier voice, she added, "And get yourself killed."

"Where's your curiosity? Don't you want to know why Simkins hasn't left the territory after all his robbing and killing? That'd be the smart thing to do."

"I do not care. All I want is to see him filled with lead for what he has done to me and my family. Perhaps that is why he stays? To kill more helpless families of farmers?"

"He can do that anywhere he rides," Leif said. "There's something else. Something big to steal." The scrap of paper with railroad tracks and tiny dots and a large X haunted him. The tracks ran to the north of Kinney across the plains.

"They make a great deal of noise," Marta said. "It is a grand fiesta, as if in celebration of someone important." She smiled. "But that cannot be. You are here with me. Who else could they be celebrating?" She laughed at such a notion.

"Let's find out." He started for the far end of town. Marta grabbed his arm to stop him. He pulled free. "Stay, if you will. I won't get into a fight with him, not with a big crowd all around."

"They will greet you, the townspeople. He will know." She hesitated before adding, "Your sister will know you."

He considered this and shook it off.

"She shot me in the back without recognizing me as her brother. Too much time has passed." He wondered how many men Petunia had killed in the last ten years, and if all their faces blurred together. Or did she even know the number? Her killings merged with Luther Simkins's, so he carried the blame for them all. That would amuse Simkins, Leif thought. He dealt with murderers the likes of which he had never anticipated.

The music soared, and four squares formed into Texas stars. Leif thought the entire town had turned out. The band members sat on a stage, sweating as they produced one song after another. As they played, he edged around the crowd. He stopped when he came to the doctor. The man clapped his hands and stamped his foot with the music.

"You? You're back? I never thought to see you again."

"What's the celebration? The Fourth of July was a couple months ago." Leif stood on tiptoe to get a better look at the people milling about. The swirl of the square dancers kept blocking his view.

"We got some real royalty visiting. A Russian grand duke and his bride are on their honeymoon."

"In Kinney, Wyoming?" That struck Leif as absurd. "I never toured in Russia, but the Russians I met thought of our country as barbaric and terrible."

"That's the point, I reckon. The archduke wanted to take his bride somewhere no one else in Russia went. They got a train back in Independence loaded with servants and Indian scouts, and set out to see the sights."

"Scouts?" Leif wondered at that. "They want to see Indians?"

"That and buffaloes. The archduke heard about bison stretching as far as the eye can see." The doctor chuckled. "He's been real disappointed in that. Nobody told him the herds have been killed off and only a few thousand remain. From what I heard, his scouts haven't found but a handful."

"Leif, on the stage," whispered Marta. "I have never seen such jewels."

"Who's the woman? His bride?" Leif kept from shielding his eyes as light caught the diamonds and rubies. And those were just from the young woman's necklace. Rings and bracelets of gold and other colored precious stones dangled from the archduchess's wrists. "Those must be worth a fortune!"

"Heard tell this is only her traveling jewelry. Back on their train, she's got gems that make these look pathetic. I reckon she didn't want to lord it over the peasants by wearing the good stuff tonight." The doctor pointed. "See those soldiers all around the stage? Cossacks. Fiercest fighters in Europe, they say. Nobody's going to steal those jewels while they're with the archduke. A good thing, too, since his personal train is loaded with gold until the axles creak, or so they say. The Russians are buying a bank in San Francisco. They already have a fort along the coast and are trying to expand their influence on the West Coast. Excuse me." The doctor bowed gallantly as a young woman crossed in front of him, trying not to show her interest or to be too forward.

They went off to join the nearest square.

Leif felt Marta press closer. She hugged him as if to keep him from finding a partner of his own.

"I heard the gossip. Everyone thinks the Russians are here to build a palace. How loco!"

"The doctor had his own tale to spin." Leif watched the duchess onstage stoically smiling and waving. Every time she lifted her hand, new rainbows flashed off her jewelry. As expensive as the bangles were, he doubted Simkins was as interested in them as in the gold supposedly carried on the train to buy a San Francisco bank.

"Will they kidnap the archduke and demand ransom?" Marta strained to see the royal group on the stage. "Or will they kidnap his wife?"

"I don't see how Simkins thinks that is possible. He has bided his time, robbing and killing, until they arrived on their train. But kidnapping isn't the sort of crime that suits Simkins. It's not daring enough."

"But, Leif, if he and . . . and your sister . . . do it under the noses of everyone in town, that is very daring!"

"The soldiers with the archduke will fight to the death. Their reputation is that they never give up until they're killed in battle. Then their ghosts fight on for the honor of the czar." Leif saw a dozen of the ornately dressed Cossacks moving restlessly around the stage. A full-scale Cheyenne attack couldn't get through that squad of Russian cavalry.

"Simkins can never hope to rob the royal train. He does not have many men left, not after you shot so many."

Leif experienced a twinge in his shoulder. He had no idea how many of Simkins's gang he had shot. All he knew for sure was that his sister had drilled him twice in the back.

"There's Simkins, talking with one of the Cossack officers. Where's my sister?"

Leif puzzled over what Luther Simkins did. Money exchanged hands. The outlaw tucked away a large roll of bills in his coat pocket and slapped the Cossack on the back. The officer did not take well to such familiarity and backed off. An agreement had been reached, one that the Russian was willing to pay handsomely for but assumed no friendliness with the outlaw.

The Russian archduke drew a pistol and fired it into the air, startling everyone. The band stopped playing, and men throughout the festivities reached for their six-shooters.

"I thank you for your quaint dancing. I and the archduchess have been amused." The archduke made a sweeping gesture, as if ordering a full-scale cavalry attack. His Cossacks formed a wedge and marched through the crowd, parting the people like a plow cutting into the sod. The archduke and his wife strode along in the V, jesting at the expressions on the faces around them.

"They came here to laugh at the peasants," Leif said. "We're little better than zoo animals to them." The words caught in his throat. He had felt that way when performing with Wyoming Bob's show. Trained dogs doing tricks. He used his six-guns, and others rode their horses, doing tricks, roping and standing in the saddle of galloping horses. The few exotic animals they had were appreciated as much as the human performers. Unreasonable anger rose in his gullet.

"There is your sister. She came from . . ." Marta turned and imagined a track behind Petunia. "From the saloon. Why was she there?"

Leif itched to have it out with Simkins, but the crowd provided too much cover for the outlaw. Try as he might, he failed to identify any others from the man's gang in the crowd. Only Simkins and Leif's sister had come to Kinney.

"The money," Leif mused. He walked steadily toward the saloon and stopped in front. "Simkins steals money. He isn't a businessman."

"I hear horses," Marta said. "Around back."

Leif had to step lively when the Russians came down the street. The Cossacks again formed a wedge. The royal carriage rattled along behind the soldiers. He caught a glimpse of the royal couple. They laughed and pointed as the coach drove away from town.

"They're returning to the train," Leif said. "They've seen enough rustic scenery with wild men cavorting about." He made his way to the side of the saloon in time to watch a heavily laden freight wagon leave. At the rear, the barkeep leaned against the saloon wall, counting a wad of greenbacks. He looked up when he heard Leif approaching. His hand went to a small-caliber gun tucked into his waistband.

"You stay back, you hear?" The barkeep waved the gun around.

"I'm not going to rob you. Why should I?" Leif moved his hands away from his holsters.

"You. You're the sharpshooter."

"I'm Trickshot. I'm not here to harm you," Leif said. "Were those Russians?" He jerked his thumb over his shoulder in the direction taken by the freight wagon.

"That's the sweetest deal I ever made. I got paid to make up some special tarantula juice for them. They gave me a recipe, and I cooked it up and bottled it. Paid good money, too. I'd be rich if I could sell that . . . that bodka, I think they called it."

"Vodka? I've heard of it," Leif said. "How much did you sell them? That looked like a powerful amount."

"A powerful amount, true," the barkeep said. "Ten cases, and it's powerful joy juice, too. I tried some. Just a sip, mind you. It set me right, it did. Potent."

"Too bad the Russians are traveling on. You'd be rich, selling them that much every week or two."

"Ain't the Russians that bought it. Well, they carted it off. It was a crusty old woman, but tonight she was dressed up like she was one of them Russian princesses."

"She gave you the recipe?"

"You have a good night, Mr. Trickshot."

"Hold on," Leif called. "You kept a few bottles of the vodka. Could I get one?"

"Seeing as how it's you, and I'm rolling in the tall green right now, why not?" The man ducked into the rear door and came back with a quart bottle. "Don't you go drinking all of it. You'll go blind and never be able to stand. This is mighty potent popskull, yes, sir."

Leif peered through the bottle of clear liquid. He pried a silver dollar from his vest pocket and laid the cartwheel on the bar. He held the bottle up in silent salute and returned to where Marta waited impatiently.

"Why do you want such liquor? There is nothing to celebrate. Simkins grows richer and is no closer to justice."

"He can wait until morning," Leif said.

"You have a plan to capture him?"

Leif did.

CHAPTER TWENTY-FIVE

LEIF GUNNARSON STARED out the hotel window. The mix of energy and lethargy scared him. He had to act. He knew what had to be done, yet his once-fast hand was gone. Over and over he drew his Peacemaker and aimed it out the window. A small tremor bothered him but not as much as the weakness in his arm. And this was his left hand. His right still betrayed him. A single slap-and-draw brought that six-shooter into his hand. If his left trembled, his right quaked.

He had to face Luther Simkins now. This was his best chance and might well be his last.

"Are you afraid?" Marta asked softly from the bed.

He never turned.

"I am, but for ten years I've longed for this day. No matter what I feel now, today's the day Simkins pays for what he did to my family."

"And mine," Marta added. She slipped from bed and began dressing. Leif saw her reflection in the glass. A quick, practiced swing of her hips brought her gun belt around her waist. She fastened the buckle and settled the six-gun.

"Take it off," Leif said. "What you need to do won't require you to carry a pistol."

"I want him!"

"I'll take care of Simkins. For both of us."

He faced Marta. She glared at him, her dark eyes hot and fierce. When he did not flinch or look away, she grumbled but unbuckled the gun and dropped it on the bed.

"Let's go. We won't have a better chance than now." Leif rolled his shoulders to loosen the tensed muscles. It didn't work.

"What are you going to do about your sister?"

They made their way down the steep stairs. Leif tried to ignore the momentary light-headedness. He dared not feel this way when he called out Luther Simkins. The outlaw looked to be an old man, but underestimating him meant more than simply dying. Simkins had to be stopped. What he had done to the Esquivel family proved his taste for torture and murder could never be sated.

Leif and Marta stepped out into the nearly deserted street and headed for the only restaurant in town. Dawn threatened, and a cold wind blew down the street. The two stopped outside the restaurant, which was just opening its door for the day's first customers.

Leif said nothing. He looked from Marta to the opening door, then left her alone to circle the building.

She knew the plan they had concocted. Leif wanted to face off with Simkins away from others who might get hurt by randomly flying bullets. Going after the outlaw inside the café carried the same danger as trying to take him inside the hotel.

Moreover, Leif wanted Simkins away from his sister. He had no idea how to deal with her. She seemed to have not only ridden with the man who had murdered their parents but had willingly joined in. Finding out why would be paramount—after he dealt with Luther Simkins.

At the rear of the restaurant, Leif prowled about to get the advantage. So much of his Wild West Show act was a matter of angles, setting up the targets properly rather than being an outstanding shot. This performance was no different. He was good—usually. Now he had to turn every small detail to his own advantage. A few practice draws with his right hand showed he needed more than that. Leif kicked some crates around to provide a barricade. Standing behind it protected him without hindering his own shooting.

He sucked in a deep breath. His mouth watered at the cooking odors billowing out the restaurant's stovepipe. There would be time to have a decent meal afterward. Leif grabbed for both his Peacemakers to see how that felt. Usually, having both weapons in his hands let him keep his balance. Firing the six-shooters at the same time also gave an advantage spectators overlooked. The recoil was uniform and let him lean forward without twisting. That left him in good position for another volley.

A couple draws warned him not to try that. Left

hand only. When he tried with both, his right lagged. If he tried to make the shots simultaneously, it threw him off. He settled his six-guns in their holsters and leaned back against a wall, his eyes fixed on the door leading from the kitchen.

He had no idea what ploy Marta would use to get Simkins to come out. All that mattered was that she persuaded him to come out back and kept Sally Randall inside.

"Sally Randall," he muttered. "My sister, a notorious outlaw. What would Pa have thought?"

Would the elder Gunnarson have stepped forward to defend his daughter for all the crimes committed by the gang? He had been a lawyer. Leif thought his pa would have defended her, even as he bemoaned what his daughter had become.

The rear door creaked on unoiled hinges. Leif came instantly alert. He moved to shoot around a stack of crates. Too many decisions slowed him. Should he face Luther Simkins or just throw down on him? That failed to square with his sense of honor, but the outlaw had no honor. Treating him as an equal ignored all the terrible crimes he had committed.

The door opened a few inches, but no one exited. Leif took in a deep breath and let it out slowly. The trouble with his scheme was that Simkins wasn't the only one likely to use the door. There were also the cook, his helpers, and anyone coming out back to throw away garbage.

The door jerked open and slammed hard against the inside wall.

Luther Simkins stood silhouetted in the doorway, a perfect target. Leif went for his Peacemaker. He started his draw before the outlaw, but both men came up with their weapons at the same instant.

Lead ripped past his head and blew splinters from a crate into his face. Leif returned fire. His first shot drifted to the left and gave Simkins as good as he dished out, sending splinters flying. The next shots were wilder.

"Ambush!" Simkins called out to warn Sally Randall. He dipped down and twisted to get out of the line of fire.

Leif shot through the thin wall. His round caused the open door to swing around and knock Simkins back into sight. Leif got another shot, an easy one. Simkins jerked. The outlaw's return fire went wild. He sprayed lead everywhere, driving Leif down behind the wall of crates. Leif started to duplicate the outlaw's attack. He had a second pistol and didn't need to reload, but he hesitated. The reason he had decided to ambush Simkins like this was to protect others. It was only bad luck that Luther Simkins had paused in the doorway and spotted the trap.

"Come on out, Simkins. Give up. You stand a better chance with the marshal than you do with me, but if you surrender, I promise not to shoot you." Leif wondered if adding *again* might convince the road agent. He hadn't seen where he winged Simkins but was fairly certain he had.

No answer. Leif switched six-guns, placing the empty one back on his left hip. He reached across and awkwardly drew the Peacemaker in his right holster. A tiny bounce in his grip settled it firmly. Leif edged around the crate.

His reflexes were a beat too slow. Simkins leaped

into the doorway and began fanning his six-gun.
Lead had torn through the air in all directions before. This time the outlaw's aim was more concentrated. Leif was lifted up and thrown back as a slug
ripped into his left shoulder. He stumbled over the
crate, saving his life. The air above him filled with
death. With a savage jerk, he flopped off the crate
and landed facedown in the dirt. He dug his toes into
the dirt and scrambled behind a crate to keep from
getting hit again.

Protected for the moment, he swung around,
snatched up his fallen Peacemaker and stopped just
short of pulling the trigger. Sounds from inside the
restaurant warned that other customers rushed about.
Any shot he made that missed Simkins had the
chance of wounding or killing an innocent patron.

His ambush had failed. He wasn't going to lose his
best chance at stopping Luther Simkins once and for
all. Leif got his feet under him, then popped up like
he was on a spring. Quick eyes took in the scene. The
door was empty. A thousand thoughts flashed through
his head. If he were Simkins, he'd lay a trap for anyone entering that back door. Leif spun and made his
way around the restaurant to the front. Simkins's
other plan had to be running. The café had only two
doors. He dropped to one knee and steadied his six-
gun with both hands. His finger came back to fire
when a dark figure appeared in the doorway; then he
let off pressure and yelled, "Marta, get down!"

"They are gone, Leif. Both of them. After the
shooting started, they disappeared!"

He stood and scouted the street for the outlaws.

Citizens had begun to prepare for the day's business. If the Russians remained, the merchants had a chance to sell them trinkets and Indian artifacts. And if they didn't, the usual commerce of grain sales and bakery goods and all the rest of trade would go on as if nothing unusual had happened in their town.

"I don't see them," he cried. "Where'd they go?"

"I do not know. They ran out too soon," Marta said. She came beyond the threshold and stood on tiptoe, trying to locate the fugitives. "Without my gun, there was nothing I could do. You told me it was not needed." The bitterness in her denunciation tore at Leif's heart.

"I need to get on their trail. Go tell the deputy."

"That boy? Why?"

"He can get another posse formed. Someone old enough will take charge." Leif stumbled off. Marta caught up with him and took his arm. Pain drove into his shoulder when she did.

"You've been shot! Another bullet, in your good shoulder!"

"The lead passed through, and the holes're clotted over." Leif pulled free. He hardly had a good shoulder now, but that was not stopping him. Once Simkins hit the trail, catching him would be impossible.

"The deputy. Tell him. Now!" Leif snapped the command like a drill sergeant on a parade ground. Marta jumped at his tone. She started to argue, but he had no time. He ran. Every step toward the stables strengthened. His resolve drove him. *Get Simkins. Kill Simkins.*

He got off a shot at Simkins as the outlaw ducked

low, rode from the livery, and put his heels to his horse. Even Trickshot missed a moving target while on the run. Leif slammed into a wall, rebounded, and came around. The stable hand looked up, eyes wide.

"He took off, Mr. Trickshot! He never paid me, not for him or the woman with him."

"Here." Leif flipped the man a silver dollar. "Get my horse saddled." While the man hastily fetched Leif's tack and slung the saddle over White Lightning's back, Leif stood out in the street, watching the dust from Simkins's escape slowly sink down. The sun had risen enough to shine through the cloud, making it glow with a butterscotch light.

"Here you go, Mr. Trickshot, sir. I—"

Leif vaulted into the saddle. It took a second to get a proper seat. Then he gave White Lightning his head, letting the powerful stallion take off after Luther Simkins. In any race, Leif would bet on his horse. He bent low and flew past the scattered houses on the edge of town. Then the clean, pure air of the countryside flowed past, cutting at his flesh and catching his long hair, pulling it away from his face.

His faith in White Lightning proved well placed. Simkins's horse already flagged. The outlaw cast a look back over his shoulder, saw the pursuit, and veered off the trail into a wooded area. Leif narrowed the distance between them minute by minute. Then he lost track of the outlaw in a more heavily forested area.

Bringing the horse to a walk, he dodged low limbs and twigs that poked at his eyes. He lifted his arm to protect his face, then regretted it. His left arm tired swiftly and made him all too aware of the bullet lodged in his left shoulder. Determination had kept him alert and on the trail until now. Slowing down gave his body the chance to rebel against the mistreatment.

For a moment, he thought of turning around and returning to town. He wasn't up to a fight with Simkins. What would he prove if he was cut down?

"Cut down," he muttered. His right hand went to his neck and traced over the scabbed-over pattern left by the barbed wire noose. His parents had died with Simkins's garrotes around their throats. And so had Marta Esquivel's. How many more?

Leif slid from the saddle and walked a few paces. Blood hammered in his ears. With his breath coming in ragged gasps, he advanced. Mocking laughter echoed through the forest.

"This is gonna be a right fine day for me. The sun's hardly up, and I'm gonna kill me a Trickshot. What do you have to say about that, you murderous snake?"

Leif turned toward the voice and cautiously placed one foot in front of the other until he came to the edge of a clearing. On the far side, he saw a shadow moving. Simkins wore all black. He had pulled down the brim of his hat to shield against the rising sun at Leif's back.

If he stepped into the clearing and went too far from the trees, he would be outlined. The sun might be in Simkins's face, but the outlaw had a perfect target lit by the dawn light. Leif started to circle the clearing, but Simkins wasn't having any of that. A bullet ripped past him and made him duck into the woods.

"Yeah, that's what I thought. I figured you'd run

like the yellowbelly you are. Trickshot, ha!" Simkins stepped forward and pulled back his black frock coat. With exaggerated moves, he returned his Colt to the holster on his right hip. "Step up, and let's have it out."

"How'd you get my sister to turn her back on her family? The family you murdered?" Leif tried to circle farther. Simkins stepped back and threatened to vanish into the woods if he tried. The outlaw had the advantage and wasn't giving it up. If Leif wanted to end this now, he had to fight on unfavorable terms. He stepped into the clearing.

The sun filtering through the treetops warmed his back. He tried to guess how long the chase from town had been but couldn't. A half hour? More? What did it matter?

"She hated her life. She hated her ma and pa, and she hated you. Nothing she ever did was right. You all laughed at her because of the scar. She's too proud a woman to tolerate mockery."

"You did something to her. You lied to her and—"

"Lied? I told her the truth of the world. She saw I was right. She helped me tighten the wire around your pa's neck. You never thought she'd do a thing like that, did you?" Simkins began walking slowly and stopped a third of the way into the clearing.

"You're lying!" Leif rushed forward, then halted. Lies only inflamed him and made him careless. Or were they lies?

"She hated y'all so much, she wanted to change her name. I still kid her and call her 'my pet,' but 'Randy Sally Randall' is what she prefers now. She's notorious throughout the territory, and down in Denver, men quake at the sound of her name. Too bad she's not here to see you piss your pants because you're going to die."

Leif started to retort, then forced himself to a calm such as he felt during his show.

"Die!" Luther Simkins's shriek rang throughout the forest as he went for his six-shooter.

Leif drew left-handed as he had planned. His grip failed him. The wound in his shoulder ruined both strength and aim. He dragged out the Peacemaker and pulled the trigger. The bullet tore into the ground a few feet in front of him when he had intended it to blow off Simkins's head. He fought to raise the gun for a second shot.

A report sounded, but it came from the outlaw's pistol. Hot lead tore through Leif's side. The Peacemaker flew from his hand and crashed to the ground a yard away. He stared at the man advancing on him like an avenging angel.

"You're no good, Gunnarson. So much for Trickshot. You're nothing but a fake." Simkins raised his Colt to take careful aim.

Leif shifted left, then jerked the other direction. His right hand hadn't recovered fully from being shot twice before, but desperation drove him. The sight of the leathery face with the sneer drawing back cruel lips also drove him. All the outlaw had said about his family and Petunia and the insults and—

Leif's speed was less than usual, but he moved smoothly. His right hand reached the Peacemaker in his right holster. It felt good. It felt like he had prac-

ticed a thousand times. His numbed finger drew back
on the trigger. Recoil drove the six-shooter back into
his hand. He staggered but did not fall.

Luther Simkins did.

Trickshot once more had hit the target that counted.

CHAPTER TWENTY-SIX

Instinct. long hours of practice. Those had saved him. Leif Gunnarson pressed against the new bullet wound in his side as he stared at Luther Simkins's body. Nervous laughter started, just a little, then built until Leif was almost hysterical. The fierce jab of pain turned his laughter into tears. He gasped for breath.

"I could have shot you holding a six-shooter in my teeth." The mental image set off new peals of laughter until his sides hurt. Only then did he calm down enough to suck in a deep breath and regain a semblance of control. Too much killing. Both on his part and on the outlaw's.

At least Simkins would never torture and kill again the way he had for a decade or more.

Leif walked on surprisingly steady feet to stare at the dead outlaw. He dropped to his knees and began rummaging through pockets, not sure what he sought. A wallet with a wad of greenbacks and a folded map caused a surge of hope at finding what skulduggery Simkins was up to. He spread out the map, using a couple rocks to hold down the curling edges. The railroad tracks running from Cheyenne to the northwest were clearly marked, as was a single spot in a low pass where any locomotive had to slow because of the steep grade. He started to fold up the map and take it back to town. The chance of catching the entire gang was within his grasp!

"It figures," came a gravelly voice. "Robbing dead men is about what I expected from the likes of you."

Leif jerked around, then climbed to his feet slowly. Across the clearing stood a woman, hand resting on the gun in a cross-draw holster. The sun was in his eyes, as it had been for Simkins, but if he intended to shoot, his target was perfectly outlined, just as he had been for Simkins earlier.

"Petunia?"

"Don't call me that. I hated the name. I hated Pa's naming us all after flowers. He treated us even worse than hothouse plants, and the day Luther came around was the best of my entire life." Leif's sister took a few steps closer. She made no move to draw, but her tense muscles signaled it would happen at any instant.

"Who killed Flora and Daisy?"

"Not me. I never heard. One of Luther's triggerhappy henchmen, maybe. The boys riding with him back then were roughnecks." Petunia Gunnarson snorted and spat in a very unladylike way. "I was tougher. That's why Luther noticed me. But he was al-

ways the worst of the lot, and that's why I love him."
She fixed her eyes on the body. "That's why I loved him."

"Not once? Not once did you try to find me?"

"I thought you were burned up in the house. You
should have been." She wrung her hands together. "If
I'd known you were there, I'd've done to you what
Luther did to Ma and Pa."

Leif sagged a little. At least his sister hadn't killed
their parents. Simkins had lied about that. He wasn't
sure why that mattered when she had been riding side
by side with Luther Simkins for the last ten years,
committing heinous crimes, but it did.

"You've got what I need, Brother dear." She made
a cackling sound. "It's a poser how you survived and
how you learned to use those fancy six-guns of yours.
But I've learned a thing or two myself. Luther taught
me, and I was a good student."

"A willing student," Leif said disconsolately.

"More than that. An eager student. You can't
know how it feels to be in control. Strong men quake
when they hear the name Randy Sally Randall. I've
seen it. I've seen it when I shoot them down!"

"Walk away, Petunia. Go now, and I'll tell the law
that I never saw you."

"Now, why would you go and do a thing like that?
You're a liar as well as a cold-blooded killer. You
have the plan for the robbery. I want it." She moved
her hand back to rest on her pistol.

"Do you intend to shoot me?" Leif stood straighter.
His left arm hung limp and useless because of the new
shoulder wound. His right hand twitched and jerked
uncontrollably due to his right-shoulder wound. "You

shot me in the back before. You want me to turn around so you can do it again?"

"That doesn't matter one whit to me. Front, back, it's all the same if you die like you should have ten years back." She widened her stance. "I'm going to give you a chance to outgun Randy Sally. Make a name for yourself, get a reputation."

Leif willed his right hand to steadiness. A calm settled over him, but it was more a composure born of resignation. He had done too much over the past weeks, and it left him physically beaten down and emotionally numb.

"I'm not going to draw, Petunia. I won't kill my own sister." In a whisper, he added, "My only sister."

"You think that matters, you sanctimonious sap?" She went for her six-gun.

Leif closed his eyes and winced when the sharp crack of a Colt filled his ears.

He stood like a statue for long seconds, then realized she had missed. He opened his eyes but didn't understand what he saw.

"Petunia?" He stepped forward. "Sis?" He ran now and dropped beside the unmoving woman lying facedown in the grass. Leif touched her back, and his fingers came away wet with blood.

"Is she dead?"

Shock dulled his thinking. Leif let blood drip off his shaking fingers, then looked up and nodded.

"Good. It saves firing another bullet." Marta Esquivel came up, her still-smoking six-gun clutched in her hand. "My practice paid off, then. She was a terrible person." Marta spat.

"Don't do that! This is my sister!"

"She killed your parents. She killed mine, too. She destroyed families and deserves no mercy."

"She was all the family I had." Leif stared at Marta, still numb inside. He should have been angry at her for killing his sister, but Petunia had tried to shoot him down. Marta had saved him from the same end as his parents—and Petunia had shot him in the back before. She hadn't known who he was then, but she knew full well when she went for her Colt a minute earlier.

"You are better off without her. Remember your parents and other sisters." Marta clacked her teeth together. "We can turn them in for the reward. I found her horse in the forest."

"No!" Leif responded so vehemently that his nerves tingled and the numbness fled. He glared at Marta. "Simkins will bring enough money. But my sister . . . my sister is to be buried here."

"Your only family," she said. She reached out and lightly touched his cheek. Tears welled in her eyes. "Do what you must, Leif."

Marta slipped away, leaving Leif to his emotional turmoil. He found a spot nearby where the digging was easy in the soft dirt. He laid her between large roots from a tree and had mounded dirt over her when Marta returned. He saw she had been crying.

She watched as he finished covering his sister, saying nothing. As Leif stood, she said, "I need help getting Simkins over the horse."

Leif and the woman together wrestled the outlaw's body belly down over the saddle. He lashed Simkins's hands and feet together under the horse.

"I need to be careful. The cavalry patrol is still prowling about."

"You were found innocent. The judge . . ." Marta's words trailed off.

"The lieutenant is hardly willing to listen to how Simkins came to have my lead in him." Leif felt woozy from the new slug in his shoulder.

Marta grabbed him and pulled him to the ground. Muttering to herself, she began doctoring him again. He cried out as she cut the lead from his shoulder. She handed the bloody slug to him.

"You have quite a collection of those."

"Check the saddlebags. There might be whiskey." He closed his eyes. "Petunia bought cases of vodka for the Russians. She must have kept a bottle."

"You had some, too," Marta said. "It will help you with your pain—all your pain."

"It's in my gear. Somewhere in the forest. White Lightning." He gritted out the words. The pain from the bullet extraction wore him down. He had been shot too many times to ignore the agony. Leif sat with his back against a tree, staring at his sister's new grave until Marta returned with his horse. She took out a bottle from his saddlebags that Simkins and Petunia had ordered distilled and sold to the Russians.

"Here," Marta said. She held up the bottle, then swirled it around as she let the morning sunlight shine through it. A frown creased her forehead. "There are leaves in the bottom. Why is that?"

"Leaves?" Leif stared at what she had found. "Those look like loco weed."

"She put it in after the saloon made it?" Marta pulled the cork and sniffed. She all but gagged at the smell. "This is not fit to drink!"

"Datura," Leif said. "Cases of vodka made with

loco weed. If the Cossacks drink this, it'll drive them out of their minds."

Marta poked Simkins's body and said, "The fierce guards will be unable to fight off even a handful of bandits. It will not matter if they are the finest horsemen in Russia if they are passed out. Or become so loco, they cannot defend their master."

"Or if they are dead. Depending on how much they drink, loco weed can kill."

Marta tipped the bottle back and sipped, then shrugged.

"I do not taste the weed. The alcohol hides the flavor."

"Good," Leif said. "See that I get back to town." He took a healthy swig. All he felt was the cool numbing of the vodka and none of the crazy-making weed, but he was close to passing out.

He barely remembered Marta helping him into the saddle and riding, riding, riding. Endlessly he rode with images of his sister rising all around along the trail. Leif told himself that was the loco weed burning rational thought from his brain. He wanted more of the vodka's sedative effect but feared too much would cause him to lose his mind forever.

He even saw men in blue surrounding him as he sat astride his horse.

"Tell them of the Russians and the train robbery." Marta's voice sounded so far off. It echoed in his head.

Marta spoke and he obeyed, all will sapped.

"Give the sergeant the map you took off Simkins."

"Here's the place where they will attack. The Russians are drugged, and the train slows, and there's more gold than you can shake a stick at." Leif fumbled, trying to hold on to the map, but it was snatched from his hand. He heard distant voices, followed by the thunder of a thousand horses.

"Time to ride," Marta said. "For town. The cavalry officer said the marshal has returned. We can turn in the body and claim the reward."

"Reward? Sleep. That's a reward." Leif realized he was delirious. Or was the loco weed in the vodka jumbling his brain? The harder he tried to sort it out, the funnier it became. Then, his mirth gone, he contented himself with grimly hanging on.

The doctor and the town and the marshal and the reward were all jumbled, and he didn't care. Luther Simkins was dead.

And so was his sister.

CHAPTER TWENTY-SEVEN

I'M GLAD TO see the last of them." Wyoming Bob pushed his fancy bead-decorated hat back on his head and wiped away sweat. "We made a few dollars off them, but they were too demanding."

"It's good they didn't realize what you showed them was a herd of longhorn cattle and not buffaloes," Leif Gunnarson said. The warm Wyoming sun made him sweat, too. Since catching up with the Wild West Show a week earlier, he had recuperated enough to walk around without fear of passing out.

"You did good, Leif," Wyoming Bob said. "Your show wasn't anywhere near as good as before, but it impressed the archduke."

"They were more impressed when the cavalry swooped down on what was left of Simkins's gang. And why not? Their Cossacks were drugged and unable to fight. From what I heard, the archduke put that Sharps rifle he'd bought to kill buffaloes to good use." Leif watched the crowd carefully for any sign of the royal party. They had all traveled on in their special train, en route to the San Francisco bank dealings and eventually Ross Counter before sailing back to their country.

"I laughed when he gave you advice on shooting," Wyoming Bob said. "You! The world's finest marksman. Well, you will be again someday." The show owner studied Leif critically. "'Til then, you and the pretty lady have quite the show. She has the knack for keeping the gents' attention on her during the shoot-out."

Leif skirted the issue. He and Marta did make quite a team. Right now, she filled in the spots where he was most lacking. Her marksmanship couldn't hold a candle to his, but after a show, he was barely able to hold a six-shooter in either hand.

"The archduke," Leif said, "was quite a character. His entire honeymoon was something out of a penny dreadful, to hear him describe it."

"Too bad there wasn't a way to entice him to travel with the Wild West Show. Russian royalty all decked out in those fancy duds of theirs would draw spectators from near and far. But putting up with him and that snooty bride of his, well, it's best they had their Wild West adventure and are heading back to Russia."

Leif closed his eyes and basked in the sun. Neither spoke for a few minutes until Leif asked, "Why'd we come to Wyoming from Fargo so fast? We never put on a single show along the way."

"For you, boy, I did it for you."

This got Leif's attention.

"I heard that the Simkins gang was kicking up dust here. This was the first time in all the years I've known you and heard your family's story and how they were murdered that anyone even whispered the name Luther Simkins."

"Somebody told you?" Leif wanted to know who had given the alert to Wyoming Bob but not to him.

"A telegraph operator. He worked the Fargo key but had been raised in Cheyenne. I figured I owed you the chance to find the varmint. Only my information was faulty."

"Why didn't you tell me?"

"You're the heart of my show," Wyoming Bob said. "I didn't want you gallivanting off and leaving me high and dry."

"You didn't happen to hear about the archduke's expedition, too, now, did you?" Leif saw that the chance to cut himself into the Russian royalty's gold trove had influenced Wyoming Bob as much as any desire to let Leif bring Luther Simkins to justice. The show had traveled extensively in Europe, and stories of the vast wealth controlled by the Russian czar had always been a lure for Wyoming Bob, but the show had never "toured the tundra."

"Some mention was made of their treasure train; I admit that," the show owner said carefully. "It was a shame to let all that wealth waiting to be traded for a unique Wild West experience go to waste."

"So we made a beeline to Newell Bluff, but Simkins was after bigger game than banks and stagecoaches." Leif wondered how his life would have been different if Wyoming Bob had cut him loose to hunt down the outlaw gang on his own rather than keeping the show together. Then again, Wyoming Bob might have been lying, and the only reason they rushed to the territory was to fleece the Russians. Luther Simkins happened to have the same idea, and Wyoming Bob saw in Leif a way to remove that threat to his Russian revenue.

He would never know the truth. It was possible that Wyoming Bob Jenks had no idea what the truth was after telling so many whoppers. Leif had to chuckle at the archduke's being duped into thinking the longhorn cattle were bison. Wyoming Bob had shown off the show's lone buffalo to the archduke and convinced him it had been cut out of the distant herd.

"The Russians and their gold train were late reaching Cheyenne, so my timing was off," Wyoming Bob said, admitting a mistake for the first time in Leif's memory. "Well, they're on their way now, and we've laid claim to as much of their wealth as possible."

"And the archduke had a honeymoon second to none," Leif said. "When he and his bride return to Russia, they'll spend the rest of their days pining for their time in the Wild West. Nothing can match an attempted train robbery by a notorious outlaw, even if Simkins wasn't personally leading the stickup."

Wyoming Bob laughed. "People believe what they want to believe. It's my solemn duty to give that to them." He paused. "You made a decision about her yet?" The showman looked hard at Leif.

Leif looked around. Marta Esquivel came over, waving to the crowd eagerly waiting for the next show.

"My shoulders will never heal up right. I'm still the

marksman I ever was, but the quick draw is gone for good. She keeps the crowd attentive when I can't." Leif moved his shoulders and winced at the stiffness. The doctor in Kinney said there'd never be improvement, and Leif was inclined to believe him. Some things felt right. Some felt wrong and like they'd never get better. He was glad it felt right with Marta being part of the Wild West Show now.

"The targets are set up," Marta called. "Come on, Trickshot. We have a show!"

"Be right there," Leif Gunnarson said, making sure his Peacemakers rode easy in their holsters. He preceded her into the arena amid great cheers. Things had worked out just fine.

Ready to find
your next great read?

Let us help.

Visit prh.com/nextread

Penguin
Random
House